The Shaking

By

Braxton DeGarmo

Christen Haus Publishing

COPYRIGHT

Paperback/eBook Edition Publication Date: August 2022

Paperback ISBN: 978-1-943509-46-1
EBook (Mobi): 978-1-943509-47-8
EBook (epub): 978-1-943509-48-5

Cover design by Rocking Book Covers
For more information, go to **www.braxtondegarmo.com**

DEDICATION

To those who made a gender transition, realized their mistake, and had the courage to return to their God-given biologic gender.

And to those wearing blue, dedicated to protecting and serving despite their hands being tied by politicians.

And finally, to patriots throughout this country who willingly "fight" for our constitutional freedoms, in whatever form that fight takes place.

Three stories. Many lives.

Revelation 6:12-13

When he opened the sixth seal, I looked, and behold, there was a great earthquake . . .

Romans 1:22-32

Claiming to be wise, they became fools, and exchanged the glory of the immortal God for images resembling mortal man and birds and animals and creeping things. Therefore God gave them up in the lusts of their hearts to impurity, to the dishonoring of their bodies among themselves, because they exchanged the truth about God for a lie and worshiped and served the creature rather than the Creator, who is blessed forever! Amen.

For this reason God gave them up to dishonorable passions. For their women exchanged natural relations for those that are contrary to nature; and the men likewise gave up natural relations with women and were consumed with passion for one another, men committing shameless acts with men and receiving in themselves the due penalty for their error. And since they did not see fit to acknowledge God, God gave them up to a debased mind to do what ought not to be done. They were filled with all manner of unrighteousness, evil, covetousness, malice. They are full of envy, murder, strife, deceit, maliciousness. They are gossips, slanderers, haters of God, insolent, haughty, boastful, inventors of evil, disobedient to parents, foolish, faithless, heartless, ruthless. Though they know God's righteous decree that those who practice such things deserve to die, they not only do them but give approval to those who practice them.

ONE

"Krueger! Incoming! Heads up!"

Ryan Krueger, a field training officer for the Portland Police Bureau, raised his shield in time to divert the bottle of what appeared to be urine that had been hurled his way. Urine was the least of his concerns. The recent crowds of "protesters" had been "lively" to say the least—rolling trashcans on fire, Molotov cocktails, chunks of concrete and bricks—all aimed at the "poh-leece."

One of his fellow officers, a well-liked and respected man of color, had deflected an arrow. Sure, black lives mattered, unless they wore blue. The guy with the bow ultimately had been taken down and arrested, but that coordinated action had cost them. Their district and Central Precinct offices were within the police headquarters building on 2nd Avenue, all of which had come under direct attack as a result of pulling men away from the protection line to go after the scumbag, um, peaceful protester. They weren't allowed to call these people anything derogatory, which meant the truth was again nowhere to be found.

Day 182. Three days before Congress was expected to ratify the vote and declare Charles Henry "Po" Sidon as president-elect. One would think the Antifa and BLM crowds would have been satisfied that they'd gotten what they wanted in the election, but no. After six months of nightly protests, 30-plus "officially-declared" riots—that looked little different from the protests, and over $4 million in property destruction, downtown Portland looked like the loser in a war they had never asked for.

New Year's Eve had seen the resumption of protests with two Starbucks, a bank, jewelers, and many other small businesses once again becoming targets. Now, three nights later, Ryan and his comrades were once more suited up for "battle," except their hands were still tied to prevent them from winning.

To say this was getting old was, well, getting old.

"Kreuger, Diamonte, St. James! Push that line back. We need more breathing room."

Standing next to him, Joe Diamonte grunted. "More like maneuvering room. We're packed in here like sardines."

Ryan had to agree. Wedged between hastily erected concrete barriers, they had little space to move should they themselves become targets for more than the occasional missile.

"We shoulda cordoned off the entire block," said Jesse St. James as the three officers used their shields and verbal commands to move people farther back from the building and sidewalk.

Out of habit, Ryan nodded, not that he expected anyone to see the gesture of acknowledgment behind his protective gear. "That would have taken twice as many men. And if we took them from the Eastern Precinct, then these animals would have taken advantage of that and attacked that precinct building like they did before."

The news media continued reporting that officers were leaving the force in "unprecedented" numbers. That was an understatement. Several of Ryan's friends had left over the summer. Those who remained did so for a variety of personal reasons, but morale was so low it had nowhere to go but up or out. And in November, the outs won. Nine officers left in November alone. By Christmas, seven more had filed papers to resign and 14 put in their retirement paperwork for the end of the year. He'd overheard the assistant chief say that they'd received 25 new requests for records, which meant those officers had applied for jobs at other departments.

Diamonte had joked about it. "Between the attrition and the bureau's policy of promoting from within, I expect to be assistant chief by June." Joe had only one year of seniority over Ryan, and Ryan had been there just shy of five years.

Ryan felt resistance to his shield and turned his full attention to the people in front of him. "C'mon, move back! We don't want any trouble. We're here to protect the building."

One man, in particular, resisted his directive and stood his ground. The man's stare from within the dark hoodie appeared menacing. Perfect white teeth from within a snarl on the man's lips reflected more than the surrounding light. They broadcasted a privileged upbringing, one able to afford the best of orthodontia. And yet, here he was, in essence biting the capitalist hand that fed him.

"Sir! Move back!"

Instead of stepping back, the man lunged for Ryan's shield and pushed it aside. Within that second, the man had reached Ryan's gun and with a practiced move, unbuckled it and began to retrieve the weapon. Ryan dropped the shield and wrestled the man for control of the handgun. As he did so, three additional officers from behind the line moved forward to assist. They took the man down as Ryan secured his weapon.

He saw that Diamonte and St. James had also moved in to help, but that left an opening within the line. In that instant, Ryan knew that perfect-snarl guy had been little more than a distraction. Another man raced through the line carrying what appeared to be a two-gallon metal spraying canister. He reached the front doors of police headquarters and began to spray the contents of the tank onto and around the doors. Two other officers ran to intercept and stop him, but he turned, knowing of their approach as if he had eyes in the back of his head. As the two men neared him, he began to spray them as well. They stopped well short.

"Gasoline!"

The two policemen backed away as quickly as they had approached the man. In fact, the entire crowd, including the police line, dispersed at the cry. If the guy tried to ignite the gas, that gas-filled tank would become a bomb capable of taking out the lobby, much of the front half of the building, and everyone within 25 yards.

The man must have a death wish, thought Ryan. Ryan faced the arsonist with his gun coincidentally pointed toward the man as a result of his tussle for control. He wasn't about to shoot. An errant ricochet and spark could be catastrophic.

He flinched as the retort of a single gunshot reverberated along the avenue between the buildings of downtown Portland. And he dove to the ground expecting the fireball to come.

TWO

Aric Afton gazed out the window toward the small lake next to which the cabin sat. For the first Monday in January, the weather was warmer than he had anticipated—partly sunny with a high near freezing. He had expectations of much colder temperatures for southeastern Wisconsin. The lake had begun to freeze over a few weeks earlier, and some locals were now comfortable with ice skating on it.

He finished his breakfast, returned to the couch, and continued surfing news portals looking for anything of interest. At one article, he began shaking his head. He'd been in Portland only a few months earlier and had experienced the riots firsthand, although against his will. And now, they were protesting again? What did those people want?

Duh, he chastised himself. Did he really have to ask that question? Even silently? Despite the presidential election being challenged in numerous states, the odds were not in favor of the results being overturned, and Congress was expected to ratify the vote in two days. President Graham had been too honest and unwilling to bend to the globalist agenda.

He had been good for the country and the economy, no matter what the haters and media pundits pronounced. He had provided a reprieve for the U.S. from its ongoing march to progressivism, a temporary fence keeping the lemmings from running *en masse* off a cliff.

A totalitarian utopia was the goal of the globalists. The term was an oxymoron. The paradise expected by the elitists would never materialize. Aric had been studying the Book of Revelation with Lynch Cully, and together they had concluded that a major shaking was coming. Not in the sense of a global earthquake that many pastors taught would be coming but as a major political upheaval. Was that what they were to expect once Charles Sidon took office in two-plus weeks?

"Hey, Adam, did you see these reports about Portland? Antifa and BLM are up to no good again."

"Uh-huh."

Aric arose from the couch and walked to the nearby doorway leading to what would have been a bedroom in the lakeside cabin. His brother sat in the room, in front of four large computer monitors and two large-screen televisions mounted on the wall, engrossed in his "work," whatever that was these days. Whenever Aric brought up the topic, Adam changed the subject.

"Did you even hear what—"

"Uh-huh." Adam pointed to the television to his left.

Aric entered the room to see what was displayed on the screen. He smiled and shook his head. *Of course he's aware of what was happening in Portland*, he thought. The television showed what appeared to Aric to be real-time coverage of those very events. Compared to the previous few nights, not much was going on during the day, but the aerial view told Aric that someone was watching 24/7.

"Whose drone?"

Adam worked his mouse to pull up something else on one of his monitors. He didn't seem to hear Aric.

"Whose drone?"

"Someone else's" was the terse reply.

"No kidding. Look, maybe I should just head home to St. Louis for the week. Get out of your hair."

Adam had sold his properties in D.C. and rural Maryland, using the proceeds to purchase the Wisconsin cabin they had used as a base while investigating the human trafficking and experimentation facility run by YFM Corp near Camp Douglas. Located in the middle of a triangle formed by Chicago, Milwaukee, and Madison, the location was rural enough to remain off the grid while being heavily invested in the grid, as Adam once told him. Strangely, the phrase made perfect sense to Aric.

"I can leave first thing tomorrow morning. Even though we were there for Christmas, Mom would probably appreciate seeing me one more time before classes start."

"One sec . . ."

Adam glanced through three of his screens and pumped his fist once in the air as he smiled. Then he feverishly typed something on his keyboard. A minute later, he clicked on an icon with his mouse, sat back, and smiled with a gleam of satisfaction on his face.

"Sorry. That was important, truly important." He stood and led Aric back into the living room area before sitting in his favorite chair.

"As I said, maybe I should head home and spend a few days there before classes start. Mom is probably deep into the empty nest syndrome by now." He sat back on the couch where he had been using his laptop.

"I doubt it. She's a nana now and has a new grandbaby to dote on."

Aric had to concede that point. His oldest sister, Gwyneth, had delivered a healthy baby girl just before Christmas. "That's true. Anyway, maybe you should join me. I'm sure Rachael and your kids would like to see you, too."

Adam offered a brief frown. "Yeah, about that. We're making headway, Rach and me, but she asked me to give her time with Grace. She wants to establish that relationship before working on ours." He looked down toward the floor. "I get that. The damage done to our relationship is on me. I need to respect her wishes, but at the same time, still be available if she needs me."

Aric nodded. They had talked about this before. Washington was 12 hours from St. Louis, while now Adam was only six hours away. That had been one factor in his moving to the small town of East Troy. He resisted moving closer because the temptation to see them on a daily basis would be great.

"Up to you. My first class starts next week. After that, I won't have time to see the folks until spring break."

Aric's growing relationship with Lynch Cully as his mentor had led Aric to make two decisions. First, he had become fascinated by criminal forensics and knew he owed it to himself to explore that discipline. Second, because Lynch had been hired by the college to help take its criminal justice program to the top national rankings, Aric had decided he wanted to be part of that. He had applied to the college for its J-term, as they called their one-month intense study program in January where he would cover in that month a course that normally took a full semester. That would be followed by his first full semester.

"Yeah, about that. Um . . ."

Aric noticed the atypical face on his brother. He had been encouraging about Aric's decisions before this. What had changed?

"What?"

Adam shuffled about in his chair. "Look, I know you've developed a special friendship with the Cullys and little Joshua adores you. But, I, uh . . ."

This wasn't like Adam. His brother never beat around the bush about anything.

"What? Is something going on with them that I should know about?"

His brother was correct. He *had* developed a bond with both Lynch and Amy. They had become like family to him.

"Well, what if Lynch isn't at the college anymore? Would you still want to go there? I mean, their criminology program doesn't even have a national ranking, while UMSL's program is, like, number 11 in the country. And if you want to focus on forensics, the college here doesn't even offer that yet."

Aric had seriously considered the University of Missouri-St. Louis program. In-state tuition and the potential of living at home for the first year, maybe two, made it the soundest financial choice. Plus, graduating top of his class and having numerous AP credits and superior test scores pretty much guaranteed his acceptance. On top of that, Lynch had received his doctorate from that program and had offered a letter of recommendation, too. Was Aric throwing away a better opportunity?

Yet, it wasn't Adam's comments about the program that caught his attention. "What do you mean, if Lynch isn't there anymore?"

"Nothing concrete, but there seems to be a growing sentiment on campus to remove Lynch."

Adam knew his brother was right. Rachel and the kids would love to see him. Yet, he hadn't lied to Aric. Rach had asked for time to bond with the daughter they had named Carolyn, but who had grown up under the name of Grace after being kidnapped and then "adopted" by a French couple living in the U.S.

That woman was a homemaker, wife, and mother who knew nothing of her husband's illicit work but was aware that they had never legally adopted the little girl he had brought home with him one day. She had been unable to have children, longed for a family, and never asked where the girl came from. In a sickening reality, he was a "scientist" who experimented on children trafficked by the company he worked for. While she might see freedom and deportation within ten years, he would never have freedom again.

Well, in a just world he would never again be free. That world was about to change. The soon-to-be president had directly benefited from the man's work. And the soon-to-be "leader" of the Free World was as corrupt as they came, using his various positions throughout his lifelong political career to enrich himself, his family, and his friends. Adam held no doubts that the "scientist" would be secretly deported back to his home country and dodge his life sentence in the U.S. In fact, he had intercepted an email confirming that belief shortly after the election when it became evident that President-elect Charles Henry "Po" Sidon would be in the position to accomplish that goal.

Adam had never been the vengeful sort. His brother would repeatedly say that vengeance was the Lord's prerogative. Adam's nascent belief in God hadn't grown to that point, and this had been personal. He made sure that every inmate in the jail where the man was being held for trial knew of the man's crimes against children. They say that pedophiles don't last long in prison. Adam could only imagine what might happen to a man who used children for medical experiments to benefit the rich and well-connected.

"What do you mean, if Lynch isn't there anymore?"

How much should he tell his little brother? He had become secretive about the work he now performed, but not because he didn't trust Aric. The two of them had been through the wringer together. He had trusted Aric with his life . . . and would again if it came down to it. No, Aric had decided on a career in forensic criminology, while Adam now, well, skirted the law, as one might spin it, even if that law was unjust. Adam didn't want to jeopardize Aric's future by involving him. Plus, Aric was super smart and intuitive. If Adam gave up too much info, his brother would figure out where it came from in no time.

Adam had not only adapted and improved the AlterNet

software he had developed for his previous employer, but he had launched a viral attack against the original AlterNet program that now rendered it a useless virtual pile of bits and bytes. The new administration, its DOJ, and its military would never be able to claim it for their own gain.

"Nothing concrete, but there seems to be a growing sentiment on campus to remove Lynch."

He had no need to say more. If things panned out as he had discovered, Aric would know just what he meant soon enough.

THREE

Dillon Ingersoll's hands shook as he gazed through the binoculars across the border. He saw no signs of movement, but he knew they would show up. The weather would not deter them. In fact, they would see the severe cold as an advantage. With regional and federal law enforcement distracted by the unusual freezing temperatures and failure of the power grid, they would feel confident of their movements, emboldened to carry out their plan against the country.

If the rumors they had heard were correct. And so far, Dillon's source, whoever that was, had never been wrong.

He had once sworn to protect the country and uphold the Constitution. He was no longer held to that bond, but his allegiance remained. If those in power in Washington refused to protect the southern border, The Remnant would. They had recruited him to join their south Texas team. He had been hesitant until they told him what was coming. Despite his conflicted feelings, he could not let *that* into the country.

He, too, hadn't planned for the sudden deterioration of the weather. He had hunted elk in the mountains of Colorado and Idaho. There he had prepared for the cold and snow at the higher elevations. But this was Texas, southern Texas, near the Rio Grande River, at a point near where the construction of the new border wall had ceased for the holidays. And with the geriatric president-elect, whose strings were being pulled by who-knows-who, to be sworn in shortly, the odds were well against the resumption of construction at any point in the near future.

He rubbed his hands and breathed into them to keep them warm. Despite being midday, the sky now darkened quickly with storm clouds, and he hoped they appeared sooner, not later, so he could climb back into his truck, warm up, and skedaddle home.

As he again scanned the land beyond the incomplete barrier, on a path leading to the river, he noticed movement. *Is it them?* he wondered. He had already watched a couple of groups of illegals use the path to enter the country. He'd had to let them pass by. While being there illegally, they didn't pose the threat that his target group did. Besides, The Remnant didn't exist to defeat innocents. The drug cartels and others who would do harm to the country were their targets.

His question was answered minutes later as a group of a dozen or so men appeared. However, he felt surprised to see not Latinos, but Middle Easterners. They appeared cold and inadequately dressed. He counted five, no, six men armed with what looked like AK-47s. Eight others carried two bulky objects, each on a pallet through which two two-by-fours had been inserted to function as poles for carrying the items. Each pallet required four men, so clearly the things were heavy.

So far, everything he saw lined up with the intelligence

they had received. The location had been chosen because the construction roads gave them access. According to plan, *their* plan, two trucks would be arriving soon to transport them and their cargo deeper into the U.S. That could not be allowed to happen, so other patriots had been sent to watch for said trucks and to disable them. And, should that require dispatching those drivers to whatever paradise they expected to go to as martyrs, those patriots were prepared to assist them.

He felt the phone in his coat's inner pocket vibrate. After fumbling a bit with cold hands to retrieve it, he opened up the fresh text message . . . and frowned.

Icy roads and detours prevented our arrival. Trucks have not been disabled.

That was not the news he wanted to hear. He was just the spotter. Their goal had been to prevent the trucks from arriving, leaving the smugglers stranded so that Border Patrol officers could be alerted to find them. After all, they could not get far with their heavy loads. He wondered, would their trucks also be delayed by ice or detours?

The answer to that question also didn't take long. The rumble of engines could be heard before the headlights became visible over the crest of a small hill. Two cargo vans, each bearing the logo and information of the construction company overseeing that section of the wall, moved slowly along the snowy gravel road and approached the men. Several of the men raised their hands in a whoop of victory at the arrival of their transportation . . . and sources of warmth.

He had a choice to make. He could call in their arrival and location to the nearest Customs and Border Protection office and hope that officers arrived quickly. Two factors disfavored that option. One, the CBP would need to respond with a force capable of taking on six men armed with semi-automatic weapons. That was not a spur-of-the-moment task. Two, the weather conditions went against a timely response.

That left his other choice, dealing with them personally. He had killed on the battlefield in Iraq, but that was different. Or was it? He had no time to mentally debate the pros and cons, legalities and illegalities of what he needed to do. Still, he would be taking on six armed men with only his hunting rifle. Those odds were not in his favor. For him to fail could mean thousands of innocent deaths. The paraphrased scripture, *There is no greater love than laying down one's life for others*, flit through his mind. He had to do this.

He checked the wind and eased his way to a position of being upwind. If their intel *was* correct, he wanted to minimize his risk, and being upwind was his best option.

He no longer needed the binoculars. The first package was loaded, and the men now moved to the second. He couldn't wait any longer.

He raised his rifle and positioned his target within his scope. Muscle memory guided his trigger finger, even in the cold. The first shot hit the object, but nothing happened. The men jumped and began searching out *his* position. In that split second before they could move, however, he pumped two more rounds into the target.

He felt the pulse of the explosion almost as soon as he saw it. The nearest truck exploded, followed by the second truck and its load. He no longer worried about the threat the men might be. They were gone. He grabbed his gear. He needed to get out from under the plume of the explosions, or at least as far away as he could as fast as he could.

He thanked God that the winds of the winter storm aided him. The radioactive debris of the dirty bombs he had just prevented from moving further into the country was moving away from him, toward the river and Mexico. The radiation would be dissipated across a broad area of desolate land where it would pose little potential threat to others, other than those who chose to travel through the region for illegitimate reasons and for extended periods of time. For them, the consequences would be silent, taking perhaps years before the health issues arose.

Upon reaching his truck, he didn't hesitate but took off as fast as the terrain allowed. The explosions would have been detected. Of that he was sure. With the storm, he doubted the ever-present aerial surveillance drones were up and flying, but satellites would have caught the blasts. Plus, he'd heard that ground sensors were in place to detect the activity of tunneling under the new fence. Whether or not they had been activated in the nearby areas of completed fencing, he didn't know, and he wasn't waiting to find out. The last thing he wanted was to be found in the immediate area.

He crossed open grazing land until he reached his first fence, which he followed to its first gate. He moved through the gate, closed it behind him, and traveled along a gravel ranch road to the county's two-lane gravel road that would lead him home. No sooner was he there than a text came through. He had his truck read it to him.

"Explosions detected. CBP alerted to danger. Good job."

And with that, he knew the text would never be seen

again. He hadn't the foggiest idea how The Remnant did it, but he knew that no forensic exam of his phone would ever find that text or the one preceding it. In fact, an exam of his phone's location data would likely show him in town buying groceries or something, or at home the whole time, maybe out in his barn. Plus, any data supplied by his carrier would corroborate what was on his phone.

When The Remnant had recruited him, he had been assured they would cover his back. Even if they didn't, he loved his country enough to become one of its frontline defenders when the corrupt government failed in its duty to do so.

Still, he struggled with the taking of others' lives. He was not their judge or jury. He certainly wasn't God, everyone's ultimate judge including himself. He found it easy to draw the line at allowing the innocent, those simply seeking a better life, to pass by. They were the responsibility of the CBP, and he could assist the local agents with information without taking a life. But there were those who were far from innocent—the traffickers and drug smugglers. He hadn't come to any sort of peace in how to deal with them.

FOUR

Ashleigh Love watched in the mirror as she finished working with her hair, knowing it was going to end up in the fur-lined hood of her parka. Her makeup was perfect, and she had even avoided getting it on the cowl neck of her sweater dress. The day called for warm, long pants, but she rarely wore pants. Tights would have to keep her legs warm. Most, if not all, of the day's protest would be outside, and Kenosha was known for its cold winds, even though Lake Michigan tended to moderate the weather on campus.

She took a deep breath and worked to rein in her nerves. Her counselor had assured her that the anxiety would ease over time, as she became more confident in her new role. Still, being an "activist" had never been on her bucket list for life. All she had ever wanted was to blend in and be accepted for who she was.

She walked to the front room of her friend's apartment. Her sign was sitting on the hand-me-down coffee table that tripled as her desk and dining table. She picked it up and checked to make sure the lettering had dried. The last thing she needed on her thin budget was a dry cleaning bill to remove marker from her coat or dress when it was so easily avoided.

Ashleigh hadn't been born "Ashleigh Love." She had legally taken on that name after being "emancipated" from her parents. She had always loved the name Ashley, even though it had no meaning more significant than a meadow where ash trees grew. The different spelling, Ashleigh, came as a last-minute decision when she completed the forms for the court. As for the surname, it represented all that she stood for—loving one's fellow man, accepting all races, colors, creeds, and lifestyles. God is love, she recalled from her early Christian upbringing. She would be, too.

She found her bag on the counter in the small galley kitchen. Keys? Check. Phone? Where was her phone? She pulled it off a nearby charging cord and dropped it into the oversized, black leather bag. Pamphlets? Check. She had designed and printed the threefold fliers to detail the "crimes" of one of the college's more recent hires. She figured 50 would be more than enough for this first day of protests. Most students weren't expected back for J-term for another week. These were for curious faculty and staff members.

She rummaged through her bag and, satisfied that she had everything she needed, grabbed her parka from the back of one of the two chairs and donned it. She rushed into the bathroom for one last look in the mirror. Her hair was perfect.

Fifteen minutes later, she parked in her designated lot on campus. She slung the strap of her bag over her head and one shoulder, grabbed the sign, and rushed toward the main admin building where the top departmental offices were found. Just outside the front entrance, she met up with her faculty counterpart.

"Hi, Dr. Fry. I hope you haven't been out here long. That wind off the lake is biting."

Dr. Meredith Fry was an assistant professor of sociology and part of the criminal justice program. Her work focused on intersectionality, the theory of the overlapping of various social identities—such as race, gender, sexuality, and class—and how that contributed to the systemic oppression and discrimination experienced by an individual. She was the person who had alerted Ashleigh to a "problematic hiring" by the college.

"Hi, Ashleigh. The others should be here shortly."

Ashleigh opened her bag and retrieved the pamphlets. She handed one to the professor. "What do you think?"

Dr. Fry examined the material and smiled. "Your Photo Shop skills are excellent as always. You've always had an eye for design. And I think the info covers things pretty well. We need to convince both the department chair and administration that one Assistant Professor Carson Cully needs to go. A man like him has no place on this campus."

Ashleigh nodded. "I think we all agree on that."

Another student and a teaching assistant joined them. Each had a sign: *"Pull the Lynch-pin"* and *"Stop the Lynch-ing."* *Clever*, thought Ashleigh. Her sign was two-sided: *"Don't be cullied!"* and *"Cull the threat to freedom!"* Three more students arrived.

With enough bodies to get attention, they began to march in front of the doorway and along the sidewalk. Several chanted as they moved, using Ashleigh's slogan about freedom. Ashleigh and the professor handed out fliers to whoever would take one.

A member of security approached Dr. Fry. Ashleigh was far enough away that she couldn't hear what was said, but the professor came up to them afterward.

"Hey, we're good as long as we don't block anyone from entering or leaving the building, or from passing by on the sidewalk." They all nodded in acknowledgment.

A moment later, Ashleigh saw the man himself approaching the building. "Hey, here he comes!"

While the others obeyed the directive from security through Dr. Fry, Ashleigh walked right up to him and started screaming in his face. "You don't belong here! Resign, you . . ." Her vindictive words spewed forth. "You should have left Graham to rot in the wilderness!"

His face remained passive, which irritated her further. He tried to step around her, but she moved to block his way, despite the directions from security. As a security officer moved to intervene, Dr. Fry pulled her aside.

Cully looked at his fellow professor. "Really, Meredith, I might not agree with you on a lot of things, but have I ever shown you disrespect? I thought you were a bigger person, but I guess not. And to get students to do your dirty work. So sad."

Ashleigh felt enraged at his words and moved to hit him but stopped herself short. Reflexively, she spit on him instead.

He turned to her. "And Ms. Love, that can be considered assault, but I forgive your ignorance. By the way, I'll need one of these." He grabbed a flier from her hands. "My lawyer will review this closely for libel." He turned again toward Dr. Fry. "You know, Meredith, I've faced truly nasty people before.

Been shot twice. Faced down assassins and terrorists. You can bring your best shots, but they will all pale in comparison. A college should be a place for diverse opinions and free speech, and I will forever fight for your right to that speech. If only you could do the same for me."

He stepped away, and the crowd, which had grown to around 20, parted to let him enter the building. Ashleigh started to follow but was restrained by Dr. Fry.

"Don't, Ashleigh. You didn't help our cause. What came over you?"

Ashleigh worked to control her hyperventilation. Yes, what had come over her? She had a flashback to her parents, but to her father in particular. Something about the calm, collected attitude of Lynch Cully reminded her of her father's smug, holier-than-thou character. From what she had learned about Dr. Cully, he shared the same born-again Christian beliefs as her parents. Such intolerance. If they truly believed in God, they would show her love and accept her lifestyle "choice." God accepted her the way she was. Of that she was convinced. After all, hadn't He made her the way she was?

Yet, just thinking about that ratcheted up her anxiety. Whenever she thought of her father, she heard his words reminding her that her lifestyle was a choice and not inbred or genetic, and her discomfort level increased.

"C'mon, Ashleigh. Let me buy you a coffee. We need to talk. The others can keep up the protest and hand out fliers."

FIVE

Aric leafed through the mail, separating his from Adam's, and found what he'd hoped would be there. His first class started in a week, and he still hadn't received his parking permit for campus. So, he felt relief in finding it in that day's mail. His next step would be to move into the dorm that coming weekend. The move itself would be easy, as most of his belongings were at Adam's new cabin less than an hour away from campus. The rest of his stuff was at the Cully's home, only ten minutes from school.

After Adam's comment about their mom being preoccupied with a new granddaughter, he canned his plans for a trip home. Plus, Adam's cryptic comment about Lynch had him worried.

He glanced at the clock on the microwave and decided that he had enough time for a trip to the college. He could check out exactly where he was supposed to park and then pay an impromptu visit to Lynch, who would be working in his office all day.

He walked to the doorway to Adam's lair. "Hey, here's

your mail. I'll put it on the end table by your chair. I got my parking permit, so I'm going to take a trip to campus, check it out, and maybe pay a visit to Lynch."

Adam glanced up from his screens for just a moment. "Okay. Thanks." He turned to face the monitors again but quickly turned back. "So, what do you want to do for dinner tonight?"

"How about that Mexican place again?" It had been a few weeks since they'd eaten there.

"Okay. I was thinking pizza, but that works."

Aric smiled. His brother could live off pizza. Aric preferred a bit of variety beyond this pizza place one night and that pizza place the next time. Of course, East Troy only offered two pizzerias, so that could get old pretty quickly.

"I'm shooting to be back before dark. See you."

"Bye. Be safe."

The drive was uneventful, and less than an hour later, Aric had found the parking lot he'd been assigned to, parked, and walked toward the main building. He passed the main athletic fields and stadium, circled the chapel, and found himself on the main drive through the heart of campus. Just ahead was the admin building where Lynch also kept his office. Aric furrowed his brow at the sight of protesters on the sidewalks. As he neared and saw their signs, he realized they were protesting Lynch.

"What the . . .?"

He glanced at all the signs and took the brochure someone shoved his way and moved past the group. They didn't interfere with his movement or block his way into the building, but their presence produced an aggressive climate around that end of the building. Of course, after what he and Adam had gone through over the past year, few things or people intimidated him.

He headed up the stairs to Lynch's office and knocked on the door.

"Just a minute!" It was Lynch's voice responding.

Aric could hear Lynch talking with another man, and although the words weren't heated, both sides displayed passion. Aric wondered whether he should leave and come back later, but then the door opened and the man he now recognized as the head of the department that included the criminal justice program rushed out. The man paused long enough to take in Aric standing there and hurried down the hall to an office near the other end.

Lynch came to the door. "Oh, it's you. Sorry about that. C'mon in and take a seat." He paused and took a deep breath. "On second thought, let's go get coffee or something." He grabbed his coat, met Aric in the hall, and locked his door. "I'll drive. Follow me." He headed down the hallway in the direction away from where the main body of protesters assembled. "It's probably best we leave by a different exit."

Aric followed his mentor to a side entrance where the coast was clear. Together, they hurried across the main drive and to the faculty parking lot. Halfway into the lot, Lynch stopped and muttered some unintelligible words. Aric noted the scowl cross his friend's face and followed his gaze further along into the lot. There sat Lynch's car with two tires flattened and "graffiti" soaped onto the windows. Calling it "graffiti" understated what they saw. The words would make sailors blush, to use the colloquial phrase. Lynch pulled out his phone a dialed a number. Within minutes, a campus security car arrived.

Aric stood apart as Lynch talked with the officer. A few minutes later, his department head arrived as well. As they discussed the situation, Lynch pointed to his car and then to the two security cameras on nearby light poles. Aric could only imagine what was being said but believed he knew Lynch well enough to know that he would use his own computer forensics skills to review the security video and press charges against the instigators.

Aric watched the security officer join them. More discussion. Several minutes later, a tow truck arrived, and Lynch relinquished his keys to the driver. A short while later, as the truck departed, the trio broke up and Lynch walked over to Aric.

"Guess we take your car."

Aric pointed. "It's over that way." They began walking toward the student lot where he had parked. "So, what's the deal? If I'm allowed to ask."

"Security assured me they would review the security video and provide me with copies. I told Dr. Carter I *will* press charges and expect expulsion of any students involved. He was noncommittal but told me the college would cover any repair costs and the expense of new tires. He was quite embarrassed that this happened."

"There's my car," said Aric as he pointed out his vehicle.

They climbed inside, and Aric started the car. "Where to? Common Grounds, The Coffee Pot, or Daily Dose?" All three were favorites among the coffee crowd in Kenosha as well as on campus.

"Bob's."

"Huh?" Aric hadn't heard of a place called Bob's.

"Turn north onto Sheridan. It'll be on the left about two miles up the road. The sign says Bob's on Sheridan."

Sure enough, four minutes later, Aric saw a dilapidated sign on a rusty pole announcing Bob's Restaurant. As he turned into the crumbling asphalt parking lot, he saw the sign painted on the building that said Bob's on Sheridan. The place made most dives look like five-star gourmet establishments.

Lynch must have seen the look of disbelief on Aric's face because he smiled and said, "It's a hidden treasure. Trust me."

As they entered the building, Aric tried hard to hide his uncertainty inside. The broken linoleum floor was in such a state you couldn't tell if it was cleaned regularly or not. The old tables appeared to be second-hand, or maybe even third or fourth-hand, from the 1970s. The leatherette of the booth seating was cracked and torn, and the ceiling was water stained in numerous spots, with drywall patches evident in others.

One unique aspect in favor of the place was a hand-lettered sign offering a variety of wild game meats such as elk, bison, antelope, wild boar, alligator, caribou, and venison. Those might be interesting to try, but Aric wasn't as sure about their offerings of camel, kangaroo, llama, and alpaca.

Lynch led him to a nearby booth, where they were quickly addressed by a friendly waitress. She already had a coffee pot in hand, along with two menus.

"G'mornin', pet. Saw you comin'."

The accent and term "pet" reminded Aric of one of his mom's favorite British shows, *Vera.* She poured Lynch a cup of coffee.

"And you, luv?"

Aric nodded and pushed his cup toward her. "Thanks."

As she left them alone, Lynch asked, "Up for lunch? My treat."

Aric's stomach grumbled as if on cue. "Sure. Thanks. They seem to know you here."

Lynch nodded. "Yeah, you could say I'm a regular. It's five minutes from the house and five minutes from campus. Their breakfasts are great and inexpensive. Don't say anything to Amy, but it's become something of my morning escape from the house on the way to work. I haven't worked up the nerve to bring her here yet. I think she'd be afraid to sit down." He laughed.

Aric took a sip of his coffee. It was really good. "Speaking of campus, what was that all about?"

Lynch looked off at something behind Aric, took a deep breath, and shook his head. His gaze returned to Aric. "Look, keep this between us at this point. I'm trusting you not to say anything, okay?"

Aric nodded.

"The cancel culture is alive and well on campus."

"Oh no, I . . ." Now Aric's second thoughts about his choice to attend the college roared into his head.

"One of my colleagues discovered my relationship with President Graham which led to her uncovering, if that's the right word to use, my faith. Actually, I've never hidden my faith, so to say she uncovered it isn't right. Anyway, she took offense at my Christian beliefs and automatically assumed I would be bigoted and an improper role model for the students in the criminal justice program. She's staked her career on critical race theory, gender theory, and all the rest of that Marxist rhetoric. She called me out on it at a staff meeting, and while I remained polite, I openly disagreed and argued that students needed to have a balance and diversity of viewpoints. Well, she got a bit vitriolic at that, and now she has a vendetta started to remove me from campus."

Aric shook his head. "That's not right. I . . . I don't know what to say. And your car?"

"Well, I hope that she wasn't behind that. If she was, she'll be the one to regret it. I suspect some of the students she's worked up thought that would somehow intimidate me."

"And Dr. Carter? Let me know if I'm prying too much."

Lynch shook his head. "I will. Still, the more you know, the better you'll be able to pray about the situation. He knew of my relationship with Bradley Graham and of my faith when he hired me. The faculty at UMSL assured him that I approached everything with a superior professional standard and never pushed my beliefs on anyone there. He told me at the beginning that he was a strong proponent of free speech and that he thought I could add some balance to the program, as well as the forensics expertise they were looking for. As of this morning, he appears to be changing his tune. I'm guessing he doesn't want to be caught up in any controversy that could damage the program he's hoping to build here."

That was not what Aric wanted to hear. It was too late to back out of the class he was about to start, but he would have to seriously pray about continuing into the spring semester.

The waitress returned. "What'll it be, luvs?"

All of the breakfast skillets looked really good, but Aric

decided he wanted lunch. "Um, I want to try an elk burger. The sign says we can create a burger from any of the wild game meats, right?" The waitress nodded. "Okay, yeah, an elk burger with the fries and iced tea, unsweetened. Thanks."

"I'm game for a burger, too." Lynch grinned. "Sorry, pun intended. Have you tried the llama yourself?"

She shook her head. "Sorry, pet, but I 'aven't. Is that a probllama?" Her grin matched his as he laughed.

"I'll go for it. Thanks."

"Do you want one of the special drinks that go with it?"

Lynch replied, "Huh? I didn't see anything about special drinks."

Aric saw the gleam in the woman's eyes and knew something was coming.

"That burger is lovely with llamanade or alpaca punch."

Lynch groaned. "I'm supposed to have the dad jokes here, but I bow to a master punster."

"Work 'ere long enough, pet, and you 'ear them all."

"As long as I'm not being fleeced by ordering it." This time the waitress groaned.

Lynch changed the conversation to one of catching up on their families and the holidays. The burgers seemed to arrive in no time and proved Lynch right. The place was a hidden gem. The food was delicious, although the elk was nothing like beef in taste or texture. Still, Aric's thoughts kept returning to the decision he'd made about starting college there. And with that concern, he began to wonder what he'd be encountering with his first class, Criminal Justice 101, with Dr. Carter.

Dr. Fry worked to assuage Ashleigh's anxiety over coffee and a pastry at the harborside eatery called Common Grounds in downtown Kenosha. The sun reflected off patches of thin ice on the calm water of the harbor, and the interior offered a cozy, warm respite from the cold wind coming off the lake. The mixed aromas of brewing coffee, cinnamon, lemon, and more blended into a potpourri that on its own had a calming effect on her.

"Thank you, Mer . . ." She looked about and recognized other students there. She would need to keep things more formal. ". . . um, Dr. Fry. I owe you and the others an apology."

The professor took a sip of her latte and shook her head. "You're welcome, and no, you don't." She took a small bite of her lemon-poppy seed muffin. "If you're going to be on the front lines, you have to keep your cool. If you get all flustered and let them get under your skin, they win that battle."

Ashleigh wanted to savor the iced cinnamon roll sitting on the table in front of her. If she could have only one sweet, besides chocolate, it would be anything cinnamon. Yet, she couldn't bring herself to eat it. She hadn't touched her coffee either.

"To be honest, I don't think it was so much him as something, no, some*one* else who upset me."

She felt comfortable with Dr. Fry, confident that she could be open with the woman. She shared how Lynch Cully reminded her of her father, who rejected her because of her lifestyle. She told of being kicked out of their house because of it. However, as she spoke, she knew inside that this was a lie she told to justify herself. Such had not been the case. Yes, her parents, mom included, would not allow her to "practice" her lifestyle under their roof, but it was Ashleigh's decision to leave them when she turned 18 and to move out.

"Are you in touch with your parents?"

Ashleigh shook her head. "No. They want nothing to do with me."

Another lie, and it made her gut churn even though she tried to deny it. Her parents had tracked her down and sent her a Christmas present a few weeks earlier. Ashleigh had refused the package and had it returned, unopened. How they continued to find her, she had no idea. She had moved six times in the past two years in her effort to disappear. If she was to be honest, those moves had not been to her advantage. Each time she broke a lease, it cost her, and her most recent apartment had been a hovel compared to the dorms and her first apartment off-campus.

Dr. Fry had come to her rescue and had secured a resident adviser position for her. That would enable her to save for another apartment after graduation. In the meantime, she made use of a friend's place over the holidays. She would be able to move into the dorm in two days, three days ahead of the rest of the students.

"Well, I can see how Cully could upset you so much. He stands for almost everything that's wrong with this country, and I believe your parents are on that side of the tracks, too."

Ashleigh nodded. She and Dr. Fry were on the same wavelength when it came to open borders; unrestricted voting that included non-citizens residing in the country; restitution to the descendants of slaves; a strong, centralized government with the power to curtail hate speech and fake news; and more. Of course, her advocacy was strongest about gay and trans rights.

She looked at her food and drink, still untouched. "Thanks, for listening. I promise to be stronger and to control myself better."

Dr. Fry smiled. "Good. Look, go home and rest up. The others and I can carry on today. And when you feel you're ready, you can rejoin us."

Ashleigh sighed. She didn't like to admit defeat, but that morning's outburst felt like failure to her. She wanted to do better, but somehow, she'd lost her drive to do so. If she were honest with herself, which she rarely was anymore, she'd admit that she'd lost interest in most everything. Not eating was good for her figure, but not for her health. Likewise, her sleep patterns were off. Either she slept the day away or she found herself up all night. She'd once read that all of these were clinical signs of depression, but that, too, she tucked away in the neverland of her mind, not being willing to admit or face up to it.

SIX

Ryan awoke midmorning after two more evenings of protests that had kept him working well past his shift's end. In thinking about it, did their shifts even have set hours anymore? Today was supposed to be his day off, a day he would normally spend with his wife, Sarah. Two things worked against him.

One, the school system had called for their kids' educations to continue virtually after the holiday break. They missed their friends and were as antsy as their parents with all of the governor's stay-at-home orders. Ryan and Sarah debated homeschooling, which they seemed to be doing anyway. They had decided to investigate the idea and what resources were available over the spring semester, with a decision to be made before the next school year began.

However, the second issue was the one likely to erase the day for him—the protests. Although the bureau hadn't formally retracted days off for its remaining officers, the reality of the situation, plus their being short-staffed made it likely. Again. If called in, this would be his twelfth day in a row at work. The overtime was nice . . . up to a point.

As he padded into the kitchen to find Sarah, the home phone rang. He found that curious as the phone was a private land line provided by the bureau. It wasn't that the chief was old school. During one protest a few months back, vandals had damaged two crucial pieces of communications equipment, as well as a main downtown cell tower. Being equally reliant upon cell phones and their radios, the department had lost communication with 40% of the force, and, unable to reach off-duty officers at home, they hadn't been able to call in reinforcements. Besides work, only a handful of close friends and family had been given the number.

"Hello."

"Hi. Who is this?"

Clearly not a friend or family member.

"Who are you trying to reach?"

After a short pause, the voice asked, "Ummm, who did you say you were?"

Ryan frowned. He didn't like how this was going.

"Look, we're a bar on SE Division, and we're not open yet. Call back later." He hung up.

He found Sara preparing food for the evening meal. Between monitoring the kids' schooling, trying to maintain their home, and little time to enjoy her favorite pastime, cooking, their Crockpot had become attached to her at the hip. He slipped up behind her, wrapped his arms around her waist, and kissed her on the neck. She tilted her head back into him.

"Mornin', sleepyhead. Who was that?"

"Wrong number. Kept asking who was speaking."

She turned her head a bit. "Weird. That's the third call like that since yesterday afternoon, just after you left for work."

Now, Ryan felt concern. Was someone phishing for their number? Why?

"I told 'em it was a bar on SE Division and to call back later. So, whatcha fixing?"

"Taco soup. I—"

"Hey, that's my pencil! Give it back."

The yell crescendoed from the adjacent room. What had been a formal dining room now hosted school instead of family dinners and gourmet meals with friends.

"You have two. Mine broke, and I need one, like, right now."

"Mommmmm!"

Sarah sighed and started to put down the can opener with the half-opened can of kidney beans.

Ryan kissed her neck and backed away. "I got this." He stepped toward the makeshift classroom. "Michael, give Gabe his pencil back. Here's another one," he said as he grabbed a pencil from a nearby drawer and walked into the room.

"Daaaddd!"

Eight-year-old Gabriel jumped up from his chair and ran to his father. Ryan grabbed him, picked him up, and after a hug, turned him upside down before lowering him to the floor. Gabe laughed the whole time. Ten-year-old Michael, however, just gaped at his father with his mouth open.

Ryan turned toward him. "What? You just catching flies or something? What's that look for?"

After a couple of seconds, Michael replied, "Whoa, Dad. Did you really kill someone the other night?"

Ryan flinched at the words, as they caught him by total

surprise. "Wh-what makes you ask that?"

The man with the gas can had indeed been shot and killed, but that investigation was ongoing. It appeared that the shooter was behind and above Ryan, who never fired his weapon. Sarah was now standing next to him, her face etched with concern.

"My friends at school are saying a police officer shot and killed a man. One of 'em said it was you, but I think he was just joking around. The teacher muted them before they could say anything else. But my buddy, Miguel, texted me and said his parents said it was about time the rioters were dealt with."

"Whoa, Michael. First off, I've *never* had to shoot my gun at anyone, and I didn't shoot anyone the other night."

"Then, who did?"

At that moment, the front doorbell rang. Sarah left his side and went to answer the door. Ryan heard her talking with a man. The voice sounded familiar.

"We're still trying to find out." He tousled his son's hair and offered a wan smile. He did not like the idea that folks were saying he'd shot someone, when in fact, he hadn't.

"Ryan, it's for you. Captain Lopez."

Ryan's eyes widened. Lopez managed what most departments called internal affairs. Why was he at their home?

Ryan walked to the front hallway as Sarah excused herself.

"Captain. Good morning . . . I hope."

The man nodded, but his gaze focused on something, or someone, behind Ryan. Ryan turned to see both boys peeking around the corner of the dining room. "Back to school, you two." Ryan heard them scurry away, followed by the sliding of chairs across the floor.

"Someplace we can talk?" asked the captain.

"Sure. Follow me. Can we get you some coffee or something to drink?" Ryan walked toward their family room in the back of the home.

Lopez grunted. "What I'd really like I can't consume on duty. Some water would be great. Thanks."

Ryan wondered at the comment. Did that bode well for him or not? "Have a seat. I'll be right back. Ice?"

"Sure."

Ryan moved into the kitchen, retrieved two glasses of ice and water, and returned to the den.

"Nice," said Lopez, pointing to the fourteen-point whitetail deer head mounted in one corner of the room. "I used to hunt, before taking this promotion and, well, all the turmoil."

"I hear you on that last point. It's been three seasons since my last hunt. That trophy was one I got back home in Wisconsin just before moving here for this position. One of my uncles has about two hundred acres of farm and timber. Opening bow season is like a family tradition there. I miss it."

The captain nodded and proceeded to drain half of his glass. Ryan sensed he was stalling.

"So, to what do I owe the pleasure?" he asked.

Lopez glanced about before setting his gaze on Ryan. "It's about the other night. Bad news is, I need your gun. Good news is, well, for you anyway, 'cause you're getting some time off, the chief has put you on administrative leave for a few days, while we investigate that shooting last night."

Time off or not, Ryan didn't like the sound of this news. "Why? You all know I never shot my weapon. The shooter was behind me."

Captain Lopez nodded. "Yeah, we know. And it looks like it was a rifle, not a handgun."

"So, why am I being put on admin leave? I didn't do anything wrong."

"Well, plain and simple, it's politics. We're doing this to protect you. Have you been on social media at all this morning?"

"I don't do social media. There's little about it that's social. My wife keeps me abreast of stuff from family and friends, but she didn't say anything this morning. Maybe she's not had time for it either."

The captain pulled out his phone and called up a video. He handed it to Ryan. "This has been circulating on social media and now the mainstream media is picking up on it. Hit play."

Ryan did so and watched a video of the events from the previous evening. He suspected a dozen or more such recordings could be found with little effort. His eyes widened as the video panned from the man running with the gas can and breaking through the police line back to him with gun in hand. He had just regained control of his gun and turned his attention to the arsonist. You could make out the cry of "Gasoline" in the background and then the sound of a gunshot. Ryan flinches in the video, but it appears as if it's recoil from shooting his gun. The scene then pans back to the arsonist as he slumps to the ground from being shot.

Ryan took a deep breath and closed his eyes. The video gave the appearance that Ryan had shot his weapon and taken down the man with the gas can.

"This makes it look like I shot the guy, but that's not what happened. We all know that."

"We do. But the mayor insists on running the damage control since word is starting to circulate that the bureau is covering things up and protecting its own."

Ryan was confused. "But you just said you're putting me on leave to protect me."

Lopez nodded. "We're making it look like it's being formally investigated, which, of course, it is anyway."

"And *I'm the scapegoat?*" Ryan did not like how this appeared. Not at all. "Captain, this video makes me look like the shooter when my gun was never fired. And anybody and everybody who watches TV knows an officer in a police shooting is placed on admin leave. This makes it look like you're treating me as the shooter. All due respect, but this looks to me like you're throwing me under the bus."

The captain vehemently shook his head. "No, no, not at all. You shouldn't look at it that way. Today's your normally scheduled day off, and the chief wants to bring you back on your shift tomorrow, like everything's normal. But the mayor asked the State Police to investigate. He's nervous about how this video looks, and the way it's being presented in the media. Today's Wednesday, and the state investigators can't start until Friday, so the chief's only recourse is to put you on admin leave for at least tomorrow and Friday . . . until the state folks can announce that you're cleared and that your gun was never fired. That's why I need your weapon, so they can test it and confirm that."

Ryan sighed. He did not like this turn of events. Not one

iota. But what could he do?

"Let me get the gun." He left the captain in the den and headed to their bedroom, where he retrieved his handgun from its safe. He removed the clip, double-checked the chamber, and returned to the den. "Here's the gun and the clip. Chamber is empty."

Lopez held out an open evidence bag, and Ryan dropped both items into it. The captain closed and sealed the bag.

"Look, you should be back on duty on Saturday. Think of the bright side. Consider this paid vacation that's not counted against you, and you get to miss three days of crowd control."

"Two days. Today's my day off, remember?"

"Three days. You were about to get called in for this evening when this came up. See, there *is* a silver lining." The man grinned.

"If you *say* so, captain." The three unusual phone calls came to mind. "Tell me something, captain. Who has access to our private phone numbers?"

The captain raised an eyebrow. "Why?"

"In the past 18 hours we've had three phone calls here at home that sure seem suspiciously like someone's phishing to find my number."

Just then the phone rang again. Ryan started to get up, but the ringing stopped. A moment later, Sarah popped her head around the corner.

"Another one. I used the bar on Division like you did."

Captain Lopez raised both eyebrows this time. "I'll personally check into that. These numbers are supposed to be confidential."

Ryan nodded and ushered his superior to the front door,

and they said their goodbyes. As he turned back into the house, Sarah was right there. She looked worried. Ryan couldn't blame her. *He* was worried. Politicians always worried about *optics*, how things looked to the public. For Ryan, the optics here were not good.

SEVEN

Dillon owned about 25,000 acres of ranch land in southern Texas, a small place by Texas standards. Located in the South Texas Golden Triangle between Laredo and Del Rio, his land bordered the Rio Grande along nearly ten miles of shoreline. The newly completed section of the border fence, however, hadn't quite made it to his stretch along the river, ending about 20 miles to the southeast.

The ranch had been in his family for four generations, and he was happy to take over its operations. He'd known no other lifestyle, short of his four years at Texas A&M, followed by a four-year stint in the Marines following 9-11. At this point in his life, he could never imagine being confined to a city. Even going into Eagle Pass—population 26,250—for supplies made him claustrophobic.

The family had missed the oil riches that made multimillionaires of some ranchers in the eastern edge of the county. Years earlier, Dillon had had the foresight to diversify. Besides crops, a citrus grove, and a reasonably sized herd of Santa Cruz cattle—developed at the King Ranch in 1994 for arid south Texas, Dillon also offered deer hunting and maintained part of the property for wildlife. Two 140"-plus trophies hung on either side of the large fireplace that dominated one wall of their living room.

He walked from the nearby workshop to the house and knocked the mud off his boots before taking them off and entering their home. His wife, Roxanne, aka Roxi, stood at the counter making sandwiches. Next to her, their daughter Meghan assisted. Her husband, Jose Chacon, had become the manager of their citrus operation. Together, they lived in a home closer to the grove, which Dillon and Jose had built together.

Dillon walked up to his wife and kissed her on the cheek. He placed his hand on Meghan's shoulder and gave her a gentle squeeze.

"So, how're my two favorite ladies today?"

"Fine, Dad. Mom needed help with lunch for the men, so I came over."

Roxi nodded. "I gave Flora the day off to attend to some family matters. So, lunch won't be quite as extravagant as usual."

Dillon smiled. Flora was the ranch cook who oversaw feeding the dozen or so ranch hands every day at lunch and often for breakfast, too, depending on the season and how early they needed to start the day. Dillon knew better than to comment on Roxi's cooking, but Flora was the best hire he'd ever made, and lunch had become the meal he looked most forward to.

"I saw Rosa Rodriquez at the Catalinas Grocery this morning. Didn't you say you were at their place on Monday?

She said she didn't see you."

Dillon hated keeping his better half in the dark about some of the things he did, whether it was a clandestine afternoon off fishing or patrolling the river to assist the CBP. The former she would shake her head at while smiling. The latter she would grill him over and over about, chastising him and asking that he not get involved. That was their job, not his. The cartels and human traffickers were armed and dangerous, and she didn't like it when he took such risks. They had been fortunate so far that few illegals had used their land to enter the country and fewer still had come near the house and barns.

"I never went near the house. Victor has been having coyote problems, and I was helping with predator patrol in the south end of their land."

Both were true. He just wouldn't identify what kind of predators he'd been hunting.

"Whoa, Dad. There was some kind of huge explosion near the border not far from where you were."

Dillon nodded. "Yeah. I heard it, and both Cody and Raul told me it happened at the storage yard where all the border fence materials are sitting. They heard something about some kids taking pot shots at a fuel barrel, and one of 'em got lucky, if you want to call it that."

That, too, was true. Both ranch hands had told him that. He hadn't asked them the source of their information, and he had no need to question it when it worked in his favor.

"Well, I hope the new administration keeps building the fence," said Roxi. I'll be happy when we don't have to worry so much about the trafficking and such. I know we haven't had much trouble personally, but too many of our friends have had things stolen and property damaged." She preached to the choir.

Meghan nodded. "Not to mention keeping the drugs out. That's becoming an increasing problem at our schools." Tears began to well up in her eyes. She sniffed and reached for a tissue from the nearby box. "Sorry, it makes me think of Roberto. I miss him, or rather, who he once had been."

And that was one of the reasons Dillon had accepted the proposal from The Remnant. His nephew had been an intelligent young man and outstanding baseball player at the high school. And then someone got him hooked on cocaine, which led to heroin. Six months after his graduation, which he missed, he died from an overdose. Dillon's sister hadn't been the same since.

To be honest, Meghan wasn't the same. The two were close, like brother and sister, while growing up. As teens, they had been part of the same groups and enjoyed the same activities. She had been one of his top cheerleaders and never missed a game he played. That relationship had fallen apart as his addiction deepened. Now, she was as hardened as Dillon when it came to drug dealers and the cartels smuggling their deadly cargo into the country.

Roxi stepped over to the sink and rinsed her hands. "Okay, lunch is ready. It's still pretty cold out there to use the usual tables in the pavilion. Where do you want to feed the men?" She looked straight at him for an answer.

"I'll have 'em pull the tractors out of the garage and move the tables in there. It'll be out of the wind, and it wasn't too bad in there when I was working on my pickup. Good thing it's solar heated." He grinned.

"Yeah, you mean the sun shining on it and warming it up." Roxi nodded toward the outside. "Well, here they come. So, get 'em moving, and Meghan and I will bring out the food."

Dillon left the house, donned his boots, and walked over to instruct the men. As they moved off toward the large outbuilding, a phone vibrated in his pocket. *The* phone. It had arrived by carrier from The Remnant a few weeks earlier. He stepped into the shadows of the building and pulled it from his pocket. Out of habit, he glanced at and recognized the caller ID. Of course he would. To date, only one caller had used it.

So soon? he thought.

Adam sat at his computer station and monitored the situation on campus, out of concern both for Aric and Lynch. He had surreptitiously authorized a police drone to monitor the protest. The higher-ups would soon be asking questions about it. When they discovered that the launch direction came from someone still on holiday, that it was being used over the college campus which had its own security force, and that said campus police never requested drone backup, they would recall the device and be left to puzzle over how that authorization occurred. By then, he would have what he needed.

Now tapped into the camera for hi-def video, he closed in on those who appeared to be leading the protest and captured facial imagery. He had worked with Lynch's friend, Mike Jurgesmeyer from the St. Louis County computer forensics lab, to take their software—on the Q.T. of course—and adapt it to his own uses. Despite Mike's liberal hippie appearance, he was a patriot, and they shared common concerns about the loss of freedom and the direction of their country. Both men, separately and individually, had discovered significant election fraud after tapping into the voting machines and software in several counties in several swing states. Sadly, they couldn't reveal their findings. Their need to keep their work deep in the shadows outweighed their desire to confront the system. Besides, that same system would likely imprison them for what they discovered and how they found it.

Adam fed the images into the modified facial recognition package and waited for his system to do its thing. He felt surprised when, within minutes, his computer provided him with the first ID.

"Well, well, isn't that interesting," he spoke out loud.

The woman was identified as an assistant professor at the college by name of Meredith Fry. Her position as a professor led to her quick identification, but that wasn't what he found unusual. He wondered whether or not the college knew she had once been someone else. And that this someone else had an arrest record dating back into her teens. The earliest crimes had been the "usual" for teens—shoplifting, trespassing, one breaking and entering. And it appears that she had more than her fair share of run-ins with police. Twice she sued for use of excessive force following her arrests. Twice she lost.

No wonder she specialized in critical theory, he thought. Her experiences no doubt led her there since the whole concept of critical theory was based not on absolute truth, but on a relative truth based on personal experience, not the reality of the world. Or as Aric would put it, not based on God's truth which is absolute and affects everyone the same way, no matter what they experience. What was it that his brother had said? Yeah, the term "relative truth" was an oxymoron.

Now that his software had a name, or rather names, plural, to work with, it would keep digging, looking for more information to mine. Sure enough, another window popped up on the monitor to his left. What he read made his eyes widen.

Dillon finished lunch with the men and dispatched them to their various duties. Two of the guys started to lift one of the picnic tables to move it back to the pavilion. Dillon stopped them.

"We'll leave the tables in here until it warms up," he said. "Other than the cold temperatures, the weather forecasts look clear. So, the equipment will be fine outside."

He helped Roxi and Meghan clear the tables, and then returned to the garage. Alone, he again looked at the message on the phone.

Los Zorros Cartel moving large drug shipment your way. $multi-million. ETA Rio Grande three days. Tracking.

Three days. Then again, maybe their route will change. He could only hope. He didn't like messing with the cartels. They were vengeful against those who opposed them. Plus, they had the resources—including informers inside the CBP and Mexican police—to track down that opposition. The last thing Dillon desired was to put his family in jeopardy.

To his favor, the stretch of the river along his property had few easy access points for a shipment like that to cross.

That made it more difficult for the cartels to link him to any attack against a shipment.

He texted a reply. *Can't do that alone.*

He *had* been alone for the last task, and he was outmanned, had it come to a fight. That time his role was to be a spotter and nothing more. Their goal had been to have the CBP take down the terrorists and to highlight that operation to put pressure on the incoming administration to continue the building of the wall. After all, the smuggling of two dirty bombs into the country would be headline news. Well, *should* be headline news. While the mainstream media might have ignored it, the alternative press wouldn't, and word would have spread quickly.

The weather had necessitated a different strategy. There was no way Dillon could allow those men to succeed. He had taken a gamble that he could detonate one of the bombs, and he'd been correct. That the explosion had eradicated all evidence pointing to a gunshot having triggered it was a bonus.

But a drug shipment? That would be a whole different ballgame. The firepower would have to be more or less equally matched.

The response came quickly. *You won't be. Help will be there. Out.*

He nodded and typed *Out* in reply. An instant later, the entire conversation disappeared from his phone.

Three days. He shook his head. That would be Saturday, and Roxi wanted to drive into San Antonio for the day . . . with him. What excuse could he find to get out of that commitment? Well, he had two days to come up with a good one.

EIGHT

Saturday morning arrived sooner than Aric had anticipated. Well, it seemed to anyway. Why was it that time seemed to fly by at some times while not at others? Usually, when he *wanted* something to happen, time seemed to drag on. Was this a sign that he wasn't quite sure he wanted to start this class?

"Hey, you sure you don't want me to help?" asked Adam.

Aric shrugged. "Help with what? Everything I need is packed into the back seat and trunk of my car. It's not exactly like Granddad's days of toting bulky stereo systems, a phonograph, speakers, and maybe a TV off to college along with your clothes and books."

Adam nodded. "True. Or even Mom and Dad's days of needing a small fridge and desktop computer system."

Aric's notebook computer easily outmatched the computing power of those old systems, as well as doubled as his entertainment center . . . if he wasn't listening to *Skillet* or some other Christian group using his phone and earbuds. Plus, the dorm rooms now came with a small fridge.

"I'm going to miss your company here. D'you want me there for moral support?" Adam grinned.

Aric thought that a bit odd. True, they ate together most of the time, but that had been the extent of the "company" that Aric provided for his brother ever since Adam became consumed with whatever his new computer project was.

"If you want. Up to you. You'd have to drive separately because I won't be able to drive you back here."

Adam nodded. "Didn't expect you to. So, whenever you're ready, let me know."

Aric shrugged. "The dorms open in about half an hour and it takes an hour plus to get there. I can go anytime, but I would like to be moved in by noon."

"Then, let me set my computer to my away setting, and we can take off. I'll follow you."

Adam had no trouble admitting that he liked having his kid brother around. He enjoyed having someone to talk with at meals. Plus, he felt a certain sense of responsibility for Aric's safety. Their previous escapade to Oregon and back had put Aric in danger, and Adam took that burden upon himself. Never again.

Adam climbed into his Audi RS3 and tapped the steering wheel to the rhythm of the song on his radio as he waited for Aric to pull out. He had no idea what they might encounter today, but he wasn't about to let Aric face what *could* happen alone. His brother had become more streetwise over the past year, but he still held a naive optimism about people. He expected life to be fair, in a world where fairness was as foreign as common sense.

Reflecting upon the past year, Adam couldn't avoid thinking about Sam Renner and his death at the hands of "Buck" Buckner and Wallace Chamberlain. Justice had dealt with both of them, but Adam still felt partially responsible for his co-worker's death. He'd sworn to himself that he'd make it up to the man somehow at some point.

He heard Aric alert him with a toot of his car horn, and a moment later, their two-car caravan moved out onto the street. Adam had no trouble keeping up with his brother's lead foot.

Adam knew that the protests on campus over Lynch Cully had grown. The crowd often grew to two to three dozen, and with students returning to campus, that was bound to increase. Aric tended to speak out without understanding the ramifications of doing so. Yes, his positions were well-reasoned and intelligent, based upon fact, but those opposing him often weren't either, reasonable or intelligent. The Woke crowd saw everything through ideological lenses, and Aric would be the abuser in their eyes. To these critical theory zealots, his reasoning smacked of white supremacy. They would see his arguments as simply rhetoric designed to bolster his personal standing as a white, cis-gendered, heterosexual. They read into history their own "moral" underpinnings and rewrote that history to suit their ideology. As such, what Aric would argue as historical fact, they would discount as just more white men's history seen from white men's eyes to keep white men in their place of superiority. Even should that history have been written by a person of color.

No, Aric enjoyed debate and found a good debate to be challenging but had no real idea of what he would be facing in opponents who did not follow the "rules" of debate. Adam needed to be there today if for no other reason than to steer his brother away from trouble. If that was possible.

Aric checked his rearview mirror frequently to make sure Adam kept up. By the time they'd covered half the distance to campus, he felt assured that his brother could. At that point, Adam went speeding past him, grinning and waving, as if egging him on to a race. Aric laughed and shook his head. Nope. He'd done that once before at the taunting of his best friend in St. Louis, Dan Lewis, whose beat-up old Jeep Wrangler—with an engine and transmission that Dan had modified—could outrun many unsuspecting challengers. Aric had learned that the hard way and to top it off, had a $150 speeding ticket to explain to his folks . . . and pay for.

He kept it steady. They had plenty of time, and he'd already shown Adam on the campus map where he could park for the day as a visitor. He'd been told that campus security was pretty lax about parking on move-in weekends, but he wanted to play it safe. Plus, as someone moving in, he'd appreciate not having to compete with extraneous family members taking the close spots.

Adam's speeding by was the last he saw of him until he arrived on campus. On the main drive outside his dorm, Adam stood there looking official and directing people where to park. His brother waved him into a prime parking spot and walked around to his driver's window.

"Hey, slowpoke, I saved you the prime real estate for moving in."

Aric shook his head in disbelief at his brother's chutzpah. As Adam began to gather a load of hanging clothes from Aric's back seat, Aric noted a number of people giving Adam dirty looks. One man, whose daughter tried to drag him away approached a security officer and pointed toward Adam, clearly not happy. Aric wanted to lower his eyes and hang his head. He couldn't disown his brother, as he was busily helping Aric unload, but he wanted to look appropriately embarrassed. The officer frowned but offered only a shrug.

Together the two brothers entered the dorm and found the registration table. The young woman behind the desk smiled. Or at least, Aric thought she did. He couldn't actually see her mouth, thanks to the gray mask bearing the school's mascot, but her cheeks appeared to rise above the top of the covering.

"Good morning. I'm Ashleigh, one of the upper-class RAs, resident advisers, here in the central residence hall. Welcome."

She did not extend her hand, but with the whole pandemic thing, Aric no longer expected that gesture of greeting. Even some of the guys in the young adults' group at the church he'd begun extending elbow bumps instead of shaking hands. Aric had no fear of a virus that had a 99.9% recovery rate for his age group, but he went along with the change. It was a minor thing. Besides, he and Adam had already recovered from COVID-19. Their immunity would be robust.

"Here's your own Gray Wolves mask. Umm, does your

friend have a mask? They're required in all commons areas in the dorms and inside all other campus buildings."

Adam shook his head. "Already had COVID. We both have. We're immune. Plus, masks don't offer any protection, particularly cloth masks like those. The science is clear on that." He pointed to the Gray Wolves mask in her hand.

Aric closed his eyes for a moment. While he agreed with his brother and understood that science backed their position, he didn't want to create a scene. The mask issue, as a student, wasn't a sword he wanted to fall upon.

He noticed Ashleigh's eyes narrow, but she seemed to rebound in a flash.

"That might be, sir, but the college's policy requires masks. If you don't wish to wear one, you'll need to go back outside."

Aric half expected his brother to simply walk away and leave the building. Instead, Adam moved closer to the table, and the woman stepped back in alarm. He laid the clothing in his arms on the table, reached into his pocket, pulled out a mask, and put it on. He then turned toward Aric to show his compliance.

Aric tried hard not to laugh. In bold white print across the black mask were the words "Masks Don't Work!" The young woman was not amused.

"Your name, please?" The words were curt.

"Aric, with an 'A', Afton."

"Ah, first one in the stack," she replied as she pulled the large white envelope from the pile in front of her. "Your room number, 412, is there on the front. Curtis Ehrlich will be your RA . . ." She said that with a sense of relief in her voice. ". . . and your student ID is inside, along with other orientation material. Guard your ID at all costs. The ID doubles as your room's key card as well as your meal ticket for the cafeterias. You are expected to take your meals in the cafeteria here, in this residence hall, but the ID covers all of the college's food services, so the occasional meal with friends in other dorms is not a problem. That said, I think you'll find *our* cafeteria the best on campus anyway. That's why I asked to be a RA here." The tops of her cheeks rose above the top of her mask again.

She pointed to her left. "The elevators are over there."

"Thanks. See you around, I guess."

She offered no response.

Aric and Adam walked to the elevators and were blessed with one opening upon their approach. Now, if only they weren't slowed down by the lifts, Aric estimated his car would be unloaded within fifteen minutes.

As they approached room 412, Aric saw that the door was propped open. He stepped into it to see a fellow his age sitting on one of the two beds. No mask.

"Hey, you must be Aric, with an 'A.' They told me downstairs who my new roomie would be. I'm Tom, Tom Wise." He reached out his hand. "And don't worry about masks around me. Already had the bug. Plus, my dad's a doctor, and he says they don't stop viruses." At that point, Adam stepped into view. Tom grinned. "Dude, where'd you get that mask? I need one of those. We should start a movement here on campus."

Aric knew already that he was going to get along just fine with his roommate. He said a silent prayer of thanks. God had his back.

Ashleigh's gaze followed Aric Afton and his friend to the elevators. Both exuded an air of confidence that she found appealing. Yet, she decided they would not appreciate her lifestyle any more than her parents accepted it. She had a way of gauging people in that regard. To date, she had not been surprised by discovering she'd been wrong.

The friend looked to be older, but there was a strong resemblance between the two, so she decided the wise guy must be an older brother. If that were true, then he likely wouldn't be around much. That was good. He irritated her.

The younger one, Aric, the student, would bear watching. Her antennae went up about him. Was he going to be trouble? Probably.

She checked the time on her phone. The protest against Lynch Cully had already resumed for the day. They had determined that a strong turnout over the move-in weekend would be crucial to their cause by getting not only more students involved but parents as well.

"Hey, Ashleigh, you going to the protest?" She turned to see her like-minded friend Lateesha heading toward the front doors.

Ashleigh shook her head. "Can't. Still have 25 students to sign in. Maybe, if they show up soon, I can join everyone later."

"Sorry you can't come. We were at 40-something people when I left to get this from my room." She held up a megaphone. "Gonna need it soon."

Ashleigh was familiar with that megaphone. She had marched with Lateesha and her Black Lives Matter friends in protest of the Jacob Blake shooting the previous August. She had, however, left that group when several of the men started burning things. Such violence was the antithesis of what she believed, no matter how badly someone was wronged, herself included. Her gut had told her the night would not end well for some. She didn't know how she knew that, but time had proven her right.

She sat down behind the table. While she hoped the remaining residents would all arrive shortly, she knew better. A few might yet trickle in, but the odds were in favor of most of them arriving the next day. *Bummer*, she thought. She'd love to be at that protest.

NINE

"Just a few days. You'll be cleared by Friday," Lopez had said. Ryan woke up Saturday morning having heard absolutely nothing from his superiors or the State Police. They were throwing him under the bus. Of that he felt confident. He finished dressing, left their room, and joined his family in the kitchen. Sarah was making pancakes, and the boys sat at the table, forks in hand and drooling.

"Hi, Dad," they said in unison.

Ryan walked up to Sarah and gave her a quick kiss on the cheek. He turned to their sons.

"Didn't you guys just have pancakes the other day? We went to Cadillac Café two days ago."

Their home in the Irvington neighborhood, east of the Willamette River, was older but spacious, and the area was perfect for them. Ryan had quick access to Interstates 5 and 84, as well as downtown. All of the shopping opportunities they needed were close by. Among a slew of nice eateries, the Cadillac Café was their favorite breakfast joint.

"And as I recall, you didn't finish your pancakes there."

"Yes, we did," protested Gabriel.

"Yesterday morning," added Michael. "We're going for three days in a row. It'll be a new record."

"And her pancakes are way better, anyway," said Gabriel in a serious tone.

Ryan laughed and glanced at Sarah. She shrugged her shoulder.

"I had just enough eggs to make my homemade batter, and we're out of their cereal. I need to go to the grocery today."

"Ugh," replies Ryan. The stores were so much busier on weekends. He did his best to avoid them on Saturdays, which had been easy up to then, thanks to his crazy work schedule. "Did I hear the phone ring again? Who was it?"

His wife nodded. "Same thing. The guy kept asking who I was, and I kept asking who was he looking for, without giving my name. He asked that three, maybe four times."

"Four times, Mom," said Michael. "I heard you ask him that four times."

Both parents looked at their young eavesdropper. Ryan was reminded that they needed to guard their conversations. While the walls might not have ears, both boys did, and he was convinced they had super hearing . . . until it came time for chores.

No sooner had Ryan sat down, a loud crash sounded from the front of the house as the front door shattered.

"Police! Hands up where we can see them!"

Six armed members of the SERT—Special Emergency Reaction Team—flooded into the house. Ryan was so shocked, he sat there unable to move. The terror in his sons' eyes spoke more than he wished to acknowledge. Tears welled up in

Sarah's eyes as she tried to control her breathing. Two of the armed officers kept the family seated at gunpoint while the others cleared the house.

"Hands up!" one of them yelled.

All four complied. With the house cleared, the team sergeant entered the kitchen, took one look at Ryan and dropped his jaw.

"Krueger? What the . . ." He looked at the man to his right. "Do we have the correct address?" The man nodded. "Guns down guys. This is Ryan Krueger, one of our own, and he's clearly not holding his family hostage."

Ryan stood and hugged both boys for reassurance. He put his hand on Sarah's shoulder. She was still shaking.

"Swanson, did what I think just happened, happen?"

Sergeant Jim Swanson nodded. "Yeah, I think so. You just got swatted. Man, I'm sorry. We got a call about a man with a gun holding his family hostage and threatening to kill them all."

Anger rose within Ryan, and he struggled not to take it out on his fellow officers. They had followed their training, which is what Ryan would hope he'd do under similar circumstances.

"Hey, the bureau will replace the door. I . . . I, well, I don't know how I can make it up to you all."

"You can find out who did this. That's what you can do." He took Swanson aside. "If my boys end with nightmares because of this—"

The man held up his hands in front of his chest. "Man, what can I say? We're sorry. I feel awful."

Ryan took a deep breath and counted to ten, still

struggling not to take out his anger on these officers.

"Hey, I'll personally swing by with some plywood and help you secure the door, and make sure someone gets out here ASAP to replace it."

Ryan nodded. "Thanks. I've got enough on my plate right now."

After further apologies, the SERT left the house, and Ryan did his best to close the front door. He returned to the kitchen to see four plates full of uneaten pancakes. That in itself said something about the boys' state of mind.

"I'll give Lopez a call after we eat." He encouraged the boys to sit back at the table and reheated their breakfasts in the microwave. They sat there, unmoving, as the food again went cold. Ryan knelt down and opened his arms to them. Both rushed to him, and the pent-up flood of tears began as he embraced them together.

TEN

Aric tested the mattress. It would do. He had Adam hang what clothes he had on hangers in the small closet on his side of the room. He had a chest of drawers to call his own, and he filled it with little room to spare. The shelves over the desk would be the only problem he'd have to correct. He didn't have nearly enough space for the books he'd brought.

"Wow. I started classes in September and don't have that kind of library. The RA told me this is your first time here, right?" asked Tom. Aric nodded. "Why so many books? I mean, if you've just arrived, you don't even have your textbooks for this class yet."

"Actually, it's right here." He pointed to the Criminal Justice 101 text. "And these two supplement it." He pointed to the two books to the right of the large text. "The others are criminology and other assorted books recommended to me by a friend who's a professor here. He's the reason I came here."

His roomie offered a small shrug along with a half nod.

"Speaking of whom," said Adam. "Maybe Tom here has some info on what's happening on campus."

Tom furrowed his brow. "Me? I . . . what do you mean?"

Aric nodded. "My professor friend is Doctor Cully, and someone seems to have organized a protest against him. Have you heard anything about that?"

Tom sighed. "Nothing good, that's for sure. My major is accounting . . . well, for now anyway . . . so, I'm not in the same classes or crowd. I won't be taking any of his classes, but a friend took his class last semester and really enjoyed it." He took a deep breath. "Anyway, there are people going from dorm to dorm trying to drum up interest and get people to attend their protests. Evidently, they don't like the fact that he worked for and supported President Graham. Some of 'em even think he should have left Graham stranded in the wilderness and the country would have been better off. Bunch of sore losers in my opinion. I wasn't old enough to vote for the man for the first time, but my folks loved him. And they think he got a raw deal in this last election. Personally, this last election was the first where I could vote, and I feel like my vote was stolen."

Aric understood the sentiment.

"I'm pretty sure they're out there today. I think one of the organizers is a RA here, but I might have heard wrong. And they got the BLM crowd here on campus stirred up to join 'em. You'll learn who they are soon enough, too, since their leaders live in this dorm."

Aric groaned inwardly. He'd had no illusions about what kind of people he'd find in the dorm. He kept telling himself that he needed to look at the dorm as a mission field. Yet, now that he was here, he began to realize that he might need a much bigger tractor for plowing.

The timer on Adam's phone sounded its alarm. "C'mon, we need to move your car."

Aric nodded. "I'll be back in a while," he said to his roommate. He made sure he had his ID, and together, he and Adam moved the car to his designated lot. Climbing out of the vehicle, he could hear the chants of the protest outside the admin building. Somebody had a bullhorn to lead them on.

"Let's go see what's happening," said Aric.

"You sure you want to do that?"

Aric thought about that for a second. No, maybe he didn't *want* to, but he felt he had to. They walked to the same location where Aric had encountered the protesters five days earlier, just outside the main admin building. This time, instead of maybe a dozen people, there was a group numbering at least 50 by Aric's initial reckoning. The size of the crowd stunned him. Were all of these people really against Lynch, or were many just bandwagoning, going along with the organizers "for fun?"

"This campus has no room for the likes of Lynch Cully!" blared the shrill voice coming through the bullhorn.

"Fire him!" echoed the crowd.

"We have no place for racists here!"

"Fire him!"

"We have no place for white supremacists!"

"Fire him!"

"We have no place for homophobic bigots!"

"Fire him!"

Two young men, holding hands, held up a large poster showing Lynch being hung in effigy. When the crowd cheered, the two kissed and smiled back at the group.

Aric had had enough. "Hey! You're exercising *your* right to free speech, what about Dr. Cully's rights? How many of you have even talked with him! How can you call him a racist, or white supremacist, or bigot if you've never discussed it with him?"

Several students nearby began to boo. One heavily tattooed young man approached Aric menacingly, but Aric stood his ground and Adam joined him. Tattoo-man backed off.

"Go home, racist! We don't need you here either!" came the bullhorn.

Adam nudged Aric. "You're not going to win. These people have no interest in honest debate. They have no interest in anyone's rights unless it's about *their* rights." Adam gently tugged on Aric's arm to pull him away.

"But they're wrong. Lynch isn't any of those things, and they can't support their arguments through anything he's ever said or written."

"You and I know that, but do they care? No. Brother, you can't win. When it comes to intersectionality, which is what they clearly believe in, *you* are in the wrong. You're white, heterosexual, cis-gendered, and privileged. You're the abuser, and they're the victims."

Aric wanted to respond in a less-than-Christian way, but that inner voice he was learning to understand and follow urged him off. He turned toward Adam.

"C'mon. Before they ID and tag you. You heard Tom. A number of these people live in your dorm. Do you want life to be a living hell?" he whispered.

He was right. Aric was glad he'd put his hood up against

the wind. It also partially shielded his face and identity. He turned to leave with his brother, but Adam had moved away toward a woman Aric just now noticed. She was not a student, maybe a faculty member, and Aric now saw that she paid close attention to him. He pulled his hood closer to his face and left the area. Adam would catch up.

Adam spotted Meredith Fry at the front of the protest, standing next to the black woman with the bullhorn. Periodically, a student would approach her, say something, and walk away. One was a young man who openly flaunted his homosexuality. After talking with her, he returned to his boyfriend, and together, they lifted a placard. It appeared to Adam that she called the shots.

As soon as Aric spoke out, the woman began searching for the source of the voice. Thanks to the jerk with more ink than clear skin, she zoomed in on Aric. Adam spoke to his kid brother. They needed to clear the scene pronto.

However, he saw that she now walked their way and would intercept them quickly. He had to intervene, for Aric's sake. Yet, doing so would require him to expose himself in a way he preferred not to do. He liked working behind the scenes, not on a public stage. He caught up to the woman about 15 feet away from where they'd been standing.

"Dr. Fry, or should I call you Isabella? Maybe you prefer Fatima."

The woman stopped in her tracks, and her face blanched. That partially answered one question he'd had. The college likely knew nothing of her past.

"Who . . . how . . ." she stammered.

"Neither of those questions matter. Just understand I have the ability to end your life as you know it. Personally, I think you'd look good in prison orange, but I won't pull that trigger unless my hand is forced."

"Those records are sealed. You have no—"

"Nothing is sealed to me. Nothing. And your lefty billionaire friends can't save you. I know *why* you're here, *who* planted you here, and have a pretty good idea how you plan to go about it. That playbook is as old as the hills. Canceling Lynch Cully might not be as good an idea as you think. Maybe it's time for you to stand up for free speech and the need for diversity of ideas on college campuses, even conservative ones."

Her lips formed a snarl. "We'll find you. You won't last long." Her tone bordered on a hiss, which didn't surprise him, the snake that she was.

He looked about. Aric was halfway to the visitors' parking lot and Adam's car. No one appeared to follow him. Adam would take a less direct route to his vehicle, to make sure no one followed.

"Men more powerful than your friends have tried. They're either dead or in prison now, not by my doing but by the hands of those they failed. I suspect your benefactor doesn't like failure either."

She started to say something but stopped short.

"Have a nice day." He offered her a smile, but the gesture was not returned. He decided to mess with her a bit more. "By the way, I'll be in *all* of your electronics before the day is done. Your phone, your laptop, your college workstation, your Ring doorbell. Even your interactive refrigerator and car's computer system." Yes, she had all of these. A little paranoia would be good for her.

ELEVEN

What in the world is going on with the weather? wondered Dillon, as he broke the ice in the watering troughs closest to the house. First, light snow and now ice. In south Texas. What was God up to? In his 46 years on that ranch, he'd never seen ice on the water troughs. The nighttime temperature had dipped into the 20s.

Still, he thanked God for the ice. Reports of icy roads between their place and San Antonio had changed Roxi's mind about driving to the city for the day. He wouldn't have to renege on his promise to join her.

He moved to the main barn and climbed onto his Deere 6120M. He felt thankful that he'd ordered it with the closed cab configuration and AC for their hot summers. Today, that cab would be heated. He lined up the rear forks with a large, round bale of hay and impaled it. With it lifted into position, he transported it half a mile away to one of the lots where his cattle were now impounded. He broke the bale and spread it across the ground for the cattle to eat. While there, he broke the ice in that trough as well.

He repeated the process with a second bale and then did the same for a second paddock. He found no ice in the troughs there. The temperature had already warmed into the 40s. His gut began to grumble. Flora was back, and he looked forward to lunch, whatever it was she decided to prepare that day.

As he started to climb back into the cab, the phone dinged. He'd been wondering if the weather had fouled the plans for the drug shipment. No such luck. The message read:

> *Drug shipment on schedule to cross the river at dusk. Three ATVs. 20 men. The ford just east of Pablo De Luna. Meet at El Indio Gas Services at 1700 hours. Out.*

Dillon knew the place. The river narrowed and shoals made it possible for an ATV to cross there. If the water was low enough, even a four-wheel-drive pickup could traverse those shallows. There was easy access on the Mexico side along farm lanes through bottom lands along the Rio Grande. Once across the river, a gravel road followed the river and rose up through an arroyo to reach the top of a plateau that sat about 75 feet above the river. Trucks could meet the ATVs at the river, or the ATVs could follow the road to a point where transferring their loads would be easier. Either way, county road 263 came to within two miles of the crossing point.

He typed a reply, *Got it. Out.* As before, the messages disappeared. Again, he wondered how they did that.

He pondered the information he just received. Was it simple luck that this ford across the river wasn't in common use? Well, to his knowledge anyway. Word in town was that the cartels preferred areas with rapid access to the interstate system. Traveling along county and state roads through sparsely populated areas like Maverick County made them too noticeable. The completed sections of the border wall must be forcing those people to more remote areas like this one, he concluded.

He considered that location again. That was the Cantu spread, and their home and main buildings sat high above the river just upstream. If he recalled correctly, they had a clear view of the shoals from the house. Surely, they'd be aware of activity there, whether it be traffickers or drug mules. He knew Jose Cantu fairly well. He doubted the family would be complicit with such activities. His son, Eduardo, had been an Army Ranger. Dillon saw no way that Eduardo would allow such action on the family's land.

Raimondo Castillo Saucedo paced in his room at the Barrokas Hotel & Suites in Piedras Negras. El Espectro had placed his trust in Raimondo to find new routes for their product. Near-completion of the United States border barrier from Brownsville past Laredo had made crossing the border more cumbersome. Either the river was too deep or the land too rugged to move large quantities, and moving smaller loads was not economically feasible because of the manpower and vehicles required.

He checked the time. His men should be nearing the river.

Understanding the reluctance of many people to help the cartels, he had pretended to be a fisherman interested in new fishing spots along the river. He was amazed at how readily people offered him tips on where to fish, places to avoid, and how to deal with the U.S. Border Patrol if stopped. That was how he'd learned of the shoals not far from Pablo De Luna. With easy access right off Carretera Federal 2, the free Mexican federal highway that ran along most of the U.S. border, he wondered how they had missed it before.

His phone beeped. *En posición.* They were at the river and waiting.

Espere hasta la puesta del sol, luego muévase mientras todavía tiene luz. Sin faros, he replied. *Wait until sunset, then move across while you still have light. No headlights.*

He checked the time once more. Thirty minutes until sunset.

Dillon took no chances. He arrived at the parking lot of the gas services company 20 minutes early and parked out of sight. He took his binoculars and watched the road in both directions, as well as scanned the sky above periodically. He had no idea who would be joining him, nor how many there would be. He assumed they would have a party of at least a dozen men, all armed, if they were expected to go up against 20 men, most of whom would be armed. His side would have the element of surprise, as well as the high ground.

Yet, Dillon felt that same internal conflict he had fought at the previous intervention. He was not a murderer. To take out unarmed men simply trying to feed their families, even if that job was illegal, was something he had no taste for. Often the mules doing the actual "heavy lifting" did so under duress. Much like the human trafficking issue. Dillon could not fault those wanting a better life, but the scum who preyed upon such people? He was being asked to rationalize the taking of their lives, that to take out armed men intent on harm was patriotic and acceptable. Was it? Were they disposable?

Sometimes he felt that they were. He knew that wasn't a Christian way of thinking, but that's how he felt . . . at times. He found himself having to acknowledge that they, too, were humans. Afghanistan *had* changed him, whether or not he would admit it.

The rendezvous time rolled around, and two other cars arrived at the lot. Two. Not the platoon he anticipated. He gave it another five minutes and watched the road and sky. No sign of anyone following the two. Should he wait for more?

He decided no. More men or not, they needed to coordinate and plan their mission and get into position. He walked into the lot from behind. One man climbed out of each of the cars. Dillon shook his head. Three against 20.

As he neared the men, he recognized one as Eduardo. That was encouraging. Someone else highly trained in the art of war. The two shook hands but did not speak the other's name. The third man was someone Dillon had seen in town while getting supplies, but he'd never met the guy. They shook hands as well.

In that instant, all three men's phones beeped. Dillon read the message: *Good, all of you are here. The targets are already assembled on the other side. I know you're all armed, but I know you need help. Check the crate on the back side of the building. 179924*

As if reading each other's thoughts, all three men looked up and then around. Dillon saw it first and pointed at the security camera on the corner of the building. He showed his message to the others. They, in turn, shared theirs. They were identical.

Eduardo led the way to the back of the building where a rough, but solidly constructed, wooden crate sat against the cement block wall. The lock on the clasp required a numerical key.

"Well, let's open this up and see what kind of gifts we've been given," said the third man. "My name's Rick, by the way."

"Dillon."

"Eduardo."

Dillon entered the numbers from the text, and the lock opened. After he flipped up the clasp, Eduardo did the honors of opening the crate. From under the brown, shredded packing material, he pulled up an unusual-looking weapon. Below that were rounds for the weapon. Deeper into the box, Eduardo pulled out a long rifle that made Dillon cringe. Memories from Afghanistan.

"Whooee. Christmas has come again," said Eduardo.

"What are these?" asked Rick.

Dillon knew that weapon all too well. "This is a M110C SASS or semi-automatic sniper system complete with quick detach sound suppressor. It fires 7.62 NATO rounds and has long-range capabilities like few others. With this baby, one guy could probably take out the entire cartel crew by himself."

Eduardo smiled, too. "So, you clearly know this weapon."

"I do. This was my baby in Iraq and Kuwait. She never left my side." That was true, but he also realized that self-preservation demanded it as much as anything else.

Rick pointed to the first rifle. "And that?"

Eduardo answered this time. "And that was my favorite back when I was a Ranger. It's a XM25 CDTE. That stands for counter defilade target engagement. It fires 25-millimeter air burst grenades. It has a laser rangefinder that automatically communicates the range to each round so that it detonates at the right distance. It was quite a bit heavier to tote around, but it ended skirmishes so quickly I never gave that a second thought. We called it 'The Punisher.'"

"I read about those, but they came out after I left the Marines," said Dillon.

"Yeah, they were introduced in 2010 but had some misfire issues and were taken out of the field in 2013. The developer improved the weapon and fixed the issues, but the senate armed services committee had soured on its use and pulled the plug on it in 2018. This puppy costs about $35,000 and each round is handmade to the tune of a $1,000. Looks like we have two options." He held up one grenade. "This one is thermobaric. We can destroy the drugs with it." He lifted a second that displayed a different color code. "This one is a high explosive air-burst grenade. We can take out the smugglers with it."

Dillon shook his head. "Let's take out the drugs as a priority."

"I'm good with that," said Rick. "If they put up a fight, then we target the men."

Dillon nodded as Eduardo chuckled. "Put up a fight? They won't know what hit 'em or where it's coming from. Both of these puppies can target them from up to half a mile away."

All three men's phones beeped again. *Like my presents? Take care of them when you're done. But now, you better get positioned.*

"Guess I'm the rear guard and get-away driver," said Rick. They piled into his Jeep and headed toward the target. With the new weaponry, Dillon and Eduardo settled on a location to set up. Upon getting there, they adjusted their plan a bit to the east and settled in.

Sure enough. Just as the sun settled below the horizon, two SUVs and three panel trucks appeared near the river on the Mexican side. Men poured out of the vehicles and quickly unloaded fully packed ATVs from the trucks. At the same time, three panel trucks lumbered down the gravel road on the American side. At a wide spot in the road, they each turned around and spaced themselves along the road. Men opened the rear doors and lowered ramps for the ATVs.

Dillon whispered, even though he doubted the sound could carry that far. "I'll take the trucks on this side, going for the fuel tanks on the side."

Eduardo nodded. "I'll take out the drug loads on the ATVs." He loaded a thermobaric grenade into the XM25. "Ready. Three . . . two . . . one. Go."

With each weapon's sound suppressor only a fast "fffftttt" could be heard. A second later, the lead truck on the American side exploded and blocked the road. A blink later, the grenade destroyed the load on the last ATV, blocking an escape back to Mexico by the other two whose drivers now dove into the water. In less than a minute all six targets were destroyed. Four men on the U.S. side began firing blindly up the hillsides around them, but Dillon and Eduardo were well out of range.

Dillon chose not to take their lives and grabbed his gear, including his spent shells, and scurried away from the edge of the hill. He tapped Eduardo on the shoulder to follow but noticed that the young man had loaded a HEAP grenade into the XM25.

"Don't. A bunch of dead bodies with distinctive grenade shrapnel inside will let the authorities know what killed them. We don't need a bunch of feds combing the area looking for military hardware."

It was an excuse he knew the others would accept. In reality, though, he didn't want to face having a role in killing those men.

Eduardo lowered the XM25 as he nodded. Together they hurried back to the Jeep where Rick kept watch. Once inside and heading back to the other vehicles, all three phones beeped.

Well done. Out.

Each man replied, *Out,* and the message threads disappeared.

When Raimondo's phone rang, he expected the message to signal his men's success in delivering the drugs to the other side of the river. What he heard instead made his knees weak and his heart race.

"*Fuimos atacados, jefe.*"

Rito was his best man—competent, faithful, reliable, and strong, physically and emotionally. Yet, now, his voice sounded panicky. Raimondo could hear the fear.

"*¿Atacado?*" he replied. Who would attack them?

He continued in Spanish, asking, "What happened, Rito?"

"Everyone was in place and the trucks on the other side

were ready to load the ATVs. As soon as all three ATVs were in the water, one of the trucks exploded, and then fire from hell exploded over the last ATV. It destroyed the load and ATV and badly burned Ricardo and Jaime. The others dove into the water to save themselves. In under a minute all three loads, the ATVs, and the receiving trucks were gone." There was a slight pause. "*Fuego del infierno*," he muttered again. "*Madre de Dios.*"

Raimondo sat on the edge of the bed, baffled. A good sniper with a rifle could take out the trucks with a well-placed aim on the fuel tanks, but what could destroy their loaded ATVs like that? He'd never heard of such a thing being in the U.S. Border Patrol's arsenal. If truth be told, he'd never heard of such a weapon, period.

However, figuring out what weapon was used would have to wait. Or should he focus on that? He would have to report back to El Espectro. How would he explain their loss? He couldn't simply blame it on some unknown weapon. Then, a more important question entered his mind. How would anyone else have known about the shipment? Did they have a traitor in their midst?

Yes, that would be how he framed the problem. That was a critical question because he needed to identify who was responsible for their loss of a $15 million shipment or else, he, personally, would be held accountable . . . with his life.

TWELVE

"Good morning, class. For those of you who don't already know me, I'm Dr. Ron Carter, head of the sociology department as well as the criminal justice program. Welcome to what everyone likes to call Criminology 101. This is the first time we've offered this course over the short winter term, so prepare to hunker down because we'll be covering a lot of material this month."

Aric's eyes began to glaze over as the man began a litany of the topics he hoped to cover. Monday hadn't come soon enough. Aric had reflected more than once over the weekend on how wild and crazy his best friend back home could get. More than once, Dan had gotten them both into trouble. Not with the law, but at school and with their parents. His new roommate, Tom, made Dan look like an introverted, self-reflective monk in the cloisters of a monastery. Tom reassured him that he would buckle down and get serious once class actually started, but at one a.m. that morning, the prospect of such seemed unlikely.

He yawned, wide and audibly. The professor looked his

way.

"Are we keeping you up, young man?"

Aric shook his head, embarrassed and more awake after being called out. "Sorry, Dr. Carter, I'm adjusting to a new roommate who thinks sleep is unnecessary."

The man nodded as the rest of the class chuckled.

"So again, by the end of this month, I expect you to understand the three major components of the criminal justice system, as well as the concepts of policing, corrections, courts, the juvenile system, probation and parole, and victimology."

Another student raised her hand. "Will we be discussing local issues like the Jacob Blake shooting by the police?"

The academician waggled his head a bit. "Perhaps. Time allowing. Cases like that are topics for a more advanced class. We'll be covering the basics here."

"What about the pros and cons of capital punishment?" asked another.

The professor nodded. "Yes, we will cover why capital punishment has no place in our society."

"It goes against the Bible in my opinion," replied the student, smiling.

"Actually, there is nothing in the Bible that rules out capital punishment," answered Aric. "It clearly—"

Dr. Carter interrupted. "We will have no talk of the Bible in this class. The Bible is full of contradictions. For example, it contradicts itself when it says 'eye for an eye' and 'tooth for a tooth' in one place and then says to 'turn the other cheek' someplace else."

"Sir, that's not true. The Bible is not contradictory here."

The professor raised his brow and replied, "Oh?"

Aric did not miss the menacing look aimed his way, but he would stand his ground.

"To think that, shows a lack of understanding of the Bible." He heard groans from other students and realized that maybe he had just accused the professor of not understanding. "Sir, no disrespect intended. I'm sure you're familiar with the term *lex talionis.*"

"I am. Please explain for the class." The smirk on his face spoke to his hope that Aric would embarrass himself in front of the class.

"Well, um, *lex talionis* is the principle of making a punishment fit the crime. The Bible says it's wrong to, say, put someone to death for simply stealing a loaf of bread, or for even insulting the king. Thirty-five hundred years ago this was incorporated into Hebrew civil law with the concept of an eye for an eye. In the 17th century, the Puritan influence in England incorporated it into English common law, which we inherited. Turning the other cheek, however, talks of not seeking revenge or retaliation. The two have nothing to do with each other, apply to completely different circumstances, and don't form a contradiction."

Dr. Carter cocked his head in what Aric hoped was at least half approval.

"Sir, I can give a contemporary example—not giving a student a bad grade for simply disagreeing with the professor." With that, Aric blushed, and the class laughed.

The laughter accomplished exactly what Aric had hoped for. It defused the tension that appeared to be developing between him and Dr. Carter. And on his first day at that. Maybe

Adam was right about needing to think more before opening his mouth.

Aric could feel the professor assessing him but felt the tension between them lessen. Or perhaps the tension was all in his head, and Dr. Carter was more reasonable and open to debate than Aric was giving him credit for.

"So, what's the Bible say about capital punishment?" asked the student who first mentioned the Bible.

Unsure about answering, Aric looked to Dr. Carter for direction.

"We'll discuss capital punishment in more depth, but if our *expert* here can keep it brief, he can answer." There was a slight air of disdain in the word 'expert.'

Aric felt the spotlight once again. "Um, yes, sir. Well, I started to say a moment ago that the Bible clearly gives the state the power over life in certain circumstances. Murder, for example. The Ten Commandments outlaw murder, not simply killing. Murder is killing someone with intent. Manslaughter is an accidental killing. The Bible says that a person convicted of murder should be put to death. But for someone guilty of manslaughter, God set up a system of refuge cities where that person could flee and be kept safe from family members intent on seeking revenge."

Dr. Carter chuckled. "See, another contradiction. The Bible teaches setting up refuge cities to protect someone from revenge while also teaching not to seek revenge."

"Not at all, Dr. Carter. That shows an understanding of human nature. People don't always do as they're taught. The two are also 1,500 years apart. The refuge cities were set up under Moses and Joshua, while it was Jesus who taught us to turn the other cheek."

"Well, good thing we have progressed beyond the point of needing the Bible. It's barbaric to think we still need to execute people when we have excellent rehabilitation programs instead. But, as I said, we'll discuss this at another time. Turn to the second chapter of the text."

Aric decided he'd better quit at that point. He was pushing his luck, not that he believed in luck. However, the professor was wrong. Mankind hadn't progressed beyond needing the Bible. It needed its guidance more now than ever. Only the hubris of humanism could lead one to conclude that the Bible no longer applied to life, but Aric thought back to his experience at the protest two days earlier and his brother's warning. If he wasn't careful, he would become known as a 'Bible thumper,' an abuser, and never right about anything he'd say.

Aric turned to the second chapter and looked up. Dr. Carter stood right in front of him.

"Young man, see me after class."

THIRTEEN

Ashleigh finished her class, stopped by her dorm room to drop off her books, and headed straight to the sociology department where Dr. Fry's office was located. She had heard about someone challenging the protesters and wanted to hear the straight scoop directly from her. She knocked on the office door. There was no answer, so she knocked a bit louder a second time, just to make sure she'd been heard. Still no answer.

She felt confident that Dr. Fry held open office hours at this time and decided to check with the department secretary to confirm that. The department's office door was open, so she knocked on the door frame and leaned inside.

"Hi. I thought Dr. Fry had open hours right now. Do you know if she's available?"

The woman looked up and quickly donned her mask. "Uh, she's around. If you're not in a hurry, maybe just stick around for a few minutes. I'm sure she'll be back shortly."

Ashleigh nodded and said, "Okay, thanks. I'll hang out by her office for a few minutes."

Sure enough. No sooner had she turned back toward the professor's office than she saw the woman exiting the women's lavatory. She hurried toward the office.

"Hi, Dr. Fry. Do you have a few minutes? I hoped to hear about the protest on Saturday. I heard that someone spoke out to defend Cully."

Dr. Fry settled into her chair behind the desk and motioned to Ashleigh to close the door and have a seat. "Well, he didn't so much defend Cully but spoke up for Cully's right to free speech, just as we are exercising our right to free speech when we protest. There is a fine line there."

Ashleigh tried not to show how stunned she felt at the professor's conciliatory tone. Was she agreeing?

"Are you saying we need to give him the right to speak his mind, to speak up against us?"

Dr. Fry shrugged. "That's just it. He hasn't spoken up *against* us per se. If anything, he's defended *our* right to free speech and to protest, while we try to deny him his right."

Ashleigh tried to wrap her mind around this change in her mentor. "Who are you and what have you done with the real Dr. Fry? I can't believe what I'm hearing. Just a few days ago, you were gung-ho about getting rid of the guy. We don't need someone like him on campus. A lot of us don't feel safe with him here."

Dr. Fry sighed. "It's just, well, I'm not sure we should be going about this the way we are. It could backfire on us."

Ashleigh's eyes widened. "What's happened to you?

The professor turned away and peered out the window overlooking the chapel. Her right hand moved up to her face.

Has she just wiped away tears? wondered Ashleigh.

Something *had* happened.

She decided to move into a more familiar mode. "Meredith, is there something I can do?" she asked softly. "Can I help you somehow?"

The professor shook her head. After a moment, she turned back toward Ashleigh.

"No. There's nothing you can do. I . . . I . . . no, nothing."

Ashleigh decided she would need to take over the protests. Something had clearly happened to Dr. Fry. Ashleigh knew some of the woman's past. Had someone gotten to her? If so, what kind of leverage did they have?

"Okay. I'll take over." She paused. "With your blessing that is."

The woman nodded.

"Do you know who it was who spoke out? Is he a student here?"

Dr. Fry shook her head. "I don't know. He's not someone I've seen before on campus."

Ashleigh nodded. That likely meant he was new to campus, or not a student. The latter was a real probability since it had been a move-in weekend. She became aware of her heart rate accelerating. She needed to remain focused.

"There were videos recorded. Would you recognize him in a video?"

The woman hesitated and then shook her head. "I've looked at four videos already. No one else has volunteered one. You can barely hear his voice much less see him at the back of the crowd."

Ashleigh did not doubt that. She had watched one friend's recording, and her video didn't catch the event at all, except for those in the crowd screaming their rebuttals at the guy. Her friend had, however, mentioned that another older guy had stopped the counter-protester and seemed to send him away. No one followed as far as her friend knew.

"I'll keep asking around for recordings. With as many people as were there and everyone having a cell phone, someone is bound to have caught him on video."

She spoke confidently, but her words were more bluster than anything else. With a flash of panic, Ashleigh felt as if her world now collapsed around her. Even if she discovered the person's identity, she had no authority to deal with the guy. And if he was a student, from what Dr. Fry and her friend had said, he hadn't said anything that could be used to force him into the college's sensitivity classes. Just knowing there were others on campus like Lynch Cully swept away her sense of safety there.

Sure, people on social media made fun of students like her, calling them snowflakes, but she had only recently begun to feel safe in her new role. The campus had become her refuge from a world that stared and made her uncomfortable. She wanted to fit in, to find her place in a fair society, but the real world didn't want to make room for her kind. One of her old friends had called her a freak. That was how the world viewed her.

Her father's words rushed back to her. "God didn't create you like this. He doesn't make mistakes, but *we* do all the time. You're making a big one." Those were his last words to her before she left their house. She hadn't made contact with them since, despite their efforts to remain to keep communication lines open. Those were the words in her mom's most recent card. Not that they accepted her lifestyle or that they could live with her choices. Yes, they said they loved her, but the words rang hollow. They loved their image of her, not the reality of who she was.

"I, uh, well, I gotta go. Bye, Dr. Fry."

Before the professor could respond, Ashleigh bolted from the room. The walls were closing in on her. Something had sucked the oxygen out of the room. She had to leave. As she ran down the hall, she heard her mentor calling.

"Ashleigh, come back. I can help. You're having another panic attack. Come back. I can help."

No, this was more than her hyperventilating or the feeling that her heart was about to jump out of her chest. Both were present, but so was something else. An inner voice taunted her. *Your dad is right. Life will never be fair. Maybe you'd be better off ending it all now.*

Aric finished placing his text and tablet into his backpack and looked up, preparing to stand. Dr. Carter stood right in front of him in the same spot where he'd previously asked Aric to see him after class. And he wasn't smiling.

"I remember now where I'd seen you before. You were standing outside Dr. Cully's office last week when I came out from meeting with him. What's your name?"

"Um, yes, sir. I'm Aric, with an 'A.' Aric Afton. Lynch, I mean Dr. Cully, is the one who got me interested in criminology and forensics. This is my first class here, and I'm glad you decided to offer it for the short winter term."

Aric felt uneasy under the man's glare.

"Well, Aric, you were quite articulate in here, but we won't be including the Bible in any of our future discussions. It no longer has a role in our justice system."

Aric felt that same boldness he'd felt earlier in class arise within him.

"Dr. Carter, all due respect, but how can you say that? Without the Bible, we wouldn't have a justice system. All of our western common law comes from the Good Book. Prohibitions against murder, stealing, adultery, and more come from the Bible. All of the most basic laws for dealing with each other come from it."

The professor shook his head. "They come from a variety of ancient codes. Hammurabi. The Medes and Persians. Ancient Greece. Rome."

Aric once again disagreed. "Sir, I'm no expert in those ancient legal codes, but I do know that Moses preceded all of them. I also know that our western standard of law came into being through men like Oliver Cromwell who looked to the Bible as the source of just law. They forced the king of England into accepting what we now consider common law."

Aric wanted to stand and look the man in the eye. He understood the "power play" being displayed by the professor standing over him, keeping him seated in a subservient position. He moved to stand up, but the professor still blocked him.

"Sir, I'd like to stand up, please."

Dr. Carter took a step back and allowed him to rise.

"Aric, we won't be using the Bible in this class, so please don't bring it up again."

Aric tried not to sigh in frustration.

"Doctor, I didn't bring it up this time, if you'll recall. Another student did. I simply defended the Bible and its place in our current laws."

The man took a deep breath before conceding that point. "Um, yes, true."

Aric hoped he hadn't been too forward. He had been captain of his high school debate team and loved an honest exchange of ideas. He had always looked to colleges as champions of free speech and as places where a host of differing ideas could be discussed. In less than a week, those beliefs and expectations had been dashed.

He reflected on Adam's comment about his continuing at the college if Lynch were ousted. He now realized that technically it wouldn't be Lynch's removal from the faculty that would drive him to leave, but rather the same close-minded, postmodern thinking that worked to eliminate Lynch from campus. They both were targets for the progressives' darts.

FOURTEEN

Ryan hadn't slept well. While some of his peers would be joyous at having the time off, the reason for those free days ate at him. Not only were they continuing to get probing phone calls, but he found his supposedly confidential email's inbox flooded with phishing attempts and, as of last night, death threats. He didn't want to think the worst of the bureau, but someone had outed him. Someone in the mayor's office seemed more likely.

The bus had run over him, backed up, and now gunned its engine to repeat the process.

Two more days had passed without the slightest word from the bureau or the state police investigators. At a minimum, he had expected those officers to ask him to give his account of what had happened that night. But, nada, no contact at all.

Through his friends on the force, he had learned that the state had sent two detectives to look into the event. One's name was Owens and the other's, Fitch. They had spent their time asking questions about Ryan, not about the incident.

Diamonte said he'd taken them to task about their lack of findings about the shooting and had stood up for Ryan. For that, Ryan was grateful. Joe also told him some of the questions they'd been asking about Ryan. They sounded like questions one would ask when looking for a scapegoat. That's what had kept Ryan tossing and turning throughout the night.

As he gazed through the half-drawn shades of a front window, he watched as yet one more car drove slowly past their house. Was its driver rubbernecking to look at his home? Two news vans had already been chased away by local officers. The boys were forbidden from playing in the front yard and from riding their bikes. Those restrictions had not been easy for Ryan to make, and although both boys seemed to take it in stride, Ryan knew that both were in fear of going outside without one of them accompanying them.

He backed away from the window as another news van pulled up to the nearby curb. His cell phone rang. It was Lopez.

"Captain, good morning. I hope you're calling with good news."

"Hey. I wish I was. Sorry."

Ryan sighed. That was *not* what he wanted to hear. The captain had called him two days earlier to let him know he'd been hitting brick walls trying to get resolution for Ryan. The frustration had finally taken its toll, and the man had turned in his retirement papers.

"I told you I'd get this fixed before I left, but somebody higher up had other ideas. I planned on my last day being the end of the week, but they put me on leave starting today. Somebody doesn't want me getting in their way, it appears. I'm hearing rumors from the chief's office that the mayor and governor want to play up this incident to support their desires to defund the police. They can't do that if they find the shooter and it's not a police officer. My best advice is to get the union involved. Call your rep this morning and get the lawyers in gear."

Ryan took a deep breath as anger began to rise. He'd been a loyal officer on the force, going beyond the call to fill in for others and take extra shifts to help make up for the shortfall. When others had moved on, retired, or just plain quit, he stood firm. And how was he being rewarded?

"Ryan, you don't deserve this, but then few officers involved in stuff like this ever do. I managed to send you a few things before they shut down my computer access. Check your email."

Ryan decided not to use his cell phone to do so. The bureau had issued him the phone. What was to say they couldn't monitor it at any time? Maybe with the cars driving past his home, along with everything else, he was getting paranoid. No. The news vans confirmed that he wasn't.

"I will, captain. As soon as we hang up."

"Call your rep. I think you're gonna need him."

Ryan felt his gut grumble, but it wasn't from hunger.

"I will. Thanks for keeping me in the loop."

"Least I could do. And if I hear anything more, I'll let you know."

"Thanks. Enjoy retirement."

Ryan went to his office and pulled up his email account. Lopez had sent him copies of the forensics reports that had been created so far on the incident. In the collection, the ballistics report of the slug taken from the body showed it to be consistent with a .30-06 round, a common size of ammunition for hunting rifles. It was definitely not fired from a handgun. Other forensics confirmed that the round came from above and behind the crowd which meant the terrace of the building directly across from the bureau's headquarters building.

He thought about that for a moment. That terrace offered easy access, and a shooter could emerge behind the crowd that was focused on the police building. However, that terrace was supposed to have been secured and used by the police to monitor the protest. Had that somehow fallen through? With the manpower shortage, Ryan could see where that task might have been neglected. If so, the police bureau, not him, *did* have some culpability in the incident because it provided the perfect perch for a shooter. The department should have secured that location no matter the cost.

However, a new thought entered Ryan's mind. Had he been set up? The guy hassling him and going for the gun. His position upon regaining control of his weapon. The angle of the video that Lopez had shown him earlier. Why hadn't that video been focused on the gasoline bomber? Everyone else's attention was sure centered on that guy. What if the "defund the police" folks had staged the whole thing? What was the taking of one man's life if it could further the cause?

No. Ryan shook off those thoughts. The old adage floated through his consciousness—just because you're paranoid doesn't mean someone *isn't* out to get you. Why him? Had he simply been in the wrong place at the wrong time?

From his desk, he retrieved a business card. Sergeant Rick Holleran, Representative, Portland Police Association. Ryan dialed the number on the card.

"You've reached Rick Holleran. Leave me a message."

"Rick, it's Ryan Krueger. You probably already know why I'm calling. Looks like I'm going to need legal assistance to clear my name for something I didn't do. Please call me ASAP."

FIFTEEN

Dillon saw the white SUV approaching the house a good quarter mile before it would reach them. He didn't need to see any signage on the vehicle to know it was Customs and Border Patrol. As with the black SUVs of the FBI, or the black sedans of the military, the CBP had its customary vehicles, and every rancher along the border knew them instinctively. He moseyed on from the barn to the house, waiting for whoever was coming.

As the federal officer pulled up by the house, Dillon recognized him. Dwayne Harris. They had worked together to tighten Dillon's security along the land he owned next to the border. He touched the brim of his Stetson in greeting as the man exited his vehicle.

"Dwayne, good to see you again. To what do I owe this visit? I haven't had any troubles, well, that I know of."

The agent touched the brim of his hat in return. "Hey, Dillon. Not here about any troubles on your land."

Dillon motioned with his head toward the house. "C'mon in. Still too cold for my liking out here. Coffee?"

The man nodded. "I'd love a cup. Thanks."

The two sat in the kitchen at the big table. Flora had two mugs of coffee waiting for them. How she did that, Dillon still hadn't figured out. Had she installed a security camera system he knew nothing about?

"So, what's up, Dwayne?"

The officer took a sip of the coffee. "We had an incident over on the river at the Cantu spread last night."

Dillon nodded. "Yeah, I heard about that. A couple of the men were talking about it this morning when they arrived for the day. Drug smuggling or something they said."

Harris nodded this time. "Yep. But it was how they were stopped that we're looking into. Three trucks on our side of the river were disabled, blown up. And three ATVs full of drugs were incinerated *in* the river. *In* it, not on either shore. Never seen anything like it."

Dillon raised his brow. "Wow. Incinerated? Any ideas how?" He hoped he looked innocently inquisitive. He'd never been much of an actor.

Dwayne took another sip and raised his cup toward Flora at the other end of the room. "Great coffee, Flora. As usual." He downed another mouthful. "One of the guys is ex-military, and he said it looked like a military thermobaric device. You're ex-marine, right?"

Dillon smiled. "You know what they say, once a marine always a marine." He paused and took a drink.

"So, you ever have any experience with anything like a thermobaric weapon? Ever seen one when you were on active duty?"

Dillon shook his head, glad that the man had phrased it

that way. "Not when I was in." He refused to lie, but he could work around the truth. "I heard about some weapons that made it into the field after my time. Grenade launchers and such with thermobaric grenades."

"How do they work?"

"Well, from what I recall, they ignite when they contact oxygen. So, as an example, they would use them to clear tunnels and caves. They'd suck all the oxygen out of the tunnel and produce a high-temperature explosion. I have no idea what kind of range they're designed to have."

That, too, was true. He had, however, witnessed their range over the Rio Grande, but that was not to be mentioned.

"Well, we know the military wasn't involved. So, you hear anything on the grape vine about anyone around here picking up any fancy weapons like that? Your men always seem to have their ears to the ground."

Dillon shook his head. "Nope, haven't heard of anything like that on the grape vine. Unlikely that anyone around here could afford to buy anything like that, even if they were inclined to use it. I remember reading somewhere that those grenades are like a thousand bucks apiece. Who around here has that kind of deep pockets? We're lucky to afford the rent on our harvesting rigs."

Dwayne nodded. "That's pretty much what our guy said. This investigation is gonna take a while, for sure." He finished his coffee. "Thanks, Dillon. If you hear anything, please let me know. We have reason to believe two men were killed on one of the ATVs."

"Much left of the bodies? Being killed by a thermobaric charge would be mighty gruesome, but it would be quick."

"Actually, no bodies at all, but that's all I'm able to tell you. I suspect they'll wash up along the river at some point."

Dillon took his last swig. "Probably. The river tends to do that."

He saw his guest to his SUV and watched as the agent headed back to the county road. Then he walked back to the machine shed to complete a welding task. As he moved, he debated making a call on his "private line." To date, he'd only *received* calls on that phone. However, he wanted to call Eduardo to find out what he knew about the investigation. He decided to try it and pulled the phone out of his coat.

He dialed Eduardo's number, but nothing happened. The phone would not place the call. He started to return the phone to his inner coat pocket when it vibrated with a message.

No voice calls between operatives for 72 hours after an action. They can be eavesdropped. Why do you want to talk with Eduardo?

Dillon frowned. The phone was too smart for its own britches. Yet, he had the attention of whoever manned the other end.

Just had a visit from CBP. They're working on the premise of a thermobaric weapon being used on the drug smugglers. Need to warn him.

A moment later, the reply came.

Already alerted. CBP talked with him earlier. And to cover tracks, some material has been added to the CBP investigation files to steer them elsewhere. Stay calm. Don't communicate with others in our group unnecessarily. We don't want unwanted attention drawn to us.

Dillon felt as if he'd just been scolded. The last thing he wanted was to draw attention to himself . . . or any of the others for that matter. Eduardo was a friend. Meeting or talking with him would not be out of character.

Good. No problem. Out, he responded.

The message disappeared.

Raimondo paced along the veranda of the palatial hacienda overlooking the Gulf of Mexico outside of Tampico Alto. The area was not one frequented by the rich and famous, or even typical American tourists. The city had once been Mexico's leading oil export port. Although the oil fields had dried up 100 years ago, the metropolitan area continued to support a population nearing a million. Yet, one aspect of the city's heritage remained. It had once been a busy waypoint for the illegal smuggling of African slaves into the southern United States after slavery had been abolished there. Smuggling, of both drugs and people, provided a lucrative business for El Espectro, Roberto Benito Felix Beltrán, and his Los Zorros Cartel.

The helicopter had made excellent time in flying Raimondo from Piedras Negras. His palms were sweaty, reflecting the anxiety he felt inside. However, he knew better than to try to report a loss this major to El Espectro over the phone, much less by email. Indeed, there were better than 50-50 odds that the man already knew the shipment had been destroyed, but Raimondo had to show that he had not shirked his duty. He needed to take responsibility and assure his boss that he would find the perpetrators.

To fail to take ownership of the problem was a guarantee of a shortened life. El Espectro, the Specter, lived up to his name as a source of terror. Many men had found their eternal resting place at the bottom of the Tamiahua Lagoon south of the city. Raimondo did not wish to join them.

He turned at the sound of the door opening. One of El Espectro's many female *sicarios*, beautiful and deadly, walked toward him. "El Espectro will see you now. He is in his study." Her Spanish held a hint of a Chilean accent.

Raimondo walked briskly into the house and toward the study. He had been there many times before and did not need directions. The door was closed, so he knocked.

"*Pasa.*" His leader's voice held no hint as to his mood.

Raimondo entered the room, bowed, and stood in his place. He would make no move until directed to. "*Buenos días*, El Espectro. I am afraid I have bad news," he continued in Spanish. He knew he needed to come straight to the point of his visit. The boss would have it no other way.

Beltrán did not smile but pointed to a group of chairs. Raimondo had attended several briefings seated in one of those chairs. He knew which one *not* to sit in.

"Come. Take a seat."

Beltrán waited until his lieutenant sat down before taking

his own chair.

"So, bad news. I suspected as much by your coming here personally."

Raimondo nodded. "Yes, sir. The entire shipment was lost."

The man raised his brow, questioning.

"Destroyed, El Espectro. Not stolen or confiscated but destroyed. In the middle of the river, before it ever touched U.S. soil."

Now his boss looked concerned.

"Explain. How could it be destroyed in the river?"

Raimondo went on to explain what had happened. He had recorded a video of Rito explaining the fire from hell and showed the third-degree burns of the two men hit by the first explosion. He offered this video to Beltrán on his phone. The man took the phone from his hand and watched. His face remained passionless.

"So, $15 million literally gone up in smoke. That is what you are telling me?"

Now, anger etched El Espectro's face. The man rose from his chair and began to pace.

"Tell me, how? What did this, and more importantly, who?"

Raimondo took a deep breath. He had come prepared. "Sir, I may have the answer to the first question. One of my contacts within the CBP told me this morning that their investigation is looking into some kind of thermobaric weapon, likely military in origin."

"You told me that this new route was safe, that it remained off the radar of the U.S. authorities, as you put it.

How did they learn of it?"

Raimondo could see that the man was controlling his anger, but just barely.

"El Espectro, I was reassured that the U.S. authorities had nothing to do with this. I was told they are speculating about the weapon that was used but have no idea who was behind it."

"What is this thermobaric weapon, as you call it?"

Raimondo repeated what he had been told.

"So, again, who did this and how did they know about the route?"

Raimondo needed to regain Beltrán's trust.

"Sir, that is what I aim to find out. Only you, me, and Rito knew about the route. Rito is totally loyal and would never divulge such information."

Beltrán scrutinized him with the lifeless eyes of a demon.

"Sir, the shipment was destroyed, not stolen. To what purpose would I or Rito seek to *destroy* the drugs?"

"To ruin me. Another cartel would pay handsomely to achieve that."

Raimondo did not like where this conversation was headed.

"Never, El Espectro. You pay us both very well. Plus, what cartel would have access to such U.S. military-grade weapons? If they had them, would they not have used them before?"

"There is always a first time."

Now more than Raimondo's palms felt sweaty. His heart rate picked up, and visions of a lonely boat ride into the lagoon danced within his head. He had to convince El Espectro.

"Sir, I swear on my mother's grave that neither of us

would betray you."

No immediate response came. Raimondo could practically smell the water of the lagoon now.

El Espectro shook his head. "Your mother still lives." He walked behind Raimondo, who dared not move or flinch. He half expected a fatal wound to be inflicted from behind, but the other half believed his boss would neither soil his study nor his own hands with Raimondo's blood. When the cartel leader again became visible, Raimondo forced himself to remain steady and not reveal the deep sense of relief he unexpectantly experienced.

"Very well. Raimondo, I am not an unreasonable man. This could take time, so I give you a month to find out who did this and deal with them. If you fail me, you *and* your mother will occupy the same grave."

SIXTEEN

"Ryan? Rick Holleran here."

"Thanks for calling back, Rick. Give me a minute to get someplace quiet."

Ryan appreciated the rapid response from the union.

"No need. We're five minutes from your house. I heard about the swatting incident, and Lopez gave me a heads up that he was going to have you call us. I got hold of our lawyer, and we figured it was time to come to—"

"Ryyannn!" His wife's scream chilled him. Had something happened to one of the boys?

"Uh, Rick, can you hold? My wife's screaming for me, and it doesn't sound good."

"Sure, I'll hold on."

Ryan toward her voice and found their boys right where he'd left them at their computers. They looked puzzled and followed Ryan into the kitchen where Sarah stood propped against a counter and crying.

"What's wrong? Are you hurt? What—" She interrupted by agitatedly pointing to the garage. The look on her face scared him. He had never seen such fear in his wife.

He ran to the garage. Their cars were intact. All appeared in order.

Sarah appeared in the doorway to the house. "Outside. Our . . . garage . . . door." The words were interspersed with sobs. She *was* scared.

Ryan walked to the side door, exited the building, and turned the corner to stand on their drive. Their garage door had been vandalized. Spray painted onto it were the words "murderer" and "killer cop." The letters revealed that two different hands were involved. He put the phone back to his ear.

"Rick, I gotta go. Our garage door was just vandalized." He described what his wife had discovered upon returning from the grocery.

"We're almost there." Holleran hung up.

Ryan took his phone and began taking photos. Then he called it into the east precinct. Reassured they would have a car there shortly, he circled their home to look for other damage. Thankfully, nothing else had been damaged or taken.

He returned inside, walked straight to Sarah, and engulfed her in his arms. The security he offered seemed to settle her. She looked up into his eyes.

"Ryan? This isn't good. Why isn't the bureau clearing you of this whole thing?"

Ryan hugged her tighter. She was right, as much as he didn't want to acknowledge it. He'd always wanted to be a cop. "Protect and serve" meant something to him. But now? Who in their right mind would want this job?

Ryan's anger mounted, and he was not one to be

intimidated. He donned his protective vest, his badge, and his personal sidearm. His department-issued weapon had yet to be returned to him. With that, he walked out to his driveway and stood in front of the graffiti. If the department was upset over optics, he'd give them optics.

He paced in front of his garage paying close attention to people and cars passing by. The other thing he did not doubt was that the perpetrators would return. How could they resist? Yet, would he be able to spot them?

A minute later, a car he didn't recognize pulled up in front of the neighbor's house and parked. Rick Holleran and a man Ryan knew only from photos, the union attorney, emerged from the vehicle. Rick raised his hand to acknowledge Ryan. The other man stopped upon seeing Ryan and shook his head. They approached their beleaguered union member.

Rick reached out to shake Ryan's hand. "Ryan, this is Sam Coleridge, our main attorney."

The man reached out to shake Ryan's hand as well. "Ryan, nice to meet you but unhappy about the circumstances."

The man looked back toward the street. A second news van had pulled in behind the one Ryan had noticed earlier. Crews from both were exiting their vehicles.

"Umm, we should probably go inside. The optics here are not in your favor."

Ryan didn't care. He'd made a decision while standing and fuming in his driveway. But first, he needed to clear his name, and if the lawyer said the optics wouldn't help, so be it. After that, he could piss off his senior officers to his heart's content. He'd moved beyond caring.

Sarah was in the kitchen, while the boys peered around

the corner from the dining room. With one look from him, they scampered back to their desks.

"This is my wife, Sarah." The men introduced themselves in greeting her.

"Let's go downstairs. Might not be as comfortable, but definitely more private."

He grabbed a couple of better chairs and arranged them in his office. Sarah delivered three bottles of cold water and gave one to each man.

"So, why am I being put through this?" Ryan felt his anger resurface but controlled it. These men weren't the enemy.

Sam nodded. "Good question. We've put in inquiries about the whole thing but haven't received a straight answer from anyone. From what I've been able to deduce so far, someone higher up than the mayor is pulling the strings. Why, I don't know. What they hope to gain from this, I don't know that either."

Ryan picked up the forensics reports Captain Lopez had sent him. "I sent copies of these to Rick. Can you use them to push back? I want my name cleared ASAP."

Sam nodded. "We can, but only after I've received them through the proper channels."

"How long will that take?"

"I hope they're on my desk when I return to the office. If not, I honestly can't say."

"Do I have a lawsuit against them?"

Rick straightened up. "You sure you want to take that step?"

Sam held up his hand. "Whoa. First off, you don't yet have grounds for such. They'll just come back with a defense that they're thoroughly investigating the situation, and that investigation has not yet been completed. If they fire you or try to charge you with something, then you'll have grounds to sue."

"Can't we fight fire with fire? Those news crews were setting up as we came into the house. Seems clear to me that someone tipped them off. And I wouldn't be surprised if the other networks aren't clogging the street by now, too. What would stop me from walking out to those reporters, holding my own press conference, and handing them copies of these reports?"

Sam appeared concerned. "We couldn't stop you, but I have to counsel you that such a move would not be in your best interest."

"And you know what's in my best interest how?" The man did not answer. "I moved my family halfway across the country to help this city fill its needs in an expanding police force. We love the area. We love this house. And the friends we've made. When all the garbage hit the streets last year after an event that took place not here, but over 1,700 miles away, I put my life on the line to protect and serve. Night after night after night, we were assaulted with stuff no civilized society should tolerate, and it continues. When the politicians tied our hands so we couldn't deal with the problems according to the law, I grumbled like the rest of my colleagues, but I followed orders. When 40% of the force left, I stuck it out. And this is how I've been repaid for that loyalty."

Ryan took a deep breath. It felt good to vent, but like most vents, his was only filled with hot air. And he'd had enough hot air from the politicos.

"Feel better?" asked Rick.

He did, but somehow that comment felt patronizing.

"Ryan, I realize circumstances are different, that a fatality is involved, and that politics are interfering, but we have ways of dealing with this. Let us do our job."

"How long?"

"A couple of days at least."

Ryan relented. "Okay, but if our property is vandalized again, or if my family is physically threatened in any way, I'll move to do it my way."

Aric's morning resumed after the break, and he found Dr. Carter to be an animated and stimulating lecturer. He wondered if the professor had also talked with the student who had mentioned the Bible earlier because that student did not seem as eager to participate in the second half of the morning. Aric, on the other hand, enjoyed the discussions and even started a couple of them. Clearly, he had not overstepped Dr. Carter's boundaries since the professor pushed some of those topics even further. There was no further mention of the Bible, but then, the course material did not lend itself to such.

After the class, two other students stopped Aric as everyone prepared to depart for lunch.

"Hi, my name's Chris."

Chris looked toned and athletic, but not big enough for the college football team, if that still existed. The entire 2020 schedule had been postponed, but the word was out that those games were officially canceled. If Aric had to guess, he'd say the guy played baseball.

"And I'm Jessica, but my friends call me Jess. You must be new here."

She, too, looked buff, but what caught Aric's attention was the deep blue of her eyes. He imagined she had dimples when she smiled . . . and a pert, slightly upturned nose. He felt smitten with her, and that feeling caught him off-guard. He wondered if they were a couple.

Aric nodded. "I'm Aric, with an A. Decided to jump into J-term rather than wait until spring semester. Nice to meet you both."

"We started with the fall term, but a lot of that was still virtual. It's really nice to be back in class, even if we do have to wear these stupid masks."

Aric liked the sound of her voice, even slightly muffled. He nodded again. "Yeah, you'd think a college would have someone smart enough to know the science, which shows that masks won't stop a viral illness."

Chris chimed in. "Yeah, well, if you haven't figured it out already, the place is pretty liberal. We liked your defense of the Bible earlier. That's why we wanted to meet you."

Aric silently thanked God. He had asked the Lord to bring some fellow believers his way. Was this God's answer?

"Um, are you both Christians by chance?"

Jess replied, "We are, but chance had nothing to with it." She laughed.

Aric blushed. "Sorry, figure of speech. I don't believe in coincidence, or chance either."

"Look, there's a Christian group on campus that meets, well, a bit irregularly this term. There's more structure in the two main semesters. We're supposed to be getting together two nights from tonight, Wednesday, but I don't have the details about where and when yet."

"Sadly," Jess said, "it's kind of like house churches in some countries. The where and when are last-minute announcements. "Last fall, we had people show up to disrupt our gatherings a few times. We found that the last-minute thing helped stop that."

"And we keep the day close to the vest, too."

"Got it," replied Aric.

"If you want to give me your cell number, we can add you to the message chain."

"Sure." Aric shared his contact info with both of them and received theirs in return. He noticed they shared a last name, Larson.

"Hey, same last name. Are you . . .'"

"Fraternal twins. PKs, too." She laughed.

"Uh-oh, the wild ones, huh?" Preacher's kids had a certain reputation for rebelling and later becoming prodigal sons and daughters. Clearly, though, these two hadn't been tempted.

Chris laughed, too. "Yeah, wild, if you like great praise and worship. Have you found a church, yet?"

Aric had been to church with Lynch and Amy a few times. It was a large Assembly of God congregation where praise and worship seemed, well, a bit reserved.

"Not really."

"Well, join us on Sunday. I think you'll find it lively and the teaching solid. Lots of guys our age."

"Give me the details, and I'll plan on it."

They exited the classroom and headed outside. Aric started toward the central residence hall, removing his mask as he walked.

"So, what dorms do you two live in?"

They stopped on the sidewalk, and Jess and Chris removed their masks, too. Aric could see the family resemblance now.

"We live in town, at home," replied Jessica.

The words didn't sink in. Jess had Aric mesmerized. She had that pert, up-turned nose he had imagined, and deep dimples formed when she smiled. Just as he had envisioned her while inside the building, but much prettier. Had God shown him a vision of her? He caught himself staring and broke his gaze away.

"Yeah, we're locals. The college offers a nice tuition break for local residents, and living at home makes it even more affordable."

Jess nodded. "And Mom and Dad are cool about it. They give us more space to do what we want and don't have as many demands on our time. You'll get to meet them at church."

"Great." Aric's attention had returned to her. He hoped he wasn't terribly obvious.

"Which dorm are you in? We can come pick you up on Sunday, if you want. After church we can do lunch and show you around town," said Jess.

Aric was about to decline and let them know he'd been in the area for several months already but stopped short. He looked forward to having Jess, um, both of them, show him around town. No doubt they'd know about places even Lynch hadn't discovered yet, he reasoned. Yeah, right. Who was he fooling? He was indeed smitten.

Oh. She asked me something. What . . . ? Oh yeah . . .

"I'm in the central residence hall."

Both frowned. "Sorry," came in unison.

"What?"

"Some of us call that activist hall," answered Chris. "The LGBTQ and BLM folks consider that dorm their headquarters, and their leaders all live there. They've made living there intolerable for more than one of our Christian friends."

SEVENTEEN

El Espectro's displeasure was confirmed when Raimondo found himself having to arrange his own transportation to Piedras Negras. He had expected a three-and-a-half-hour flight back but instead had to rent a car . . . at his own expense. He did not look forward to the over-ten-hour drive.

Yet, he found the time in the car calming, almost mentally relaxing. And that helped him think more clearly. Yes, he had multiple distractions at various points along the road—a farm truck with hay flying from its bed, numerous drivers more focused on their phones than the road, and the ever-present *puercos* with their radar traps aimed at supplementing their income not improving road safety. Only one of the latter actually caught him, but the expected bribe made the stop a short one.

Halfway through the trip, he had a plan formulated. Each step, however, depended upon information he had yet to obtain. With five more hours in the car, he hoped to reduce that paucity of data. With his phone set up for hands-free use, he made his first call.

"I thought we had an arrangement that you do not call me during the day." The whispering voice on the other end was curt.

"*Buena tarde* to you, too. And do not argue with me. I pay you well and can provide much information to put you in jail for many years."

The other end remained silent.

"I need to know—"

"Now is not a good time." The whispering continued.

"When is it ever a good time? I need five minutes. Break free from what you are doing."

Raimondo paid well for information from the CBP. He also had leverage, more so than just the threat of prison. After all, an informant could turn, provide false information, and arrange things to Raimondo's detriment—like a double agent. Money alone was not a guarantee of compliance. Money plus the threat of imprisonment was not adequate insurance. The man's daughter in college, however, was.

"Elizabeth has been doing so—"

"Okay, okay. Give me a minute."

Raimondo could hear voices in the backdrop. His informant appeared to be in some sort of meeting, perhaps a briefing on the very topic Raimondo wished to discuss. The background noise went silent.

"Alright, you have my attention, but I can't stay away for long."

"Then I will come right to the point. What more do you know?"

"We've confirmed that it was a thermobaric weapon."

"That much you told me earlier."

"Yes, well, a munitions specialist has confirmed it, and the explosive residue he tested was consistent with a weapon no longer in the army's inventory, the XM25. Soldiers who used it called it 'The Punisher.' While in use, it was a game-changer in Iraq."

The man went on to brief Raimondo about the weapon's capabilities. Its nickname appeared well earned, and its use against Raimondo's men was worrisome. If used once, it could be used again.

"Who would have such a weapon, and how did it end up at Pablo De Luna?"

"That is the $64,000 question. The army is searching its records for every soldier who ever fired one. That list could take a while because they were decommissioned in 2018. The specialist believes they were all destroyed. Clearly, they weren't."

"Clearly." Raimondo pondered that info. Did he have anyone who could expedite that search?

"Anyway, we don't see anyone local as having one. Those things cost over 30 grand and each round is a thousand dollars. Folks over here fight for every dollar their ranches earn."

Raimondo knew that to be true, but affording one and knowing how to operate one were two different things. The former would need the latter. So, more concerning was who could be behind the curtain pulling the levers. He already knew that the U.S. federal government would not do this. The ramifications of a lame-duck president with but days remaining in office authorizing such an attack were great. And the new administration, with its promise of opening the borders, would not hesitate to prosecute the perpetrators.

"Do you have any idea who is behind it? Was this the State of Texas?" The state's governor was already making noise about taking over border security if the new administration followed through on its intentions to abandon the wall construction. Yet, this, too, seemed unlikely. A state government would not sanction the murder of men, not even a single man. Besides, if the authorities knew of the smuggling ahead of time, they would simply have arranged for the state police and others to be there waiting to intercept the shipment and arrest the people involved.

"Not likely. The CBP would have been alerted to the shipment and ordered to stop it. No, this was not likely any sort of government operation. We're looking for some rogue, nationalist group, but right now we have zero leads."

Raimondo nodded as he heard that. The words were confirmation of what he believed, and that worried him even more. Who did this? How did they know about the shipment? Are his next shipments also to become targets? Finding the answer to that question required starting somewhere, and that somewhere was to find the shooter, the man who used the XM25.

Aric had become accustomed to the dark of night arriving around 4:30. What seemed strange was being released from class at that time and walking back to the dorm at night. True, the campus was well-lit, to the point someone might not realize it was dark. Tonight, though, Aric felt impervious to the dark. The memory of Jessica's eyes and the depth of her dimples when she smiled filled his mind. He sure hoped she didn't have some other boyfriend waiting in the wings.

Lost in thought, he entered the dorm and made a beeline toward the elevators.

"Mask!" someone yelled at him.

He took a deep breath and sighed. Getting accustomed to walking back to the dorm in the dark was one thing. Being forced to don a useless piece of cloth while indoors was another. He wanted to yell back, "Show me the science that proves they work, and I will," but he was in no position to make waves over the requirement. As a freshman from out of state, he was required to live in a dorm unless staying with local family. His only "local" family, Adam, lived too far away to make that feasible.

He stopped, pulled his mask from his pocket, and adjusted it over his face. Two minutes later, he unlocked and entered the door to his room where he again removed the mask. Mask on, mask off. Mask on, mask off. This was only day three on campus, and the tediousness of that cycle wore thin.

He glanced about the room. His side of the space appeared just as he'd left it after lunch. Tom's side, however, looked as if an F3 tornado had torn through it. It hadn't looked like that after lunch.

I hope this isn't as routine as his late-night habits, Aric thought.

No sooner had he tossed his backpack onto his desk than his roomie appeared at the door.

With his mask in hand, Tom said, "Hey. Sorry about the mess. I needed my mask for class after lunch and couldn't find it. Ended up being in my backpack all along." He began to pick up after himself and toss things back into his desk, as well as his chest of drawers.

Aric nodded. He wondered how Tom could forget where his mask was. Every undereducated progressive on campus reminded others to wear them. He chose not to ask.

With his side of the room tidied, Tom asked, "Ready to eat? The cafeteria opens in five minutes."

Aric had considered reading for the next 30 minutes before heading downstairs to eat, but his gut grumbled at the thought. Plus, eating now would allow him to study uninterrupted afterward.

"Sure. Just want to hit the john first."

A few minutes later, after bounding down the stairs instead waiting for an elevator, Aric and Tom joined the growing line outside the doors to the cafeteria. Despite a plethora of signs reminding them to "social distance," none did. That crowd flowed into the facility as the doors opened, but soon the doors would be shut again, once the facility's occupancy reached 25% of max. No one wanted to be at the tail of that first wave and forced to wait. The college had attempted to assign seating times for each student, but too many complaints of time conflicts arose. So, they returned to first come, first served and the craziness that followed. Still, complaints had fallen 95%.

The place was divided into multiple food bars, each with its distinctive style of food, as well as a beverage bar, a central stash of trays and silverware, and another for condiments. Aric swiped his ID for "payment," headed toward his preferred lines, and worked his way through the stations to get what he wanted for dinner. Tom did the same, but Aric made it to an empty table before his roommate.

With his head bowed, he said a silent prayer of thanks over his meal.

"You still pray over your food?" asked Tom as he sat opposite Aric.

Aric nodded. "Every meal. I thank God for everything he provides for me. Even in restaurants." He would never be shamed over his expression of gratitude to his Provider.

"Whatever. If that works for you, that's cool."

After three days of sharing a room, that comment was all Aric needed to understand that Tom was like the majority of self-identified Christians whose beliefs included the postmodern concept that "whatever works for you" is acceptable. To the postmodern thinker, there were no absolute truths, only relative ones. What was true for you was based upon your life experiences and what made you happy.

"Hey, you're that guy!"

Aric looked up from his food to see a guy—at least he thought it was a guy—pointing a finger at him. The person had pink hair, earrings, and a nose ring, and appeared to be wearing subtle eye makeup. His voice sounded as effeminate as he looked. Aric fought looking surprised and tried hard to keep his composure.

"Yeah. You're that guy from the protest." The young man looked about the room. "Hey everybody, this is the guy from the protest!"

Aric didn't like the way he emphasized "the guy" and could feel a dozen or more sets of eyes now riveted on him. At that moment, he also remembered the person in front of him as half of the gay couple fawning over each other at the protest against Lynch. He decided that being friendly might de-escalate the growing situation. He extended his hand.

"Hey. I'm Aric. Nice to meet you."

The person jumped back as if Aric was about to pounce and refused the handshake as if he carried a plague. Four others joined the, um, man, or whatever he decided to identify himself as. A meme he'd seen recently came to mind: "Men are from Mars, women are from Venus, and the other genders come from Uranus." He caught himself smiling and hoped the man hadn't caught him.

"Are you laughing at us?" asked one of the others. She was a hefty black female who clearly had the butch vibe going. She truly looked menacing, and he noticed Tom edge away a few inches.

"Not at all," Aric replied, hoping he sounded persuasive.

"You're the dude who stood up for Professor Cully the other day."

Aric wanted calm and reason to prevail. The last thing he needed was to get in trouble his first week there by getting into a fracas in the cafeteria. Not that he started it.

"I'd stand up for you, too, if your right to free speech was being infringed upon. That's all I said there."

"So, you admit it," stated another person standing there. This one he *really* couldn't tell its gender.

"I admit I spoke up for free speech, yes. A college campus should be a place where different ideas, ideologies, and beliefs can be discussed openly. The campus should be a bastion of free speech. You were exercising your right to free speech while trying to deny those of a professor here."

The quintet moved closer to his table, and the black

lesbian appeared prepared to dump his food tray on the floor. At that point he stood . . . and towered over all five. They backed off, just as one of the RAs appeared. She looked at Aric and then the others. Aric remembered her from move-in day.

"Is there a problem here?"

Pink hair spoke first. "Ashleigh, this is the guy from the protest."

Aric didn't wait for her to say anything. "My roommate and I were starting our meal when *he* confronted me. We were just sitting here talking and eating."

Tom, who had made a concerted effort to steer clear of what was happening, nodded in confirmation. "That's true. Aric didn't start this."

Aric noted several others around them nod in agreement. He heard another "That's true" from behind him.

Ashleigh folded her arms across her chest, which Aric noted was unremarkable for a woman her height. She seemed to study him.

She addressed the gang of five. "You guys go sit down. Don't get into trouble here." She turned back to Aric. "Aren't you the guy whose friend, or brother, or whoever, had the stupid mask that he wore in protest?"

"Stupid mask? I don't think so. My brother had one that spoke the truth, but nothing stupid."

"Well, this dorm honors diversity and the freedom to be who you are. If that's a problem for you, I'm sure we can get the college to find you another dorm."

"So, that's how your friends there honor diversity and freedom, huh? Strange way of doing so." He sensed that he would have to be more assertive from that point on and not shrink away from the cultural debate that appeared to be living within the dorm. The Word said he was to be salt and light. He figured he was going to have to be salty before any light could shine through.

"Don't cause trouble here."

"I didn't. Talk to pink hair over there. He started it."

She looked him up and down, frowned, and left. Aric sat down and took a drink. He picked up the burger he'd ordered for dinner. It was cold.

"I need to go get another burger."

He stood, grabbed the plate, and walked toward the food stations. He dumped the burger into the trash, placed the dish on a dirty tray on the rack, and proceeded to get another meal. By the time he returned to the table, Tom had finished eating.

"Um, I need to get to studying. See you up in the room."

Aric sighed as he watched his roommate stand and leave. Now he'd have to eat alone. He never liked eating alone. As he started into his burger, he felt a tap on his right shoulder. He turned to see a fellow he'd seen around the dorm but had not yet met.

"Mind if I join you?"

Aric pointed to the chair vacated by Tom. "Please do. I'm Aric, with an A." He extended his hand.

His handshake was returned with a grip he'd rarely encountered. "I'm Mitch, Mitchell Johnson. I think we're on the same floor. Fourth floor, right?"

Aric nodded as he chewed. After swallowing, he said, "Yep. 412."

"I'm in 422. I applaud your standing up for free speech. Not many on campus will do so as boldly as you have. Pretty much everyone in this dorm has heard about 'the guy from the protest.' So, if you're that guy, I salute you." He offered a quick salute with three fingers.

"Thanks."

"But I need to warn you. You might have just painted a target on your back. The queers, if I might use that term, in this dorm are the most intolerant lot on campus. Most folks just steer clear of them."

"Have they bothered you?"

"Naw. I'm a starting end on the football team, and they're afraid of us jocks." He laughed. "None of us want booted off the team, so we'd never start anything with them. But our size intimidates them, and we just let them think we'd beat the crap out of anyone who messes with us. We wouldn't but don't tell any of them that." He grinned. "Anyway, I'll do what I can to help protect your back, and I'll pass that on to the other guys on the team."

Aric wasn't sure what to make of that but any help keeping life in the dorm tolerable was appreciated. He reflected on what Chris and Jess had told him about this dorm. 'Activist hall' they'd called it.

"By the way, you're pretty good-sized yourself. You ever play football?"

EIGHTEEN

Dillon pulled up to the feed store in his Silverado and climbed out. He rubbed his hands against the cold and hurried into the store. The owner's son greeted him.

"Hey, Dillon. We got your order 'round back if you want to pull in at the dock."

Dillon nodded. "Thanks, Jared. Say, what've you got for a black lab puppy? My daughter just got one and asked me to pick up some food for the little fur ball."

The young man pointed. "Second aisle, on the left, near the back. We got Orijen and Ollie Fresh on the high end, and Purina Pro, Nutra Pro, and Iams Smart Puppy on the low end. Far as I'm concerned, they're all pretty decent, so save some money by going with one of the cheaper ones. Don't forget to check any age recommendations. You didn't say how old the puppy is."

"Thanks." He wasn't sure he knew how old the animal was either. "Don't rightly know, to be honest." He hoped that Meghan was available by phone if he had questions.

Dillon hadn't made it halfway down the aisle when

Wallace Griffin, the owner, caught up with him.

"Dillon, glad I caught you."

"Hey, Wallace. What's up?"

The man had concern etched upon his face. "Just thought you should know. Someone's been going around town asking folks about who in the area are military vets. Not sure what any of the other business owners told 'im. I claimed ignorance. Didn't share anyone's name. I think folks shut up after it got around that the guy was hitting up every store in town, askin' the same question. But I don't know what he learned. He just seemed suspicious to me. Figured I should warn you, Rick, Justin, Rito, Roberto, Eduardo, and the others I know."

Alarm bells rang in Dillon's mind. "Thanks. Did he seem dangerous or something? Why would he be askin' about local vets?"

"Yeah, like I said, he seemed fishy."

Dillon didn't like the thought of someone asking around about his brothers in arms. He could only think of two reasons for that.

"I was talking to Gerardo at the hardware store. Word's floatin' about that some type of military gear was used to take out that drug shipment in the river near the Cantu spread. Seems to me someone's fishin' around to see if anyone in these parts could have done that. Far as I'm concerned, more power to 'im if it is. Sure not going to give up any info on someone doing what our government is failing to do."

Dillon nodded, unsure just what to say to that. A simple "Amen" seemed an appropriate response.

After a moment of contemplation, Dillon continued. "I heard that rumor, too. Well, not so much a rumor. Dwayne

Harris stopped by the day after, said they thought it looked like some kind of military-grade weapon. The kind that costs way much more than anyone around here could afford." He expected that it wouldn't take long for that info to spread about town. Wallace wasn't exactly a town gossip, but he had his network of buddies who spread any and all local news efficiently.

"You don't say. Well, that confirms what folks are sayin'. Anyway, like I said, more power to 'em, whoever they are. Things are sure gonna get a whole worse around here once this bogus president takes the office, so it don't bother me none that some patriots are takin' things into their own hands."

Dillon nodded again. Everyone he knew agreed that the election was fraudulent and that corrupt actors had stolen the presidency. Of course, proving that was another story.

"Wallace, thanks for the heads up. I hope it's just some news reporter looking for a story. The other option, well, I'd prefer not to think about that. Could get messy."

The feed shop owner slowly shook his head from one side to the other. "That's for sure, if I catch your drift. Umm, we are thinkin' the same thing, right?"

"Probably. The cartel might be looking for revenge and wanting someone to blame."

The man nodded. "Yep, that's my thinkin', too. Like I said, I'm trying to get the word out to our vets. The more recent ones I know, anyway."

"Appreciate that. I'll make a few calls myself. Right now, I need some puppy food."

Dillon's concern for the latter option grew as he pulled

around to the back of the store and watched them load his truck with his main order. With his bill settled up, he took off toward home. Yet, he hadn't so much as left the town limits when he decided he should make a short detour and head toward the Cantu ranch. He needed to talk to Eduardo in person, not by a phone call that likely would be intercepted.

As he turned off the road onto the gravel lane to their home, a shadow crossed over the hood of his truck. He slowed and took note of the sun's position. He kept one eye on the drive as he scanned the heavens to see what might have cast that shadow. He was less than halfway to the house when he spotted it . . . a drone.

As he pulled into the area near the house, he spotted Eduardo moving one of their tractors into a barn. His friend and comrade-in-arms saw him, too, and waved. Dillon pulled the truck up to the barn door and lowered his window.

As the younger man walked toward him, he yelled, "Room in there for me to pull in?" Eduardo gave him a questioning look. "I'll explain inside." His friend waved him in, where he parked behind the tractor and climbed out of the truck.

"Dillon, what's with—"

"You have a visitor outside." He went on to explain his conversation with Wallace Griffin and about the drone he spotted over their property.

"A drone? Over our place?"

"Cartel is my guess. I figure the guy asking questions in town is one of two things, a reporter or a cartel lackey. Both would be fishing for information, but in my mind, a reporter's likely to introduce himself as such and entice people to talk by saying they'll get their name in the story. A cartel flunky probably wouldn't be smart enough to think up such a story as a cover. Plus, a reporter's likely to just drive up to the house and identify himself. He wouldn't resort to a drone."

"Why our place?"

"Closest to where they lost their shipment."

Eduardo nodded. "Sure. Makes sense." He turned and walked toward the tractor he's just been driving. He pulled a rifle from inside the cab. "Might be time for some bird hunting."

Dillon shook his head. "Wouldn't advise shooting it down. You might have the right to do so, but if you show off your marksmanship, you're likely to draw more attention here." He stepped to the back of his truck, lowered the tailgate, and climbed up onto it.

"Good point."

Dillon began to shift feed bags around in the truck bed. "I pulled in because I want to make it seem like I picked up some feed from you. Make it seem like a normal workday. If I pull these bags from underneath and put them on top, whoever's running that drone will see different colored bags than the ones I drove in with."

Eduardo nodded. "Sounds like reasonable subterfuge." He laughed.

"I suspect that when I pull outta here, that drone'll be right above us. If you see it, run back in here, grab your gun, and then look right at it, make sure it's looking at you and not following me. Wave it off with the gun, or maybe shoot and miss. Let 'em know they've been seen, but don't let 'em know you're an excellent marksman."

"I like that idea. 'Course, *you're* the one who could take it down at long distance better than I could."

Dillon grinned. "Heck, that thing's only flying, what, maybe a hundred yards up? At that distance, it'd be like shooting tin cans off the fence with a BB gun for either of us. Much as I'd love to do that, not while they're looking. Last thing we need is to show off any skill that might get them suspicious. But you need any help, call me."

Dillon climbed into the cab, backed out of the barn, waved through the open window, and slowly headed down the lane. Just as he'd suspected, the drone hovered a few hundred feet over the house. He looked into his rearview mirrors and saw Eduardo play the part he'd suggested. He nodded as he watched the drone appear to evade a bullet that would never come close to it—as if the operator could actually see the bullet coming. It was a reflexive dodge followed by its speeding away toward the river, back to Mexico.

As Dillon turned back onto the main road, his "special" cell phone rang.

"You had instructions not to contact the others for at least 72 hours."

"Circumstances changed. How did . . . never mind. You must be tracking this phone."

"How did circumstances change?"

Dillon proceeded to tell the anonymous voice on the other end about the man asking questions in town and about the drone over the Cantu's home. He also voiced his concern that the cartel was snooping around. There was a slight pause on the other end.

"Okay. Good decision and good intel. We'll see what we can find out from our end and let the other man know to be careful. Out."

The line disconnected. Dillon reflected upon the call. So, whoever it was, wasn't as all-knowing as they came across. Plus, he'd said *we'll see* and *our end.* So, there was more than one person on the other end. Still, whoever *they* were sure seemed to put the NSA, CIA, FBI, and military intelligence to shame. Or maybe those alphabet organizations simply had a different agenda, one in which their country did not come first.

Raimondo watched over the shoulder of his man operating the drone. The ranch closest to where his shipment had been attacked seemed the most likely place to start, although its obviousness also ruled against it. Who would be insane enough to attack the cartel right next to their home? After 30 minutes of observation, they had seen nothing suspicious, just a typical working ranch.

His cell rang.

"*Si.*" His man in Eagle Pass reported in. Had he learned anything useful? "*Que has aprendido hasta ahora?*"

"*Si, jefe. Tengo los nombres de una docena de veteranos militares. Te los enviaré por mensaje de texto.*"

"*Excelente. Buen trabajo.*" Raimondo made a mental note to reward the man for his good work. His phone dinged to alert him to a new text. "*El texto acaba de llegar.*" He scanned it quickly. Yes, a dozen names. "*A ver si puedes averiguar más sobre estos hombres.*"

"*Si, jefe.*"

The man would continue to delve into the names he had

just provided them. With luck perhaps Raimondo would move several steps forward in his quest. He looked at the property map in his hand to check the name of the ranch owner, and then cross-checked it with the list of names he had just received. There was no match.

"*Jefe, un camion se acerca al rancho.*"

Raimondo turned his attention back to the drone video to watch the truck approaching the ranch. A Silverado with a load of what appeared to be feed sacks had turned down the lane to the ranch. He watched with interest. Perhaps this was just a friend or neighbor. Maybe someone doing business with the ranch.

"Can you get the license plate?"

"I can try, *jefe*, but it is so dirty the plates might not be readable from our distance. Do you want me to fly in closer?"

"No. I do not want the drone to be spotted."

They watched as the truck approached the house and then turned toward one of the barns where a tractor had just driven inside. The men exchanged greetings, and then the truck also entered the barn.

"*Maldecirlo!*" They dared not get closer to the barn, but he wanted to see what was happening in there.

Several minutes later, the truck emerged. There appeared to be a different cargo in its bed. The men waved in parting, and the truck drove off.

"It looks like he picked up more feed from the barn."

Raimondo had to agree. Simply more ranch work, nothing clandestine.

"Uh-oh, we have been spotted."

They watched as the man from the barn looked directly

at them, turned, and ran back into the barn. He exited the building with a rifle in hand and began waving it at the drone. Seconds later, he aimed and appeared to fire upon the device. They could not hear a rifle retort, but clearly, he didn't like their presence there.

"Ha. Not much of a shooter. My 14-year-old nephew could have picked us off at this distance."

Raimondo responded only by saying, "Bring it back." His man's words rang true. At just over a hundred yards, a skilled shooter could have nailed the drone. And in his experience, most of these ranchers had honed their shooting skills by hunting coyotes and deer. Without hearing the retort, they could only assume he had actually fired his rifle. Maybe he hadn't.

If he had, he likely meant it to be a warning shot. Yes, Raimondo decided it had been nothing more than that, a warning. After all, the family's name did not appear on the list, assuming the list was complete. Perhaps they would revisit this ranch in the future.

COL Michael Southworth, Ret, stared at his comrade, Mike Jurgesmeyer. Both were good friends with Lynch Cully and staunch patriots. The past November's election had stirred concern in both, one that they could not share in any real depth with their friend. The CIA had coined the term they preferred—plausible deniability. The least Lynch knew, the better, particularly since they didn't want anything working its way up the chain to Lynch's old boss, soon-to-be ex-President Bradley Graham. Neither could be linked to them should their efforts be revealed.

Colonel S, or simply "colonel," as some called him, paced. That last conversation with an operative in Texas had triggered a thought that disturbed him. Mike J, as he was known in their social circle, sat at his computers. The older man reflected on how they had come together.

On a leave of absence from the St. Louis County Computer Forensics Lab, Mike J had put his significant talents to use creating a network that could monitor the southern border. As border incidents and smuggling—both human and drugs— increased in anticipation of the next, more compliant administration, he knew something had to be done. And he knew that this "something" would have to be clandestine and skirt the law, if not break it outright. But some things required extraordinary action.

He also knew he needed a military tactician with the appropriate background to help plan the required activities. It hadn't been easy feeling out the colonel about such an operation. Subtlety was not one of Mike J's strong suits. But in the end, the two found they worked well together, had a strong, common love for their country, and would do what they could to keep their country safe. With the world going crazy around them, they called themselves The Remnant.

It didn't take long to build a corps of like-minded individuals with special talents they could utilize. Some were warriors. Others had access to high-grade weaponry. A few offered access to federal and state surveillance systems, access that Mike J found particularly helpful. And some stood in the wings, covering their backs should certain authorities begin sniffing about for those disrupting their plans to open the border. These patriots were on the alert, now that the first operation involving military weapons had been completed. Proving the use of such weapons would not be difficult. Each left behind its own chemical signature and characteristic form of destruction.

To date, The Remnant could claim success in stopping over $100 million worth of drugs, mainly fentanyl, from entering the country, securing more than a few routes into the country, and preventing two dirty bombs from causing death and fear in whatever target cities they were destined for. Three illicit terrorist camps—one each in Texas, Oklahoma, and Missouri—had been destroyed. While the FBI was aware of the camps, they sat on their duffs and simply surveilled them—much as they did Antifa groups—upon the orders of higher-ups. The Remnant's operatives had eliminated them as threats, all under the nose of the FBI "observers." To say that ruffled some federal feathers was an understatement.

Colonel S sat down in a nearby easy chair. He covered his eyes while using his thumb and long finger to massage his temples. He needed to think. While they had some cover from federal scrutiny, the power and finances of the cartels were proving harder to restrain.

"You know, we talked about the eventuality of one or more cartels seeking retribution. If anything, we should be thankful it's taken this long for them to start."

Colonel S nodded. "I know, and I am. Thankful, that is. That's not really what's worrying me at the moment."

"Oh?" Looking concerned, his friend and compatriot swiveled away from his computers and faced him. Face on, you couldn't see the man's silky, long ponytail hidden behind his bulked-up shoulders on a six-foot, two-inch frame. His forehead had a receding hairline that hadn't been there when the two first met through Lynch, but little else appeared changed.

"Yeah, maybe we shouldn't have deployed the XM25 so quickly."

"Okay, but cell phone chatter says we took out a $15 million drug shipment."

"True, there's that. But it's also alerted the feds to our use of a weapon that was decommissioned by the army. They won't be as aggressive as the cartel, but they have better records on people trained to use it."

"And if that gets to the cartels, we have to be concerned about our people." Mike J completed his friend's thoughts.

The colonel nodded. "Last thing we want is to endanger our people and their families. That is definitely *not* what they signed on for."

"So, we turn our focus onto the southwest border, away from Texas, and not use the military gear for a while."

Colonel S stood and paced across the room. "Or we figure out how to keep those names from passing on to the cartel. But how?"

Mike J shook his head. "Not something my system can handle. But . . ." His voice trailed off.

"But what? There's always something after the word 'but.'"

The younger man played with his ponytail. "Well, word on the dark web once talked of a PsyOps software project in Afghanistan that morphed into this mastermind surveillance program called AlterNet. Rumors linked Wallace Chamberlain and his company to it, but folks who seemed to get close to it had a habit of dying."

The colonel chortled. "That alone gives credence to the rumors. But Chamberlain himself died in a car accident last year."

"Yep. And that's when chatter about AlterNet stopped . . . until recently."

"You think it's been taken over by someone else? If it actually exists."

Mike J smiled. "Well, if it has, it's been taken over by a white hat."

The colonel raised his brow. "Really? Why do you say that?"

"Saw something about it being used to take down that international child trafficking ring. The one harvesting blood products from kids. Can't remember the name. Fronted by some company using three letters."

A sense of amazement filled Colonel S as he recalled meeting two young men at Lynch's new home in Wisconsin a couple of months earlier. Aric with an 'A' was the name he remembered, and that the older brother was some kind of computer whiz. Had AlterNet been mentioned? He couldn't recall, but the gist of that conversation involved taking down a child trafficking ring. "YFM Corp?"

"Hey, yeah, that's it."

The colonel pulled his phone from his pocket and rushed toward the door.

"Hey, where're you going?"

"Have a call to make." He needed to call Lynch and get more information on Aric and his brother.

NINETEEN

In the course of two days, Jess and Chris had introduced him to a dozen young members of their Christian group. Two of those were also taking Dr. Carter's class, and they all now sat together. The previous day, Lindsey and Theresa had snagged the seats on either side of Jess, to Aric's disappointment. He was determined to change that seating arrangement today.

He arrived early and found a nest of seats for their group, in which he claimed the central seat. A few minutes later, Jess and her brother entered the room. He waved and caught their attention. He noticed Lindsey had joined Jess at the door, and the two talked.

Had he imagined it, or had Lindsey pointed to him with her head, while smiling and talking. Did Jess blush? Were they talking about him?

The trio—Theresa hadn't appeared yet—approached him, and Aric was happy to see Jess claim the seat on his right. He was then surprised that Lindsey took the seat to his left. He had expected Chris to sit there. The ladies got settled in and prepared for class.

Then, Lindsey surprised him again as she leaned toward him and spoke. "So, we hear you're already a celebrity on campus."

He turned his head toward her, only to feel conflicted as Jess joined her, closing in from his right.

"That's right. On campus, what, five days now and already folks are talking."

He swiveled his head to the right . . .

"Yeah, they either hate you or applaud you."

. . . and back to his left.

"At least you're in the right dorm if you plan on being an activist."

. . . and to his right.

He heard Chris laugh behind him. "Looks like my folks watching one of my tennis matches." Aric glanced back to see that Theresa had joined Chris in the row behind them.

Aric put his hands up to stop the back and forth. "Okay, okay. What's up? I have no idea what you're talking about."

"Really?" asked Lindsey.

He resisted the urge to turn to face her.

"Really."

"You're THE GUY," said Jess.

She placed her hand on his, and he felt his face flush.

Lindsey laughed. "I have a friend on the football team and word is out that you're the guy who stood up for free speech at that protest last Saturday."

He took a deep breath and sighed. "Wow. That didn't take long." He now understood the comment about being hated or applauded. He started to say something when the professor walked in and took to the podium. The room suddenly hushed.

Dr. Carter looked directly at Aric and had a look on his face that Aric couldn't quite interpret. The man appeared ready to say something to him but appeared to change his mind.

"Class, let's get started. This morning, we're going to look at the Magna Carta and its role in our modern jurisprudence system."

The class droned on for the next ninety minutes before letting up for a break. As soon as they could, both ladies began to pepper him with questions. It quickly became clear that the football team wasn't very good at the game of telephone. The reality of what had happened in the dining hall two nights earlier had been changed and exaggerated in several ways. With their break time almost over, he proceeded to straighten out the story Lindsey had been told.

"Well, that black lesbian you described is named Lateesha. I've seen her 'at work,' if you want to call it that. She can be outright dangerous."

Eric chuckled at the idea. "After what I went through last year, nothing she could come up with would seem dangerous."

As soon as he'd said it, he regretted it. He'd just opened up a conversation he would be better off avoiding. As his brother liked to tell him, he needed to control his mouth better. What was it that James wrote in his epistle? ". . . but no human being can tame the tongue. It is a restless evil, full of deadly poison."

"What?"

"What happened to you last year?" they asked in unison.

The prof called the class to order.

"Saved by the bell," said Chris, smirking. "But I'm looking forward to this story, too."

Aric rolled his eyes. He'd have to figure out just how much he could share with them, but for now, he had a reprieve.

After another hour of lecture, the class broke for lunch. After the group had packed up, Jess took Aric's arm, smiling. "Now, we can all go out for lunch and hear the rest of this story."

Aric looked down at her and grinned. He loved that she'd taken his arm without hesitation or waiting for him to offer. Maybe this whole thing would be to his advantage.

"Okay, but I have to swing by my dorm room first. Where can I meet you?"

Chris nodded. "We'll wait outside the dorm."

As they walked toward the dormitory, they discussed where to go for lunch. Well, the others discussed it. Aric hadn't heard of half the places they mentioned.

"Be right back," he said as he left them outside the building.

He ran up the stairwell rather than waste time waiting on and taking the elevator. As he neared his door, he spied two things right away. Some kind of poster had been taped to his door and a brown paper lunch bag sat at the base of it. He frowned as soon as he could make out the poster. It was a poster of the cross with a big red circle painted around it. Through the middle, a red line divided the circle and on the line was written "HATE." As he stood before the door, he didn't need eyes to see what was in the bag. The smell of feces—human or otherwise—was strong.

He debated what to do. Calling the RA was one option, but

this was more than a prank. He grabbed his cell phone and dialed Campus Security. "I need to report a hate crime."

As he waited, he debated whether or not to open the door. Did something else await him inside? He hoped Tom wouldn't wander back to the room. After the dining room incident, their relationship had seemed, well, strained, although Aric could not understand why. Tom, of all people, knew that incident wasn't of Aric's making.

Several people passed by. Some snickered. Others groaned and frowned. He used his phone to both take photos and text Chris and urge them to go ahead to lunch. *Something has come up*, was all he shared at that point. He then set the phone to record video and placed it in a spot where it would record his encounter with security.

An officer arrived just a couple of minutes later.

"I came back from class to get something, and this was here."

The woman frowned. "You called it a hate crime."

Well, isn't it? Whoever did this even used the word." He pointed to the poster. "Is this the type of thing you do to a friend? So, yes, I want it reported as a hate crime."

"We see this kind of stuff as pranks frequently. I don't know that I'd classify it that way."

A year ago, Aric might have given in to her authority status as a police officer, but he'd been through enough, seen enough, and toughened enough that she wasn't going to find him some compliant freshman.

"Ma'am, I have no desire to get you in trouble, but this is an outward display of hatred for my religious beliefs and an attempt to curtail my first amendment rights. If I have to take this beyond Campus Security, I will."

The woman donned gloves and opened the bag, wincing as she did so. All she accomplished was to confirm its contents.

"Don't toss that. It could be DNA evidence pointing to precisely who did this."

She gave him a look, but he knew that she knew that he was correct. If it was human excrement, its DNA could point to its origin, which would point to at least one person involved.

"Look, I'll report this but not as a hate crime—"

He interrupted. "Why? Because the college doesn't want it on record? Look, I know hate crimes have to be reported to the FBI under the UCR Program, and many police departments shy away from such because they don't want the stats showing up for their jurisdictions."

The Uniform Crime Reporting Program required all Part 1 crimes to be reported. Initially, such crimes included things like murder, rape, kidnapping, felony theft, and more. Fifty-two crimes were reportable, and in the mid-1990s, hate crimes were added. Colleges were required to report such crimes just as their municipal counterparts had to.

"If something like this had happened to one of the black or gay residents, you folks would be all over it. But, because I'm a white Christian, it's just a prank? How do you draw the line? What's fair and right for one should be fair and right for all."

He couldn't tell whether or not he was helping or just getting under her skin. She stepped away from the area and made a phone call. He couldn't hear what she was saying, but he guessed she was getting guidance from a supervisor. After a moment, she turned and walked back to him.

"We'll file a report, but not as a hate crime."

"Then the college leaves me no option." He retrieved his cell phone, which caused a look of dismay on the officer's face when she realized she had been recorded. In reality, when Aric also looked about, he saw that he wasn't the only one recording the event. Mitch and some of his friends all had their cell phones out.

Aric opened his contact list and pulled up a specific name and number, which he dialed. A moment later, the man answered.

"Special-Agent-in-Charge Wiese, hey, this is Aric Afton. . . . Do you have a moment? . . . Yes, sir, I'm well, but an incident has happened here at college." As he described the situation to the state's leading FBI agent—a man he'd gotten to know well enough a few months earlier to have been given his private cell number—the officer's face blanched. "Yes, sir, here's the video." With that, he pressed a button and transmitted the video directly to the man. The officer breathed more heavily. "Thank you, sir. Here's the officer."

He handed his phone to the woman, who took it as if it was radioactive. "Officer Wellston. With whom am I talking?"

Aric couldn't understand the words, but the S-A-C's tone came through loud and clear. He refrained from smiling, not that it was a situation that anyone should find amusing or pleasing. But, if he was going to be THE GUY on campus, he was ready to shake it up. Between Portland, Camp Douglas, and now, college, he'd had enough.

Adam, with elbows on his desk, laid his head in his open

palms. What had his kid brother gotten himself into this time?

He would never admit to Aric that he monitored Aric's phone. Most of his calls were innocuous, and Adam paid them no attention. He sure as heck wasn't about to eavesdrop on his brother.

But this time? A call to Campus Security? Followed by a call to S-A-C Wiese in Madison? He tapped into the call in time to hear Aric describe what was happening at his dorm room. Then he, too, received the video of his interaction with the security officer. He had to admit, his brother had become bolder and tougher after their time together. He also acknowledged that Aric was correct about the "prank" actually being a hate crime and attack on his religious rights and freedom. He felt quite proud that he'd had something to do with Aric's maturity and toughening.

Maybe he was wrong to monitor his brother, but how else could he help keep him safe?

There were still those allies of Wallace Chamberlain who searched for whoever took him down and launched the viral attack that caused AlterNet to "implode." Of course, without AlterNet, they stood no chance of finding what they wanted. With AlterNet's self-destruction came his own. Of sorts. Adam Afton no longer existed as a one-time employee of Custodia Circumdant Systems. Of course, CCS no longer existed either, but all traces of records for the company, should someone other than Adam somehow discover them, pointed to one Alistair Cummings as the genius behind AlterNet. And Cummings had been killed in a fiery accident involving too much to drink. All who had firsthand knowledge of Adam's involvement now fertilized the grass somewhere.

Well, not all. Aric, Lynch Cully, and a Colonel Michael Southworth all knew. But none of them would betray him. The latter, it now appeared, had his own secrets to keep. Of such, Adam had discovered only recently by chance.

As Adam watched the video, he pondered first, should he get involved, and second, if so, how? How indeed. Aric was holding his own well. For Adam to give any inkling that he knew about this incident would expose his monitoring of his brother. No. Aric would have to come to him for help before he would assist.

That decided, he did take one more small step. He placed a tap onto S-A-C Wiese's phone. The man *did* owe them both big time. He *had* told them to call anytime they needed help, and even gave them both his private cell number. And the FBI *did* track all hate crimes. But he likely never expected either to take him up on the offer. Adam chuckled as he wondered what might possibly be going through the man's mind right now. One thing for sure, after hearing the rest of the phone call, he didn't want to be in that Security Officer's shoes right now.

As he went about his business of tracking down corrupt politicians and businessmen, a task that promised never-ending job security, his focus returned to his brother's phone when a text from that very same Colonel Southworth came through on Aric's phone. *I need to find your brother. Can you put me in touch with him?* Curious.

Aric motioned to the others in the hall to stop their video recordings. They did.

The officer handed back his phone. He put it to his ear.

"Thank you, sir. I just want the same protection as anyone else here, as well as the peace to pursue my studies."

"And you'll have it. I heard from Lynch Cully that you signed on to be part of his criminal forensics major. I wish you well, and should you want to take that major and use it for the FBI, you'll have my endorsement. We owe you and Adam."

"Thank you, sir. Again. I hope this didn't bother you."

"Not at all. Got you covered. Have a better day."

"You, too, sir. Have a great afternoon." He hung up.

Officer Wellston scrutinized Aric. "At first, I just thought you were some smug Bible thumper getting a little payback. But after that call, I'm actually impressed. We have an unsung hero in our midst. I would never have taken you as someone involved in taking down an international trafficking ring. He didn't say where, but I have my suspicions. The whole child trafficking issue breaks my heart. Thank you."

"You're welcome, but please, that's not to be widespread knowledge. And you might want to keep your suspicions to yourself. If the wrong people get wind of those suspicions and that you could possibly point them to the people responsible, you'd find out what real hell is like before you ended up anchored in the deepest part of Lake Michigan. I'm not exaggerating, and I certainly don't want that. As I told the Special Agent, I just want the same protections as anyone else and to be able to study in peace."

The woman nodded. "I'll do my best to help with that. Look, I'll file the report as you've asked, but don't be shocked if my superiors change it. You're not wrong about the college wanting to look good and avoid certain statistics. A lot of municipalities do the same."

"Thanks. And I understand. Uh, could I ask one more thing?"

"Sure."

"After finding this, I didn't want to take the chance of opening my door and finding more surprises."

She nodded. "Good thinking. Go ahead and unlock it."

He used his ID to unlock the door. The officer then took over and cautiously opened the door. But not carefully enough, as some kind of container dumped what reeked of urine onto her right shoulder. She managed to avoid getting hit squarely over the head with it. From her reaction and words, Aric wondered if she'd once been in the Navy, capable of making her comrades blush.

She looked at him. "Sorry. I shouldn't have reacted like that. I half expected water 'cause I've seen that prank before, but this takes it to a different level. Now I'm gonna write it up as an assault with a biological agent and see what my superiors say to that. I'll get someone up here pronto to clean this up."

He looked at her, trying not to step back to avoid the odor. "This also means someone gave the person access. I doubt my roommate would agree to this, so that points to a RA being in on it."

The officer contemplated that. "I'd have to agree. I will insist on an investigation into that. If a RA did give someone access to your room, to anyone else's room for that matter, it's cause for dismissal."

She stepped back into the hall and glanced about. The few who witnessed it did not laugh. She called for maintenance and began to collect the "evidence."

Aric stepped over the puddle and entered his room. It held one more surprise for him. Tom's side of the room was empty. He had moved out. Aric found a terse note on his desk.

Aric you're a good guy and I think we could've been good roomies but dude you've become a target and I don't want to be collateral damage. No hard feelings I hope.

In truth, Aric didn't know what to feel. In one sense, he felt abandoned. He and Tom shared a variety of social and political views. In that sense, they got along well. But the guy was a night owl to Aric's morning person and a slob to Aric's nearly obsessive tidiness. Maybe being in a room by himself would be best, for now. But how would the college view that? As lost revenue? Probably. Would they force a new roommate upon him? Now, Aric dreaded that potential.

Adam found that text on Aric's phone to be a distraction. His brother hadn't yet opened it, but calling Aric at midday wasn't an option. They talked in the evenings, outside of class hours, and Aric would be heading back to class shortly. He decided on discretion. Aric would likely discover the text before the next class session.

Adam stood and walked to the windows in the back room, overlooking the lake. The lake was solidly frozen to the point that part of it had been cleared for pick-up hockey games. He preferred watching the ducks, geese, and other birds on and around the water, but it could be another two months, or three, before they returned. He paced a bit, still wondering what the colonel wanted. Then he went to the kitchen and pulled a cold water from the fridge.

What he wanted was a beer, but he'd been sober for two years and counting, and he was determined not to fall into that again. Aric was underage for alcohol in the state, so that made it a bit easier to keep it out of the house. Of course, even if he was 21, Aric would never bring that temptation into Adam's house. Aric was his biggest cheerleader for sobriety.

Again, he paced. "C'mon, Aric, find that text," he murmured to the empty room. Five minutes later, the notification alert on his phone signaled a text. *Yes!* he thought. He rushed to the desk and picked up his phone. It was a local pizzeria texting him with a special discount coupon. He frowned and sighed.

He returned to the window to discover show flurries settling onto the already white landscape. He didn't recall snow in the forecast. As he took the final swig of water from the bottle and walked toward the kitchen to toss it in the recycling bin, his phone emitted another alert.

This time he didn't rush to get it. Too great a chance it was the competing pizzeria with their matching coupon. The two of them did this all the time.

Yet, as he picked up his phone, he saw the message from Aric.

*Great morning. Lousy lunchtime. Got a message
from Colonel S that he wants to talk with you. Here's
contact info. Talk tonight.*

Adam wasted no time utilizing the contact info to do a deep dive into the colonel's background. Yes, he was eager to learn why the man wanted to talk with him, but he'd learned the need for due diligence many years ago. His upgraded version of AlterNet, which he now called UltraNet, took little time before beginning to return the sought-after data.

The man's military record had been exemplary. Since retiring a decade earlier, his life had been busy with charity projects, church, and other good deeds. Perhaps, but from Adam's experience, such squeaky-clean findings were too good to be true. He added Lynch Cully as one more search factor. That, too, didn't take long, but the angelic colonel was starting to gather some rust on his halo.

There were few police records or detailed reports, but as Adam read between the lines, the colonel had no qualms skirting the law if aiming for a "good" outcome. He'd been involved in taking down a human trafficking ring in St. Louis. That was how he and Lynch had met. It was some time after that when Lynch got involved with then-presidential candidate Bradley Graham, and the colonel once again entered the picture. At that time, he'd shot and killed a man outside his home who seemed bent on assassinating someone in the home. The colonel had been exonerated by both witness accounts and the state's Castle Doctrine. He again got involved in protecting the young king of England who was being targeted by assassins while in the U.S. Clearly, the man had no qualms in taking whatever action was needed to do what he thought right.

In reflection, Adam saw the same things as being "right." With his work to bring down corrupt politicians and business leaders, he sought to save the innocent and protect his country. The colonel seemed to want the same.

In all, Adam spent over two hours combing through the data UltraNet had provided him about Colonel Michael Southworth. In the end, he felt comfortable contacting the man. Whatever the colonel wanted, Adam was well-armed with the data he might need to assess the call.

He picked up a burner phone that he could "clean" by fully resetting it to factory settings if necessary. He entered the contact number and after several rings, a man answered.

"Adam Afton, thanks for getting back to me."

How? How did the colonel know it was him? Adam shook his head. Of course, one of the easiest "tricks" in the book, and in his eagerness, he'd totally overlooked it. The number he called went to another burner, a number that only Adam Afton would have. Adam made a mental note not to get caught short again.

Yet, the fact that the man had felt the need to use such security spoke volumes to Adam. The other thing he made note of was that the man had to use Aric as a contact point. He hadn't been able to track Adam directly. That was good. However, if the tidbits of data that Aric had seen recently which pointed to the colonel were correct, that was outstanding news. After all, a man with few resources would have to use family contacts or mutual friends to find someone. That a man with considerable resources couldn't track him was what was outstanding. He would soon find out which case applied.

"Colonel, I think we have some common goals. Is that why you contacted me?"

"It is, but burner phone to burner phone isn't the ideal method. I think you should plan a visit to your family so we can meet in person."

Adam nodded. The man had resources. That was the only way he could know that Adam, too, used a disposable phone.

"Perhaps. Would it be worth my while?"

"Do you believe in securing our southern border?"

"I do."

"Then I think you'll find it worthwhile. Here's another number. Call me at that number when you get to St. Louis. You have one minute to copy it down."

A text arrived with the number, which Adam suspected went to another phone. The colonel had said to copy it, so he did, both to his phone and to paper. Sixty seconds later, all traces of the text disappeared.

That was impressive, he thought. "Got it. I'll leave tomorrow morning."

"Fantastic. We'd like to invite you to join The Remnant."

"I'll be in touch." After hanging up, he discovered that his phone had been wiped of all traces of that call. *How does he do that?* he wondered.

The Remnant? Why hadn't any of his queries brought that name to light? He set UltraNet up to find any and everything on The Remnant. After two hours, all he had was the title to some lame 1980s novel. Yes, he had the impression that this meeting would indeed be worthwhile.

TWENTY

"Rick, that's not what I want to hear from you." It had been two days since his union rep and the union attorney had met him at his home. Ryan paced in the small space of his basement office. They had told him to give them two days.

"Ryan, I understand. We're being stonewalled by the mayor's office, the governor's office, and everyone in between who might have anything to do with this issue. The forensics lab told us they've been ordered to hold any and all reports until further notice. They're sympathetic to your dilemma, and off the record, they told us that everything they have exonerates you. But they don't want to lose their jobs by disobeying orders."

Ryan sighed and shook his head. Sympathy for his "dilemma" didn't clear his name.

"Then I'm going to release the report myself." He heard his union rep mutter something on the other end but couldn't make out the words.

"Ryan, look, I'd think hard about doing that. You tick off the upper brass, and you might find yourself in worse shape.

Releasing the report might also get someone fired, and no one deserves that. Plus, releasing the report will likely instigate an investigation into how it was released, and that will lead to further delays. Like I said the other day, I can't stop you from releasing what you have, but it could very likely backfire in your face."

Ryan had to admit to himself that he hadn't fully thought that out. As he mulled over Rick's comments, he heard footfall on the steps, his wife's. As she turned the corner toward his office, the look on her face said it all. As tears rolled down her cheeks, she said nothing but handed him her phone.

Ryan's anger flared as he saw the text messages.

"Rick, you better do something and do it fast. My wife just received two death threats on *her* phone, one of which includes our boys and mentions their school."

Ryan retrieved his desk chair and offered it to Sarah. But she refused to sit. The tears had stopped, dammed up by the anger that now hardened her face as well. Ryan had seen that Mama Bear look before. She went to their gun safe near his desk and entered the code to open it. Ryan watched as she pulled out her 9mm Glock and its full magazine. She handled it like the expert that she was, clearing the chamber, and inserting the magazine. She grabbed her phone and marched back up the stairs.

"Rick, Sarah is now fully armed, and heaven help anyone who might try harming her boys. That Mama Bear is one grizzly when it comes to protecting her own."

Silence followed that brief distraction from the topic at hand. After about 30 seconds, Rick continued. "Look, shoot me copies of those death threats, and I'll roust up Sam and go to

Chief O'Reilly. We'll schedule a press conference for later this afternoon. This has to end."

At that moment, their recently installed driveway alarm alerted them that someone had come up the drive.

"Are you expecting any deliveries?" he asked.

Sarah shook her head. The alarm sounded again, its motion detector having been triggered again. Had the first intruder retreated already or had a second one joined him?

Ryan used his thumbprint to open the small gun box on his dresser, grabbed his 40mm Sig, and hurried out the side door. He wasn't surprised to hear Sarah scurrying right behind him, nor to see the Glock in her hand. He rushed directly toward the front of his house where his car was parked just outside the garage. She turned the other way, which would take her behind and around to the other side of the house.

As he cleared the side of their home, he saw two figures in black hoodies and cloth face masks vandalizing his car with spray paint.

"Drop the paint and get on the ground, or I'll shoot!"

The two figures glanced at each other, dropped the spray cans, and bolted away from him. He was right behind them but hadn't run 30 feet before he watched them stop and raise their hands. He smiled when he saw Sarah in her favorite firing stance daring them to continue.

"On the ground," he commanded. They complied. He nodded with his head toward the garage, and Sarah responded by putting her two wrists together. He nodded, and she ran off. She knew what he needed. A couple of minutes later, she returned with a handful of zip ties. While she held her gun on them, he secured their hands behind their backs, as well as their ankles. They wouldn't be going anywhere.

"I called 911 while I was in the garage. I mentioned we had them at gunpoint." She grinned.

He smiled. She'd been a police wife long enough to know the keywords needed to get immediate action. Sure enough, within minutes they heard sirens. Not one. Not even two. Sounded more like three units responding.

Under state laws, the right to self-defense falls into three basic categories: Stand Your Ground, Castle Doctrine, and Duty to Retreat. Oregon, under ORS 161.209, was like the majority of states in being a Stand Your Ground state. However, with the liberal, 'defund the police' attitudes held by most of the Portland and state politicians, you had to be very careful. Deadly force against a person, or persons, was justified only if they were committing or attempting to commit a felony involving the use or threatened imminent use of physical force against you, or were committing or attempting to commit a burglary in a dwelling, or were using or about to use unlawful deadly physical force against you.

As an off-duty police officer, Ryan's response to the vandals was a matter of training and his duty. For Sarah, however, none of those conditions qualified, and being an officer's wife did not count. She was grilled for over an hour by a senior detective who had been called to the scene. Fortunately, deadly force had not been necessary. Also to her advantage, the presence of death threats on her phone made her armed reaction to the vandals appear to be a reasonable one—an action any sane person might be expected to take.

Still, Ryan's rage mounted at her treatment by his own

force. He couldn't help but think that this was somehow directed at him. Sarah found him standing in the front room staring out the window.

"Enough is enough. Are we going ahead with plan B?"

"After the way they treated you today, you bet we are. Call your friend Monica, and I'm calling Joe."

The afternoon rolled along and by three p.m., he had convinced himself that the union had failed him yet again. But at 3:15, his cell rang, and Caller ID revealed Rick as the caller.

"Rick, I was beginning to think you had gotten nowhere with the department again today."

"Sorry. Hey, I see you had more trouble today, but you caught the vandals."

Ryan gave him a synopsis of the events and mentioned his displeasure over the treatment of his wife.

"I'll make a formal complaint if you wish."

Ryan shook his head, even though Rick couldn't see it. "No need. We're going to deal with it differently, but to return to the reason for your call. Where do I stand?"

"Yeah, right. You need to get into uniform and head straight here to headquarters. We talked with the chief and told him about the vandalism, the death threats . . . all of it. While we were meeting with him, we got word of your property being vandalized again. That was the final straw, I think. He as much as admitted that people above him were dragging their feet for political reasons and that he'd had enough. He's going to stand by you, release the reports, clear you for duty, and wait to get fired. His words, not mine."

Ryan sighed in relief. Finally, his name would be cleared.

Ashleigh waited outside Dr. Fry's office once again. She had called her mentor several times over the previous two days but had received no reply. The protest had been only four days earlier and had been a success in Ashleigh's mind. She knew the protests would taper off as classes began and people focused on their studies. Instead, at Dr. Fry's urging, they just stopped, like going cold turkey with cigarettes—which Ashleigh had never been able to do. What had happened?

She had only one answer. Someone had gotten to her. Somebody had something on Meredith Fry. But who? And what?

She heard the clip-clop of a woman's heels walking down the hallway from behind her. She turned to see Dr. Fry heading toward her office and stepped aside to allow her mentor to unlock and open the door.

"I don't have time to talk, Ashleigh. Can you make an appointment through the department secretary?"

What? she thought. She had never been told that before. The professor always made time for her, and she respected that by not taking up a lot of Dr. Fry's time.

"It's just that you've not returned my calls. I'm worried—"

The woman grabbed some papers from her desk and hurried back to the door, ushering Ashleigh away from it to close it. "I'm sorry, but I really am in a hurry. Please go ask Sheila to make you an appointment with me." She shut and locked the door.

"Has something happened—"

This time the professor sounded stern. "Ashleigh, make

an appointment." With that she hurried down the hall, and Ashleigh saw her knock on and enter Dr. Carter's door.

Dejected, Ashleigh turned in the opposite direction and headed toward the nearest exit. She would call the department office and make that appointment when she felt better. Right now, she was too upset to think about it. Dr. Fry had been rude to her. True, that was uncharacteristic of her, but Ashleigh felt as if her biggest ally in all the battles she had faced and continued to face had just abandoned her. She needed the emotional support Dr. Fry had once offered but seemed uninterested in providing.

She plodded back toward the dorm, wanting to cry but forcing herself not to. Others looked up to her for support, and she didn't want to look fragile to them. Still, she felt as if the world crashed in upon her. It was an emotion that was all too familiar to her.

As she neared the dorm, she saw Lateesha and Toni walking toward her. Toni, who identified as they/them, must have redyed their pink hair because it stood out like a neon sign in the dark.

"We did it, we did it," said Toni.

"Yeah, thanks, Ashleigh. We couldn't have done it without your help."

Ashleigh felt puzzled. Couldn't have done what?

"What?"

"We got him. You know, *the guy.* What's his name, Eric."

Ashleigh thought of Aric with an A. "What do you mean, you got him?"

"Yeah, we made it look like one of those frat-boy pranks." They described what they had done. "We also made it clear to his roommate that he'd receive some of the fallout if he stayed. We used one of your reassignment requests to help him move to another dorm."

"You what?" Ashleigh's mood plunged deeper into darkness. "H-how did you get into the room to . . ."

Lateesha smiled one of her rare but devious smiles. "We borrowed your master key card. We knew you wouldn't mind."

Ashleigh felt faint and fell to her knees. The others looked shocked and rushed to assist her.

"What's wrong?"

"You okay?"

Tears fell from Ashleigh's eyes. "Y-you m-may have just g-gotten me kicked out of the dorm, maybe even the c-college."

"Huh?"

"The misuse of that key card c-could get me kicked out. At the minimum, it could get me removed from the RA program, and without that, I can't afford to stay here. Without that, I have no place to live."

"How will they know? It's not like anyone saw us do it. We made sure of that," said Toni.

Ashleigh shook her head. "It's not like you used an old key. Every swipe of these cards is registered. If campus security decides to look into this prank, as you call it, one minute at the computer will show them whose cards were used and when."

The two looked aghast at the thought. "Hey, maybe it's not too late. Maybe we can get back to the room and remove everything, clean up." Lateesha appeared ready to run back to the dorm to accomplish just that, although using the verb 'run' with Lateesha didn't fit the woman's manner. Ashleigh had never seen her lesbian friend move any faster than an amble.

As the trio looked toward the dorm, they let out a unified moan. A female security officer had exited the building carrying a bucket, 2x4, and other evidence of the "prank." Ashleigh began to hyperventilate.

TWENTY-ONE

Adam divided his attention between preparing for his trip back to St. Louis and monitoring a situation in Portland, Oregon that had caught his attention a week earlier. After their experience in Portland several months earlier, he had set UltraNet to work trying to identify individual Antifa members, outline the loose hierarchy of their organization, and prepare a package of data for law enforcement should they ever return to enforcing the law instead of looking the other way. Even for his software, it had not been easy. The group's aversion to technology for communication made it difficult to isolate and track individuals. With their use of hoods and masks, facial identification had been impossible. The few people he'd identified through facial recognition appeared to be those simply caught up in the moment and not dedicated members of the cause.

During his continued surveillance, however, he had witnessed the shooting of a protester at the city's police headquarters via a variety of traffic cams, security cameras, and cell phones. Two of those cell phones proved to be those of the actual shooter and his accomplice. Although they were burner phones, the individuals had continued to use them long enough that UltraNet had tracked their location data for the past week and developed a list of probable owners based on the most frequented addresses and the time spent at those addresses.

Yet, while he prepared his anonymous "tip" regarding the shooters for the police, the vague incrimination of a police officer as the shooter was what caught his attention. Analysis of available video confirmed he had never fired his weapon, and the forensics lab had cleared him but had been ordered to hold their reports by people in the governor's office. UltraNet had ferreted out communications and money transfers to those people from a certain Hungarian-born billionaire known for funding far-left radical causes. These same people thought they had provided the governor with plausible deniability, but his software had thwarted that effort as well. In a different political environment, he had enough data to bring down that state's executive branch and imprison many of those people for a long time. But not in the current political environment.

Yet, considering all of that, it was the identity of the officer that next caught his attention. Under this or any other political circus, he could, and would, help that police officer. He was prepared to do so. At first, the most recent cell phone intercepts between the officer, his union rep, and another officer told him that his intervention might not be needed in the immediate time frame. In fact, it was the police chief who would need assistance first. And the city was in for a rude awakening.

Adam smiled as he thought about how he could help the officer. He prepared a short text to be sent anonymously to Officer Ryan Krueger.

Contrary to his expectations, Ryan felt uncomfortable in his uniform. He had given up much for his adopted city, and they had done nothing to support him in return. Not just the high muckety-mucks in the department, city, and state, but the people themselves. He and Sarah had made some good friends in the area, and most of them stuck with them through the ordeal. But not all. And more acquaintances than not refused to associate with them. Ryan had come to experience firsthand the liberal tradition of guilty until proven innocent.

Their meeting with Chief O'Reilly had gone well. The man had been candid about the treatment Ryan had received and that it had not been of his doing. He was about to go behind the backs of certain city and state leaders by reinstating Ryan to full duty and releasing the forensics reports. He suspected he would not have a job by day's end. But push-come-to-shove, he was fine with that.

As Ryan, Rick, Sam, and a few others stood behind the chief, the man organized his notes and waited for the clock to hit 4:30. Ryan felt his phone vibrate—either a call or a message—and his first thought was that it was Sarah and something else had happened at home. He pulled the phone out and found a message from an unknown number. That puzzled him, but the message confounded him even more.

Do not worry about Chief O'Reilly. I have his back

. . . and yours.

Truth be told, he had been worried about the chief's future. The man had Portland's best interests at heart. The riots had deflated him, but the orders to stand down and not enforce the law had taken a greater toll.

Thirty seconds after reading the message he glanced at his phone to read it again and it was gone. *How in the . . .* he wondered. He hadn't deleted the text. He didn't think it possible for the sender to delete it. And who was the sender? How did he have the chief's back? His thoughts were interrupted by the chief.

"Ladies and gentlemen, thank you for coming. I know the press has been speculating for a week about the shooting of January third, right on this very spot."

Ryan glanced around. He hadn't thought much about it, but the man was correct. They were holding the press conference in that same spot. He looked up at the second-floor terrace where the real shooter had been and saw an obvious police presence there. He offered himself a subtle nod. He wouldn't have tempted fate by leaving it open again either.

"I know you've been clamoring for the formal report, and that it's been somewhat delayed in coming. We turned over the investigation to the State Police, and while the forensics reports were completed days ago, they insisted upon being thorough."

That's what Rick had told Ryan. Ryan felt a subtle nudge in the ribs from the man.

"And to be honest, they wanted to hold out a bit longer before releasing them. I felt, however, that doing so was not fair to an officer who had gone above the call of duty for this city. Social media, as well as some of you, have pegged Officer Ryan Krueger as the shooter. Yes, I'm using his name . . . not to confirm your speculations but to announce that he is not responsible. Forensics has proven not only that his weapon was never fired, but that the fatal round came from a .30-06 rifle fired from the second-floor terrace right over there." He pointed to the location. "We will provide a more detailed report with the packet of information that most of you should be receiving electronically right now."

The chief paused as reporters began to check their devices for the data. Ryan watched their faces. Some appeared assured while others actually looked disappointed.

"We do not have any suspects at this time, so again, I encourage the public to come forward if they have any information that might help us. And as of this afternoon, a reward of $10,000 has become available to anyone who provides information leading to the arrest and conviction of the shooter."

That got heads turning and tongues wagging.

"At this point, I'd like to ask Officer Krueger to step forward."

Ryan did so, feeling a bit nervous over what he was about to do.

"Officer Krueger, I thank you for your service to our community. I know this past week has been hard for you, but I want to publicly state that you have been cleared of any wrongdoing and to publicly reinstate you to full duty. In addition, I'm promoting you to Police Sergeant. You have been the type of officer that Portland should be proud of."

Ryan's heart quickened. He had not been forewarned of the promotion. Plan B was going to seem like a kick in the teeth to the chief, and he didn't deserve that. He hoped that whoever sent that mysterious text truly had Chief O'Reilly's back. The man handed Ryan his badge, service weapon, and a set of stripes for his uniform.

As he accepted them, he whispered to the chief, "Sir, I apologize in advance for what's about to happen. It's not a reflection on you."

Ryan stepped up to the mic. "Thank you, Chief O'Reilly, you have been an outstanding leader and someone we all look up to. Sadly, not all departmental decisions have been yours to make. I thank you for the promotion. I was not prepared for that, but at this point, I'm afraid I must decline."

The chief's countenance looked more crestfallen than irritated.

"I moved my family from the upper Midwest to Portland five years ago in search of the career I'd always dreamed of. We love the area and the people we've met are, well, friendly and gracious are two adjectives that always come to mind. But then, politics got in the way. And the pandemic with its politics. When the riots started over an incident that occurred not here but 1,700 miles away, we thought they'd be short-lived. But they continued, and the department was ordered to stand down, to protect only government buildings—not the businesses and the people, and not to enforce the laws of this state and this city. The toll that took on our police cannot be overstated. As 40% of our force slowly left, I stayed out of love for this city and its people. I worked overtime and double overtime because we were so short-staffed. It took a tremendous toll on my marriage and my family. And then the incident of January third took place. Despite having never fired my weapon, I became the face of police evil, a murderer, and the poster child for a reckless defund the police movement. My home was vandalized. My wife and children received death threats. Just this morning, my car was vandalized."

He looked about. He had most people's attention. The few who ignored him he could readily identify as part of the problem, not part of the solution.

"While I truly appreciate my name finally being cleared and being reinstated to full duty, as well as being surprised by a promotion, my wife and I made a decision that should it ever come to threats against our family, that would be the end. Chief, as much as I appreciate your going out on a limb to do this for me, I formally resign, effective immediately."

Ryan looked about again. This time he saw Joe Diamonte, Ethan Auch, Jaden Wright, and a dozen other officers in the crowd, all moving forward. One by one, they came up to the chief and handed in their badges.

"For the people of Portland, you voted in people who seek to defund the police. We're honoring your wishes. The leaders of this city have shown their lack of support for their police, and now they no longer have to pay for 16 officers. We quit."

Ryan joined the end of the line and handed his badge back to the chief. "Chief, I'm sorry it came to this, but don't rush to pack up your office. You have a guardian angel watching your back if you wish to stay." Ryan hoped that text message was real.

Without waiting for a response, he turned toward the

building. The armory sergeant would be busy. Ryan was about to enter the building to turn in his weapon and gear, when he heard the chief take the microphone and say, "Make that 17. I'm retiring. Have a good night, everyone."

Adam watched the Portland press conference on three different news feeds. He had learned of Plan B through an intercepted phone call between Ryan Krueger and Joe Diamonte. And as he anticipated, the press corps went into overdrive as the 15 other officers lined up in solidarity with Krueger.

Adam always liked a good fireworks show.

And the chief's announcement that he was retiring, well, that was a suitable grand finale.

As he continued to watch the aftermath of that press conference, one that would be at the top of the news cycle there for weeks, he checked UltraNet. That intercepted phone call had given him the names of the resigning officers, and he put his program to work to find them their ideal jobs. The software not only developed personality and career profiles, it then scoured the Internet to find jobs that would fit them best. The list was ready.

He figured Krueger would still be in line to turn in his gear, so he proceeded to text him.

Good show. I still have the chief's back if needed.
As for you and the other 15, check your email. I have
potential jobs for all.

A minute later, his program alerted him to the fact that Krueger had indeed received and opened the email. A moment later, a text came through.

Who is this?

He replied,

A friend. When you come back to Wisconsin, I'll get in touch.

Even though the police chief had announced his retirement, Adam decided to cover his back as promised. He didn't want anyone interfering with the man's retirement. Plus, it would be "fun" to put the fear of God in some people. For each of the people involved, he put together a packet of incriminating evidence of their corruption and illegal actions, as well as a warning. Routing each email through a dozen international email servers and adding a few roadblocks to further prevent back-tracing, he sent them their information. He had little doubt that they'd behave.

TWENTY-TWO

Colonel Southworth had arranged to meet Adam at Sugarfire Smoke House in Olivette for lunch. The place had outstanding bar-b-que and was close to both Adam's parents' home and The Remnant's "secret lair"—as he and Mike J liked to joke. The main drawback to the place was that its shared tables offered no privacy. There would be no business discussion.

Waiting outside in the cold, he recognized Adam as soon as the young man emerged from his car. He met him at the end of the walkway and extended his hand.

"Colonel, nice to see you again," said Adam as they shook hands.

"You, too, Adam. Ready for some good bar-b-que? My treat."

"You bet I am. Wisconsin is pretty backward when it comes to que. They still confuse grilling with true bar-b-quing. And where I'm located, it's more of a battle between two pizza joints. My diet has been a bit lacking."

Colonel S laughed. "I've been down that path before,

before I met Mary. She's the whole foods, organic, gourmet chef that I could never be."

"Sounds like my mom. By the end of the day today, she'll have a week's worth of meals prepared for me to take home."

They took their place in line and examined the menu on the wall. With food in hand, they found an abandoned end of one large table to stake out as theirs.

"How are Rachel and the kids?"

Adam gave him the eye. Their only previous conversation had been one of legalities and how best to provide information on criminal activity to the authorities.

"Lynch keeps me up-to-date about you and Aric. I hope you have a chance to see them while you're here." He wasn't going to reveal that he had called Lynch to get all the information he could on Adam. He hoped his suspicion about the young man was correct.

With his mouth full, Adam nodded. He finished chewing and replied, "They joined us for dinner last night, and I'll go to her house this afternoon."

"Well, I hope that your relationship is becoming what you want it to be." He hoped that came across as diplomatically as he intended it to be.

The young man nodded again.

"So, you mentioned Wisconsin. Where in the state are you living now? Lynch wasn't quite sure."

Adam downed a few sweet potato fries as he scrutinized the Colonel. "Well, let's just say not too far from Lynch and the college that Aric's attending."

Colonel S nodded. The vague answer was what he'd expected. He wouldn't probe any further. The time for details might arise later, or not at all. He decided to take the conversation into the realm of current events, to get a feel for the young man's political and social stances.

"So, what'd you think of the election results?"

Adam leaned toward him, and the Colonel responded accordingly. Their voices took to lower volumes. Colonel S could read between the lines. Although Adam did not give specifics, he appeared to have information that could prove the election had been stolen from Bradley Graham. How? If Lynch had more detailed info on how Adam had taken down that child trafficking ring, he hadn't shared it. All the colonel knew was that Adam had been searching for his kidnapped daughter and found her.

"Tell you what, let's finish eating and find someplace private to talk."

Adam seemed hesitant.

"I think we share common views on a lot of things pertaining to our country and our freedoms, and you'll find what I have to say interesting. Actually, why don't you just follow me to my home, and we can continue with a beer or two."

Adam waggled his head. "Well, maybe some tea or a soda. I'm 18 months sober and don't want to go back to that. I try to avoid all temptations to drink again."

"My apologies. I didn't know that. I'm sure we can come up with something suitable to your liking. Mary keeps like 20 varieties of tea on hand, and I'm partial to Coke products . . . despite all the fuss over high fructose corn syrup."

Adam nodded. "Lead the way."

Fifteen minutes later, the colonel ushered his guest into

the front rooms of his historic Ferguson home. Adam glanced about.

"So, this is where you hid the king of England. Nice place."

"This is it. This way to the butler's pantry, not that anyone who ever lived here had a butler. That's where Mary keeps the teas. She's not home right now, by the way. I don't know if she'll return before you leave or not."

While their teas steeped, Colonel S built and started a fire in the library's fireplace. With drinks in hand, they settled into the chairs facing the fire.

"So, now we can talk. You should know that this house is swept routinely for electronic bugs, and the windows were treated to eliminate any risk of a listening device being used through them."

Adam gave him a strange look. He understood. If someone who was basically a stranger invited him into their home and told him that, he'd think the guy was looney tunes.

"I know. You're probably thinking who is this guy, some whacko conspiracy nut. Well, the windows were dealt with because President Graham was a frequent visitor here, and we discussed many issues quite openly. As such, I still have a high-level security clearance, although I expect that to be revoked with the incoming administration. I've kept up the electronic sweeps for other reasons, which I think you'll come to understand."

"Okay. I didn't realize you were that close to the president."

"We became very close friends, and it pains me to see the election stolen from him."

The two men sized each other up, again.

"I'm going to be up front. I knew Wallace Chamberlain back in his military days. Didn't care for the man, at all. Lynch told me you once worked for him, at his company. That's all he knew. I also know he participated in a major PsyOps program in Afghanistan. Another friend of mine, who is quite comfortable on the dark web, has told me about chatter he's seen about the software from that PsyOps program finding its way to Chamberlain's company. That chatter stopped when the man died but has resumed recently. Current chatter links the program to a white hat operator."

He paused to see if his words produced any reaction in the young man. Most wouldn't have noticed, but Adam developed a twitch, tapping his left thumb and index finger together. It was subtle, but it was there.

"I think you know my friend. Mike Jurgesmeyer. And, from what I know about the take down of YFM Corp, I'm putting two and two together. I think you now have AlterNet and are that white hat."

Adam clenched his left fist while taking a sip of tea from the cup in his right hand, trying to look nonchalant. The colonel didn't expect him to own up to his claim. This wasn't some British crime show where the perpetrator is confronted, immediately spills his guts with a full confession, and is led to a squad car without handcuffs. This involved truly evil men who wouldn't hesitate to kill to gain such information.

"Are you aware of any recent events along our southern border?"

"You mean the growing crowd of illegal aliens waiting to cross over when the new administration takes over?"

At this point, Colonel S knew he had to be cautious.

"Well, yes, there's that, and it's about to become a flood. But I'm referring to the prevention of a terrorist cell smuggling in two dirty bombs between Laredo and Eagle Pass near where the border wall construction has ended." He paused again to assess Adam's reaction. "Or of several drug shipments that were destroyed along the border, the most recent being a $15 million load of Fentanyl from the Los Zorros cartel out of Tampico."

There was that twitch again.

"What if I told you there's a growing company, in the military sense, of patriots who wish to protect our southern border from the rising tide of drugs and other threats to our nation."

"I would applaud their efforts, but also warn them that there are powerful, global forces that will come against them with everything they can. If they can rig the U.S. elections, you know they have incredible resources at hand." He took another drink of tea. "I can put two and two together, too. You must be part of this group. You need to be careful. I mean, *really* careful."

The colonel smiled inwardly. Had he just tacitly admitted to being AlterNet's white hat?

"Give me a minute. I'll be right back." Colonel S arose and walked into the kitchen where he dialed Mike J.

"Hey."

"Mike, I think I've found AlterNet's white hat."

"You sure about that?"

"Maybe 95% sure. Even if he's not, he's got skills we could use. I want to bring him to the lair." He still smiled every time he called it that.

"Do you trust him?"

"He's the one who took down YFM Corp, and yes, I trust him to be discreet."

"Well, I'll go on record as saying I'm not sure this is a good idea, but I trust your judgment. You've not been wrong yet. I'm here."

"I think you would trust him, too. You know each other."

"What? Who?"

"See you shortly." Colonel S disconnected and pondered his decision. Mike had said he hadn't been wrong yet. He hoped this wouldn't break his streak. In the meantime, he looked forward to surprising Mike J with his mystery guest.

Adam couldn't explain it, but when he met the colonel again outside the restaurant, he felt as if they were meant to work together. His deep dive into the man's past had intrigued him. The man had been entrusted with the life of the king of England and his family, and Adam felt assured that he, too, could trust the man. Yet, that didn't come easily.

He had survived the goons sent by Wallace Chamberlain only by his remaining in the deepest shadows of anonymity, by keeping tabs on every communication and contact he made, and by placing virtual alerts everywhere he could think of. That was easy when only he and Aric knew of his endeavors.

Adding one more person into that circle complicated things. Adding even more people made his security exponentially harder to maintain.

That the colonel was security conscious had been evident

from that first contact with the burner phones. That these people had the expertise to remove text conversations from phones meant computer skills perhaps as good as his own. Now he understood whose skills those were.

Still, as he ate lunch and later had tea at the colonel's home, he couldn't bring himself to reveal anything about the work he did. Why? What held him back?

Now, they drove to another location, to meet up with yet one more person Adam would be expected to trust.

"You mentioned your invitation to join something called The Remnant in our first conversation. Am I correct in thinking that this is that company of patriots you mentioned?"

The colonel nodded. "You are. It's a small group right now, and I can't say anything further unless I know you're part of us. Even then, some of the contacts we have are known just by me, some just by Mike. It's not so much a need-to-know thing but simply a way of limiting exposure should anything happen to us."

"What do you mean by 'us'?"

"Mike and me. I will tell you that we are the hub of The Remnant. That way we keep things close to the vest, you might say. I help develop strategy, but Mike is the brains behind the tech. I think you two will hit it off well."

Now Adam was truly encouraged. The man had helped perfect facial recognition, technology that Adam had built into UltraNet. Mike also had been instrumental in developing high-level security encryptions, and more. He understood why UltraNet had been unable to find anything on The Remnant. They shared certain skills that enabled them to hide on the web, dark or otherwise. And they had worked in each other's virtual backyards without the slightest hint of each other's work. That in itself was remarkable.

Soon they came to a gated drive in the city of Ladue, an inner-ring suburb of St. Louis comprised of old money estates. The city had the highest per capita income of any community in the state. The colonel drove up to the gate, opened his window, and faced a security panel. A portion of the panel slid forward to the car. The man pressed his thumb onto the pad, which retracted into position as the gate opened.

"Both facial recognition and thumbprint required."

They drove through and headed down a driveway longer than Adam had ever seen. He glanced about and noticed that the gate wasn't the only security measure. What he assumed to be motion detectors and maybe infrared sensors dotted the trees covering the now barren, winter grounds. He held no doubt the place looked beautiful in the summer.

"Is this his home?" His question came out as incredulous as he felt.

The man nodded. "It is now. He inherited the place from his parents when his mom died a year or so ago. He's now the third generation to own it."

"Does it have its own cave?" Adam asked as he grinned.

Colonel S laughed. "It should. We jokingly call it the lair."

As they neared the front door, it opened and a man of about six-foot-two with the shoulders of an Olympic swimmer and hair pulled back into a ponytail awaited them. He and the colonel greeted each other with a brief man-hug, and then he extended his hand to Adam.

"Adam, it's great to see you again. Welcome."

The man ushered them inside. The place looked like a

museum. Adam didn't want to touch anything out of fear of breaking something. He glanced about more than once.

"Yeah, not exactly my style. My grandfather collected fine furniture. My grandmother, Chinese and European porcelains. And my dad, antique weapons. My mother collected cleaning services to dust it all." He laughed. "Come on back to where *I* live. Lot more comfortable, and I have a fire going, too. Can I get anyone something to eat or drink?"

The colonel held up a hand to beg off while Adam shook his head. "Thanks, but I'm fine."

The back half of the home was indeed more contemporary, and the type of place Adam could be at ease in. He took a seat on an overstuffed leather couch that appeared well-worn and felt like he was sinking to the floor.

"Sorry, should have warned you about the couch. It was in the basement of my old house, and I slept there a lot. Need a new one but just don't seem to get around to it. Why don't you grab that recliner there."

Adam took him up on the suggestion, after making two attempts to get up from the couch.

"So, I told Adam a little bit about The Remnant, and that you and I are the hub of the group. Not much more."

They talked for a short while as the two men outlined their goals, examples of the types of people they had recruited so far, and a brief synopsis of what they had accomplished to date. Adam had no doubt they would have their work cut out for them with the incoming administration.

"Let me show you the center of our operation," said Mike. He walked to a nearby bookcase, touched something, and a portion of the case eased open.

They both laughed as Adam's jaw dropped. "It doesn't lead to a cave, and we have no poles to slide down."

The trio walked into a room the size of a large master bedroom complete with its own kitchenette and bathroom.

"My folks had this built as a safe room after a series of home invasions in the area in the 1990s. It's largely impregnable, fire and tornado safe, and two or three people could survive in here for a few weeks if needed, and if they had the place stocked for it."

Instead, however, Adam saw an advanced operations center like some of the military command centers he had worked in at one time. Mike pointed out various aspects of the room and what he could do there. The place put Adam's computer center to shame, but then, they didn't have him and UltraNet. Yet.

Now the colonel's countenance turned serious. "Okay, we've shown you ours. We're trusting you to keep this secure and secret. Have we earned *your* trust?"

They certainly had. He sat down at one of the consoles but turned the chair to face them.

"Colonel, your suspicions are correct. However, AlterNet no longer exists. It advanced to become what I call UltraNet."

He proceeded to tell them of his software's capabilities and how he'd been using it to develop indestructible legal cases against corrupt politicians and business leaders. Many of the business leaders had been convicted. The politicians, however, were a different story. US and state attorneys seemed reluctant to proceed with those cases, and the media treated them like dead letters at the post office.

"I see how your approach works better. Cut off their

supply lines, so to speak. So, I agree that we need to work together, to combine the power of our software. I've got about an hour to give you now. Then, I have a couple of kids to go play with."

TWENTY-THREE

Raimondo read again the message from El Espectro and for the first time in a long time, felt a tinge of real fear. Yes, he had had concern for his wellbeing before meeting with the man four days earlier, but at that time, he felt confident he would be able to assuage the man's anger over losing a shipment. The loss had been unexpected, no fault of Raimondo's, and the occasional loss was considered a cost of doing business.

No más retrasos. ¿Ha encontrado quién atacó nuestro envío? Otro está listo, incluso más grande para compensar la pérdida. ¿Puedo confiar en ti para moverlo al otro lado de la frontera?

Raimondo shook his head. It had been but a week since the attack and only four days since meeting with the boss. How could El Espectro possibly expect him to have found the perpetrators in such a short time? The hit had been highly technical and well-coordinated. Those responsible could be anywhere in the U.S. but the boss expected no more delays and wanted Raimondo to move a larger shipment without fail.

The image of a watery grave in the Laguna de Tamiahua amidst the dozens of other lost souls who'd ended up there by turning on, or even just disappointing, El Espectro didn't simply flit through his mind. It touched down there with a perfectly executed three-point landing and wheeled itself into the hangar of his consciousness. He couldn't shake the dread.

To fail was not an option.

Raimondo considered his choices. The completion of significant portions of the wall limited his routes. Some might say it would be foolish to try the same route because they would expect greater surveillance there. Yet, there was a certain reverse logic to using the same ford in the river so quickly after the last attack. No one would expect them to do so, making it the perfect place to go. Sadly, his limitation was that the burnt hulls of their trucks on the U.S. side remained blocking the access road.

Another route that he'd scouted had been used by a terrorist cell in an attempt to smuggle two bombs into the U.S.—dirty bombs if his sources were correct. They hadn't made it very far. Word on the street said one of their bombs had become unstable, exploded, and that detonated the second. Perhaps. In light of the attack on his shipment, he could not help but wonder if they, too, had been attacked.

He picked up his current burner phone and dialed a number.

"Hello, Agent White."

"*Señor* Saucedo, to what do I owe this honor?"

"Agent White, I need an update on an incident at the

border." Agent White was the code name he used for the man who supplied him inside information from the CBP Office of Field Operations in Laredo. He was paid well for such information, as were others, and his extended family within Mexico was afforded a better than average lifestyle—one they would dramatically lose should he change his loyalties.

"And which incident would that be, *señor*?"

"The two bombs that exploded near the river at the end of the current wall in south Maverick County eleven days ago. I have two questions. Did the bombs go off on their own or was the explosion triggered somehow? And is the area safe?"

"To answer the second question first, no. You do not want to spend any extended time in that area. As for the first question, yes, we still believe an instability in one of the bombs caused it to detonate. However, forensics is still trying to put together the pieces they were able to recover, and if they find something to say otherwise, that official opinion will change."

"*Gracias*, Agent White. Expect a token of our appreciation."

"And thank you, *señor*."

Raimondo smiled. The rumors of the bombs being dirty appeared to be true, and that worked in his favor. He had done his reading about such weapons of mass disruption—not destruction—and knew they posed little harm to someone who was simply to pass through the contaminated area. Follow-up of Chornobyl victims had proven the studies true. Even a full year's exposure caused no real injury or illness in those exposed. The disruption occurred when hundreds or thousands of people in a city had to undergo decontamination. Such bombs proved to be great terror devices, but not as destructive or deadly as the populace was led to believe.

And that is what made the location perfect for him. The area would be secured, and proper warnings posted, but actual patrols would be limited out of concern over undue exposure.

He created his reply to El Espectro.

Sí, estoy listo para mover otro envío. Todavía estoy trabajando para encontrar a los que destruyeron el otro. Tengo varias pistas.

Yes, he was ready for the new shipment and had leads on the attackers.

He hit send and crossed his heart that his reply would satisfy the man. More importantly, he began to set up his plan to prevent another catastrophic hit. He knew better than to take chances, as he reminded himself that failure was not an option.

Dillon remained amazed at the prolonged cold spell hitting south Texas. He couldn't recall one lasting as long as this one had. He worked his cattle lots with new bales of hay and again broke the ice on the watering troughs. The area meteorologists called for another week of such temperatures. That he could weather, he thought, smiling at his pun.

What was more problematic were the rolling electrical blackouts covering all of the ERCOT grid, a grid that covered 90% of Texas. In addition, the cost of electricity had rocketed through the stratosphere—from $30 per megawatt-hour to over $9,000 per megawatt-hour. Thousands of households were about to get sticker shock over their home utility bills. He had a friend who had warned him of the issue, and he'd switched to his ranch's generator for power. It was a hassle keeping the thing fueled, but gas was cheap enough to make it pay off.

A side issue for many was that the power problems affected the cell towers as well. If he had a medical emergency, would he be able to reach 911? He found himself periodically checking his phone for a signal, and right now he had none. So, when his "other" phone beeped, it startled him more than usual.

The text read:

A new drug shipment is in the works. Will put together a team when timing and location are known.

He checked the phone. No bars. How did they get through? He responded, "*Out.*" The message disappeared. How . . .? He realized he needed to just ignore *how* they did what they did. He wasn't that tech-savvy to begin with, so trying to figure out the tech had the potential to drive him crazy.

Another shipment. He'd been having second thoughts about the whole Remnant thing. He'd never give them up to anyone else, but he wasn't so gung-ho about participating anymore.

Word was that two men died in the last shipment they stopped. That info wasn't confirmed, but it still bothered him for a reason he couldn't put his finger on. As a marine, he hadn't been one of the "lucky ones" to come home without having killed someone. On the ranch, he had no trouble killing coyotes, rabbits, and other pests, plus the occasional deer. But people? The eyes of the man he killed in hand-to-hand combat in Iraq still haunted him.

When it came to the terrorists and their bombs, he'd gone into warrior mode. Protecting a city of "innocents" from such a weapon was justifiable, and they had been proven to be dirty bombs, just as he'd been told. Yet, even with the terrorist cell, he rationalized the situation by acknowledging that his shots hit the bomb, not any person. They were killed by their own work, not directly by a bullet from his rifle.

And with the drug smugglers, he reasoned that it wasn't *his* shots that killed anyone. He'd taken out the trucks. Who were the men? Were they active smugglers or just men trying to support their families? He realized that the line between them was blurry. How long would it be before he was forced to kill someone directly?

God forbade murder, and the Bible was clear that this pertained to first-degree, premeditated murder. It didn't refer to manslaughter. God had provided cities of refuge where someone involved in manslaughter could flee to get a fair trial. Defending one's country, or, more importantly, defending one's home and family were also allowable. Still . . . all men were created in the image of God, and the value of life had become paramount in Dillon's mind since returning from overseas in one piece. Others he knew hadn't been so fortunate.

Yes, how long would it be before one of his bullets killed someone, someone who perhaps was acting only to survive or to protect his own family? Maybe it was time to quit while he could still reason away what he'd already done. He looked at the phone. As long as he had it, they'd find him. Something stopped him from dropping it to the ground and smashing it under his boot. Instead, he opened the case and removed the battery. Then he stashed it and the battery in the toolbox under his tractor's seat.

Mike J stopped in mid-sentence as they talked with Adam. "Uh-oh. Might have a problem."

He had just demonstrated his technology for sending out text messages and deleting all traces of them. The demonstration served a dual role in showing how they could bounce a message or call off satellites even when cell towers were down. The phone they had contacted was a typical burner phone—with a bit of added tech—but it was not a satellite phone. And yet, the added technology gave it limited features like one.

"What's up?" asked the colonel.

"One of our phones has gone off-line. The marine vet we just sent the message to."

Mike J moved to a different console and began to work with his system.

"How can I help?" asked Adam. He'd been impressed with the setup and capabilities of their system. Maybe now was the time to demonstrate his.

Colonel S nodded. "We have the ability to comb through records to select people based upon military service and experience, locations, and more, but we can't do psychological profiles on them. If your UltraNet's origin was the PsyOps program in Afghanistan, then it should excel at that."

"It does. But it takes a while."

"What's a while?" asked Mike J.

"Depends on the person. A few hours to a few days if they're actively trying to hide something."

"Okay, we probably have that kind of time. The guy's name is Dillon Ingersoll, and he has a ranch outside of Eagle Pass, Texas. Marine vet." They provided Adam with the basic identifying info they had.

Adam pulled out his laptop, powered it up, and connected to their secure VPN leading to the Internet. He entered the data into UltraNet and set it loose to dig up everything it could find on the man.

"From what you've told me, this shouldn't take too long. What exactly are you looking for?"

Mike J pointed to his monitor. "Tapped into a drone and took a pass over his ranch. There he is working on his tractor, so we know he's okay. That means one of two things. Either the phone's been damaged accidentally, or it's been deactivated on purpose."

The colonel continued the train of thought. "If it's been damaged accidentally, we need to get him a new one. But we had one warrior near El Paso who worked one job for us and then destroyed his phone. We learned later that he suffered from PTSD, and the task had triggered it. Again, our software couldn't show us a psych profile. We would have realized he wasn't suitable for our work and wouldn't have recruited him. We got him help."

Mike J nodded. "No one is ever forced into joining us, and

they can quit at any time. We simply ask that they keep our secret if they move on. It's not that we worry about them ratting us out. They have no idea who we are, where we are, or who else might be in the network, except those they might work with on a multi-man task. But the lower the profile we can maintain, the better. Sooner or later the feds will see our shadow on their radar and start looking. We'd prefer it be later, and that our shadow be more of a ghost they can't find."

Adam smiled. "Well, UltraNet can help with that. It can alert us to anyone sniffing about and make sure they can't find anything useful to lead them to us." He checked the time. "Shoot, I'm gonna be late."

The colonel came closer and started to close the laptop. "Later. Your kids take top priority. We can work on this tomorrow."

Adam nodded. "Thanks." He closed the laptop and placed it back into his bag. "Tomorrow it is. I should have a profile on this man in a few hours, but we can review it in the morning."

They agreed upon a meeting time, and the colonel drove him back to his car. By that point, Adam had already compartmentalized his work and moved into family mode. He couldn't wait to see his kids ... and Rachel. Maybe a move back to St. Louis was in his future.

Ashleigh had barely slept during the past 48 hours since learning that Lateesha and Toni had misused her key card. She had missed a day and a half of classes and would have to struggle to make up the assignments. Every minute she expected an urgent text from the dean's office advising that she come to see him ASAP. And now that she'd forced herself to return to class, the dreaded text came. She wanted to go somewhere private and throw up.

During the break, she approached her professor. "Doctor King, I just got a text. I need to go see the dean."

The economics professor frowned. "You've missed almost two days already. Can this wait?"

The woman didn't have to remind Ashleigh about the missed time. The January term was difficult enough with its intense schedule. To miss two days of class was like two weeks of the class during a typical semester. However, she'd never be able to focus on the class until the matter with the dean had been ironed out. Perhaps, she wouldn't have to worry about the class at all.

She shook her head. "I'm sorry, but no, it can't wait. I promise to make up all the work and reading I've missed over this weekend."

The professor shrugged. "It's your education. Do whatever you need to do."

Ashleigh hurried to the admin building and straight to the Dean of Student's office. The secretary knew her and pointed to a chair before announcing her presence to the dean. The over-20-minute wait became excruciating.

"Dean Schmitz will see you now, Ashleigh."

Ashleigh arose, straightened her clothing, took a deep breath, and knocked on the office door.

"Come in."

She entered and wasted no time in talking. "Dean Schmitz, I know—"

He pointed to a chair and said, "Have a seat, Ashleigh."

She took the seat and fidgeted with her skirt.

"I think you know why I called you in."

She nodded. "Yes, sir. I think so. I didn't do it, and I didn't okay it. I didn't know anything about it until afterward."

"Then who and how did they do it?"

"Umm, I'd prefer not to snitch. I've already reprimanded them myself. It won't happen again."

"Ashleigh, we put you in a position of trust, and that trust was violated. You have a master key card for emergencies only, not to perpetrate personal vendettas or pranks."

She hung her head. "I understand that. I had . . . I still have . . . no intentions of violating that trust. They . . . uh . . . well, they found my card in my room and used it while I was in class."

"Who did? They need to be reprimanded formally. Fortunately, no real damage was done, but I have to tell you, the college is under pressure to investigate this. Some are calling it a hate crime and a violation of the student's first amendment rights."

Did she hear that correctly? "A hate crime? What does he know about hate crimes?" Her anger rose. "He's a white, cis-gendered, heterosexual male who has lived in privilege his whole life. If anyone's guilty of hate crimes, it's people like him."

She realized as soon as she spoke that she'd made a mistake. Dean Schmitz was not known as an ardent supporter of critical theory.

He leaned toward her and replied in lower tones. "Until a few years ago, didn't *you* fit that description?" He sat back in his chair. "Ashleigh, as I understand it, the victim of this prank, or whatever your friends want to label it, has never done anything to you or them. And yet, he's also been verbally accosted in the dining hall, and this is only the first week of the term. I need to know who did this?"

Ashleigh wondered. *If he also knows about the dining hall situation, does he already know who did it? Or is he speculating? Who else had Lateesha or Toni mentioned the "prank" to? Were they already in trouble and was he testing her?* She sat there, frozen in her chair.

"Well then, Ashleigh, if you aren't going to uphold your duties as a RA, I have no recourse but to remove you from—"

She sat up straight. "Please, Dean Schmitz, no. If I lose that position, I can't afford to stay here. I'd have to leave the college."

"Ashleigh, you signed an agreement to support campus security and that means complying with information requests during investigations like this one. You aren't upholding your agreement."

She was beaten. "It was Lateesha Williams and Toni Perrone. They just wanted to prank the guy." Yeah, *the guy*, she thought. *Isn't that how it all started? He had spoken up during their protest. This all originated with him. The privileged prick.*

"Thank you. We'll be talking with both of them. As for you, you're on probation. One more infraction and you're gone."

The dean rose and walked to the door, which he opened for her. "Good day, Ashleigh."

Good day indeed, she thought as she left his office. She would have to warn Lateesha and Toni if they didn't know already. Hopefully, they wouldn't learn that she had ratted them out. And if they did, she would go out of her way to make amends.

As for *the guy*, he was the one really responsible for this trouble. They were the victims here. They would figure out how to get back at him . . . without the fallout coming back on them. She wondered if one of Toni's good friends would want a new roommate.

TWENTY-FOUR

Aric seemed on Cloud Nine as he walked to class that Monday morning. Not only had he gotten some much-needed sleep without a roommate keeping him awake until after midnight, but he'd also gone to church with Chris and Jess. He met her, um, their, parents, and they seemed cool. The church service was unlike any he'd experienced before. The congregation truly celebrated God. The music and dancing had been amazing, although a few times he felt as if the floor was going to give way under them, the way it bounced as folks danced. Chris reassured him that it was checked regularly by engineers who assessed the safety of the nearly 100-year-old building.

More amazing was the people's willingness to yield to the Holy Spirit. In line with the Bible, words of encouragement and exhortation were judged by elders of the church before being offered to the congregation. One prophetic message touched Aric's heart in a way he'd not felt before. It spoke to the Spirit's gift of faith and the ability to do miracles. Aric felt as if that was in his future as he closed his eyes and asked for such faith.

After church, he had accompanied the siblings to lunch and a tour of the area. As sunset neared, he learned of Jess' love of photography and joined her in taking sunset photos at a farm west of the interstate. The location was great. The sunset, a dud, something she told him was a major hassle with taking images that were dependent on the weather.

Yet, as awesome as the day had been, that's not what had him floating to class. During that time of worship, one of the women in the church came up to Jess, and after scrutinizing Aric, leaned close to Jess and proceeded to talk into her ear on the side away from Aric. Part way through the message, both women looked at him, and Jess blushed. Once the woman left, Jess slid her hand out from her side and touched his hand by his side. Just briefly, but it felt like being plugged into a 120-volt socket.

He couldn't wait to see her in class.

As he entered the classroom, he saw that he was the last of their group to arrive. But something was different. Instead of his trying to position himself so that she would sit next to him, she had saved the seat next to her for him.

He decided to do something bold. He reached over and touched her hand as he greeted her. She did not flinch or move her hand away. She smiled, and he thought he would fall into those dimples. How in the world was he going to be able to pay attention in class?

When the lunch break came, Jess looked at him and said, "Want to join us for lunch? We're just heading home for a quick bite, so it won't be much. At least the price will be right." She smiled, but this time it was the gleam in her eyes that entranced him.

"I'd love to, but I need to switch out a book in my room before the afternoon session. I can do it now, or after lunch."

"Okay, why don't you do that now. We'll get our car and pick you up outside the dorm."

"Cool. I'll hurry."

Which he did. He made it to the dorm in record time and ran up the stairs to get to his room. When he opened the door, he did a double-take. He stepped back and looked at the room number again. Of course, how would his card have worked unless it was his room?

He stepped inside. The side where Tom had resided now had a distinctly feminine vibe to it with pinks and purples. A feather boa lay across the bed's pillow. The closet door was open and inside he saw not only jeans, slacks, button-down shirts, and two pairs of men's shoes but also a handful of dresses and women's shoes. On the shelf were a wig and a pink, plastic box that he recognized as a makeup kit. One of his sisters had the same kit.

His side remained untouched.

As he stood there in shock, totally forgetting the book, a guy about his height but slighter in build walked in. He wore pink fluffy slippers and a silky robe. His hair was bleached blond in a spiked cut. He carried a towel and toiletries and had come from the bathroom down the hall. You didn't need gay-dar to recognize this guy's orientation.

"Hi, roomie. You must be Aric with an A. I'm Bobbi with an I." He grinned. He extended his hand with a limp wrist.

Aric responded out of habit with an extra firm grip.

"Wow, and you're buff, too."

"Hey, can't chat. I, uh . . . um . . .just needed to get a book."

Aric switched out the books and bolted from the room. He was still hyperventilating as he climbed into the back seat of Chris' car with Jess. She looked at him with concern.

"You okay?"

He sat there for a moment. Had that really happened? Had the college given him a gay, cross-dressing roommate? Really? He shook his head.

"No, I don't think so." He tried to formulate what to say in his mind. "You know how I told you that my roommate had moved out? The weekend was great. I, uh, . . . the college has moved a new guy into the room, and he is gay as he- . . . well, gay as gay can be." He described what he had seen. "He says his name is Bobbi with an I. I think he was just mocking my name."

He noticed Chris shaking his head. "Nope, that's Bobbi with an I. He's known not just on campus but in town, too, for pushing the limits. He crossdresses on a whim, says he's bisexual, and can get pretty aggressive about his so-called rights."

Jess looked sad. "I'm so sorry, Aric. I can't think of a worse roommate for you. Can't you ask for someone else?"

Chris continued to shake his head as he drove. "You can ask to move out, but that's exactly what they want you to do. Jess, you remember Brad? Last October."

"Oh my gosh, you're right." She turned to face Aric. "You haven't met Brad yet. He decided against doing this J-term. The LGBTQI crowd in activist hall wanted him out, too. Pressured his roommate into moving and then moved Bobbi in. Brad lasted just over a week."

Aric felt as if he'd been hit with that old ice bucket challenge. "So, you're saying this is their way of weirding me out and getting me to move?" That sounded like a challenge.

Now Chris nodded. "Yep, we've seen this play from their playbook before. Someone's probably got a betting pool started on how long you'll last."

A small voice inside Aric's head said, "*Be bold. Put on My full armor. Show your faith through your works. I am there with you.*" And he felt emboldened.

"Well, they picked the wrong guy. We'll see who lasts the longest."

Aric had to admit he wasn't looking forward to the coming battle. He, Chris, and Jess had strategized during lunch, and both kept texting him ideas during class. They talked more during their afternoon break and sought opinions from Lindsey and Theresa. When the day was over, he wondered if any of them had any idea what was taught during those three hours of class that afternoon.

"I still can't believe you're going to go through with this," said Jess after class.

Aric still wondered about it, too. "Well, my brother is ten years older, so he wasn't around much after I started third grade. I was raised with three sisters. I'm kinda used to girl stuff. Can it be much different?"

"Yeah," both Chris and Jess said in unison.

"And I have a cousin who says he's gay. I've been around him at family gatherings and heard him spout off about being on the right side of history and all that rhetoric they use to convince themselves. Plus, I'm grounded in the Bible and my Christian worldview. I think I can do this."

"Well, we'll get the young adults group at church to surround you with prayer," said Chris.

"And I'll be here for you," said Jess. She took his hand into hers and smiled.

His heart began to race. "Thanks. I'll need that." He gently squeezed her hand.

They departed for home, and he hesitantly headed for the dorm. When he got to the room, nothing had changed since lunch, and Bobbi wasn't there. He walked down to the dining hall to get in line. Mitch found him in line and together with two other men from the football team, joined him for dinner.

After sitting down, Mitch said, "Sorry, man. I heard about your new roommate. You gonna move out soon?"

The others groaned in agreement.

As he chewed, Aric shook his head. "Nope, that's exactly what they want me to do. They're in for a surprise, especially Bobbi."

"Whoa, no way. I'd be done in a day rather than live with that weirdo," said the guy on his left, Zach somebody.

"Man, you got a pair if you think you can deal with this. I remember that guy, Brad Wilson, that they sicced Bobbi on last fall. I couldn't put up with that. I'd have been arrested for pummeling him to a pulp if he pulled that stuff on me."

Aric blocked on the guy's name, but replied, "Yeah, well, don't say that too loud down here. The college will demand sensitivity classes or something."

All three guys laughed, and Mitch said, "Yeah, well, they tried that already and gave up on him."

Zach nodded. "If he hadn't been a starter on the team, they might have booted him, but the team needed him."

Mitch leaned toward the guy. "Still, Aric has a point. We don't want to give them anything to change their minds." Then he faced Aric. "So, if you need a safe space . . ." He stressed those words in mockery. ". . . you can hang in any of our rooms."

Aric smiled. "Thanks. I'm likely to take you up on that."

They talked about other things, joking and laughing. When Aric finished eating, he braced himself for what he might find in his room and headed upstairs.

As he approached his door, he could hear someone doing a lousy impersonation of Cyndi Lauper singing "True Colors." He hesitated in opening the door, afraid to see whatever might be going on inside. He took a deep breath, swiped his key card, and opened the door.

Bobbi sat at his desk, with the makeup kit and mirror in front of him. He was in full-on drag makeup and about to don his wig. He turned to face the door as it opened.

Aric nodded in greeting, prepared to battle.

"Helloooo, Aric with an A. What do you think?" He made it sound as feminine as he could.

Aric offered a subtle shrug. "Well, if you're aiming for a garish, over-the-top drag queen, you've got it nailed. If you want to pass, the wig's the wrong color for your skin tone, the eyeshadow needs to be toned down, and the blush and lipstick need more subtlety."

Bobbi looked deflated. Had he expected Aric to gag and throw up? Or run from the room?

Aric opened his backpack and retrieved his book to begin

studying. He nonchalantly sat propped up on his bed and turned to the pages where his reading would start. He grabbed his notebook to take notes and his phone for background music. He looked at Bobbi.

"You're leaving, right? So, I can put on some music and won't disturb you."

Bobbi continued to simply watch him and offered a halfhearted nod.

"Thanks. Don't let me hold you up." He powered on his Bluetooth speaker, found the music he wanted on his phone, and cranked it up. *Skillet*'s lead singer, John Cooper, let loose, singing about no power on earth or in hell stealing his peace. As the song continued, Aric watched Bobbi from the corner of his eye and smiled inwardly. *I call upon the name*, he thought. Indeed, the light of Christ terrifies the dark.

TWENTY-FIVE

As Ashleigh prepared for Tuesday's morning class, someone knocked on her door. Make that two someones, as a different knock echoed the first. She unlocked and opened the door to find Toni, Lateesha, and Bobbi.

She smiled in anticipation that they were there to report on Bobbi's first day with *the guy*. She had done a bit of research on Aric Afton. He was in the top ten in his class but hadn't jumped right into college last fall. His social media was sparse, and there was a huge gap in posts following his graduation and his arrival at the college. She could find no clues as to why. Since then, most of the posts seemed to focus on topics from the Bible, things that were foreign to her. Short of going to Sunday school as a kid, she'd never paid any attention to the Bible but had heard that it was mostly a bunch of letters from long-dead men.

"Hi, gang. C'mon in."

The three clambered into the room, and Lateesha and Toni sat heavily on the bed. Bobbi, on the other hand, began to pace, fidgeting with his hands. He wore jeans and a button-down shirt this morning for class, in stark opposition to his attire the previous night.

"We need to keep this short 'cause I can't be late for class this morning. So, how'd it go?"

Bobbi stopped in the middle of the room and turned to face her.

"Well, I . . . "

Lateesha chimed in. "The guy didn't go runnin' from the room like that Brad fellow."

Ashleigh knew that was an exaggeration, but the mental picture of Brad Wilson fleeing from a guy in a dress brought a smile to her face.

"So, I ask again. How'd it go?"

"I was in that jungle print Donna Karan that you love so much and was putting on my makeup when he came back from dinner. He asked me what look I was shooting for. Didn't seem to bat an eye."

"What do you mean, what look?"

"Well, high drag or passing. Told me I nailed the high drag, but that if I wanted to look passable, I needed to change some things. Then, he pulled out some books and sat on his bed to study."

"That's it?"

"Yeah, well, no. The changes he suggested were on target. He was so chill, it was like I could have been his sister or something. Oh, and then he puts on some rock music about not stealing his peace and enemies on their knees and fear having no hold on his heart. Stuff like that. I think the song was called 'Terrify the Dark' or something like that."

Maybe Ashleigh had underestimated the guy. But those

Christian types were all the same—judgmental, self-righteous, intolerant. He might be able to put up a good front for a while, but they could wear him down and drive him out.

"Okay, so let's do the door treatment next. You know, make it look like you both support the pride movement. That'll embarrass him and make him do something."

They had talked about it before. They—Bobbi, Toni, and Lateesha—plus any others who wanted to help would create rainbow banners and other decorations for the door to the room in support of the LGBTQI movement. They would make it seem as if both occupants of the room supported the cause. If he tore the things off the door, they'd redo it. They wouldn't let up until he gave up.

Raimondo had been alerted in the middle of the night that his product from El Espectro's facility—in a rural area of the State of Tamaulipas just off Federal Highway 85 heading toward Monterey—had found its way to him. Now, as the sun already baked the desert causing waves of heat to ripple from the highway, he drove from Piedras Negras along Federal Highway 2 toward Guerrero, a small city of fewer than 1,000 inhabitants. Along both sides of the highway, the flat desert was filled with cacti, agave, Mexican olive trees, *frijolito*, and scrub oak. He had once read that over 120 species of plants and 34 types of trees found a home in the desert of Coahuila, some being unique to that state's arid topography. He remained amazed at the diversity of flora in such a dry locale.

The one thing not common to the area was people. It was an inhospitable environment for humans, and the few buildings he passed appeared baked and dilapidated. They also stood out like a neon sign at night. He needed a building that would blend into the space around it. He had that in his warehouse in Piedras Negras, but he had concerns about that location having been compromised. How else could someone have known about the previous shipment and his plans for moving it?

He'd had his men search for electronic listening devices and cameras inside that storehouse, and they had found nothing. Yet, that didn't mean nothing was there. Such bugs had become quite small and might have been missed.

So, he took the opportunity to secure a new building in the small city of Guerrero. No one but his top lieutenants knew of it, and that information had been passed on to them verbally with instructions to say nothing about it via any electronic device. Even El Espectro knew nothing of this facility. That information would have to be passed along in person, too.

He turned onto Calle Lic. Raúl Lopez Sanchez and a few blocks after the Iglesia Bautista El Faro and the town square, he made a left into a nondescript drive, through an open gate, and past the tall adobe wall surrounding the lot. The wall and buildings all needed paint and other maintenance, but as is, they blended right into the neighborhood—worn and impoverished.

To his right was his story-and-a-half tall, plastered brick building with a single door large enough for his vans. Next to that door was a weathered wooden door, which had been retrofitted to hide a secure, metal door. Exploding a hole in the wall would gain someone access faster than trying to penetrate the door. His understanding of the track records of rival cartels led to the security door. Reinforcing the walls would be next.

"*El jefe*, all is ready."

Rito handed him a clipboard listing the inventory and men who would make the run. He quickly reviewed the papers, saw no issues, and handed them back to the man.

"I must deal with something before anyone leaves. I will be in the office."

At the well-worn mesquite desk, he opened his laptop and pulled up his favorite map app. All of their communications had talked of using the route the terrorists had used, but he preferred caution. Someone knew of their plans. His contact at the CBP had put him on alert. Agent White had no details or names, just a rumor that a group of self-described "patriots" had banded together to protect the border. Even the source of said rumor was a mystery.

He zoomed in and out of the map several times as he looked for the route he had found earlier. He would need to give clear directions to his men before they could leave.

There were multiple shoals in the river to the south and east of Guerrero. Any one of them would provide passage across the river. It was access to the river from the U.S. side that proved problematic. His scouts had informed him—again, in person, no phones—that the only roads were simple, gravel, work roads belonging to a single ranch. There were several fence lines with locked gates on each road to divide up the grazing lands. Those locks would be no problem and using ATVs to move the goods away from the river solved the access issue.

One section of land appeared to be bordered by tall

fencing designed to keep deer either in or out. A search on the Internet showed that the landowner ran a deer hunting operation in that section. While the fencing posed no problem, the potential presence of men with guns, and hunting rifles at that, could cause trouble. He wished to avoid that land.

There was also a small dam in the river that posed two obstacles. The water remained too deep for ATVs for a good mile upstream. The water behind it also provided a source of irrigation for several farms and ranches on both sides of the river. The cultivated fields meant the potential presence of farm workers who might easily spot them and call the authorities. That forced him to remain downstream of the dam, but he had that in mind from the beginning.

What *was* a problem was finding a place among the scrub that provided enough cover along Eagle Pass Rd. that their ATVs could remain hidden until trucks on the other side could meet them. He had not thought that this would become an issue since Eagle Pass Rd. was nothing more than a two-lane gravel road. He had been surprised when his scouts reported higher than expected traffic along that road from ranchers in the area. That increased the odds of being spotted.

As he zoomed in on the map one more time, he found the route he was looking for. It led straight from the river toward the road, and to its east was a shallow, wooded ravine where the ATVs could remain until unloaded. The only risk on this route was that it came as close as half a mile to the landowner's home. The scouts reported that the road could not be seen from the house or vice versa, but noise tended to travel over the hardscrabble land along that particular path. He would have to take that risk.

"Rito!" he called.

The man responded immediately. *"Si, el jefe."* His grin revealed the missing front tooth that made his smile so distinctive. "All cell phone communications talk of the shipment going near the end of the wall. Written communications will be sent to the men with the true route. Have you decided on that?"

"Excelente. Si." He motioned for his top man to come to the desk. "Here is the way to go." He pointed along the map as he wrote down detailed directions. "At dusk, tomorrow night."

"We might have a problem," said Mike J to the other two.

Colonel S and Adam had been conferring about strategies they might use once the new administration took office in Washington. None of the men expected the status quo. Quite the opposite. The new occupant of the White House had voiced his support for open borders, and they expected him to reverse many if not all of the policies of President Graham that had taken illegal entries into the country to a record low. The man wouldn't do it overnight. The political uproar would be too great. Yet, if he lived up to his word, over a million illegal entries a year would become the new "normal."

"What's that?" asked Colonel S.

"I've been monitoring the chatter about that new Fentanyl shipment along the river in East Texas. According to what I'm getting, it's supposed to take the same route as those terrorists with the dirty bomb."

Adam shrugged. "Sounds like a good move on their part. The typical person would steer clear out of fear of residual radiation, but the actual risk is nil unless you stay in the area for an extended period."

The colonel nodded. "Yep. Pretty smart of them, but we have that area covered pretty well, don't we? I mean, the dirty bombs were eliminated easily."

"True," replied Mike J. "Even if our closest guy has quit, we have enough people on the ground there to compensate. That's not the problem."

"Oh?"

"Yeah, there's something off with the communications I'm intercepting. It's like someone is trying to convince someone else that that's the path they'll use. Previously, they might have had one call or text about the route to take. Now, it's like twice a day there's a call or text message talking about it. Seems too obvious."

The colonel and Adam agreed.

"Give me the info you're using to track this and let me see what UltraNet comes up with."

Mike J complied, and Adam worked to set up search parameters for his system to use. His fingers nimbly went about typing while the colonel watched. He had his own concerns. While the border wall that had been built to date blocked off miles of access points across the river, there were dozens of other places to cross if one was determined to do so. Few could swim across the cold waters, so most foot traffic used weirs and natural shoals for access. ATVs, however, had fewer access points, being limited to shoals they could cross safely. He needed to think like a drug smuggler, not a battlefield commander.

"Mike, can you pull up some of the high-def drone images

we got of the river between the wall and Eagle Pass?" Eagle Pass sat on the U.S. side of the river with Piedras Negras on the Mexican side.

"Sure. What about points upstream from there?"

"Might need them, but not yet."

The U.S. side of the river upstream from Eagle Pass for several miles was more densely populated with irrigated bottom lands for farming. After that, the terrain became hillier and harder to navigate almost the entire way to Amistad Reservoir. West of the reservoir, the mountains began to take over and quick access to good roads in the U.S. was sparse. No, he suspected the drug smugglers would continue to use points between Eagle Pass and the wall until forced to do otherwise.

"What about activity at that warehouse in Piedras Negras?"

They had used satellite imagery to pinpoint what they believed to be the smugglers' base of operation there. Cell phone activity from that location seemed to confirm that suspicion.

"Give me that data, too," said Adam.

"Some of the cell calls have originated there, like before, but there has been no truck traffic in or out since the last shipment we destroyed. Are you thinking they have a new base?" asked Mike J.

The colonel nodded as he perused a map of the area. "And the most likely place for that is a town called Guerrero. Can we get surveillance video of that area?"

"Working on it."

Adam looked up from his computer. "I think you nailed it, Colonel. A shell company owns the place in Piedras and another recently bought one in Guerrero. They have one name in common, a Raimondo Castillo Saucedo. I'll start digging into him."

"Good. If we want to stop this shipment, we'll need everything we can get on the new place and him."

TWENTY-SIX

Other than the guy's clothing preferences and over-the-top effeminate characterizations—which Aric was convinced was more of an act than natural, Bobbi had proved to be a reasonable roommate over the past two days. He didn't keep Aric up late and was respectful of Aric's stuff. Aric reciprocated.

However, he had started a practice that was proving to irritate the guy no end. He insisted on calling him Bob, with the occasional Robert thrown in. He'd even talked the jocks in the dorm to start the same. Aric still smiled as he recalled the first time Mitch called across the dining hall to call him Bob. If the dining hall needed extra steam tables for the food, the activists at Bob's table could have powered them.

Aric was sitting with his dorm friends at dinner. He'd learned that Wednesday's dinner special was always lasagna, so he'd grabbed a plate of it to try. One of the RAs, Drew Pierson, came up to the table.

"Hey, guys, I need to talk with you about Bobbi."

"What's Bob complaining about this time?" asked the

team's offensive tackle, Dan, as a smirk crossed his mouth. At six-foot-three and 280 pounds, nobody wanted to mess with Dan. The RA seemed to back off a bit.

"Just that. You guys keep calling him Bob and Robert. He wants to be called Bobbi."

Zach shrugged. "Well, his name is Robert, right? He hasn't legally changed it, right?"

The RA sighed as if he recognized this conversation was going nowhere. "True, and no, he hasn't changed it."

"And he still uses male pronouns, right?" asked Mitch.

"As far as I know he's not asked otherwise."

Aric watched the exchange from his end of the table and said nothing. He didn't have to.

"So, we're just calling him by his legal name. Nothing in campus rules says we're out of line."

"But he wants to be called Bobbi with . . ."

". . . an I," said the three in unison.

"Look, Drew, he already asked all of us directly. So, we know want he wants. We all told him we preferred that he address each of us as 'sir,' but that hasn't happened. There is a quid pro quo needed here."

Drew took a deep breath and gave a subtle shake of his head. "Okay, I . . . I will mention that."

Aric stifled the laugh that wanted to erupt, but he couldn't help the smile that took its place as the RA left. "Thanks, guys."

Mitch and Dan gave each other a high-five. "Hey, we told you we'd have your back."

Aric gathered up his utensils and dinnerware and piled them onto his tray. He pushed back from the table, grabbed the tray, and said, "Been fun, but now I have at least three hours of reading ahead of me. See you later."

They said their farewells and continued to joke around as Aric headed for the service area to drop off his tray. He took the stairs to the fourth floor and turned toward his room. Only ten steps were required before he saw their door and stopped.

Across the top quarter of the door was a rainbow flag, with a large-font slogan underneath that proclaimed, "On the Right Side of History!!!" The remainder of the door held pro-LGBT+ posters and slogans, as well as advertisements for various LGBT+ events coming soon to campus. Should Aric consider posting anything of his own on the door, Bob had left no room. He also discerned that Bob had been compliant and respectful over the past two days because he had been preparing for this next move.

Rather than enter the room, Aric took a photo, bound back down the stairs, and walked a brief distance outside away from the dorm entrance. He pulled out his phone and dialed Jess.

"Hey there. I was just thinking about you."

"Likewise. Just wanted you both to know that Bob has made his next move."

"Wait a sec. Let me get Chris."

A minute later, both siblings were on speaker. Aric sent her the photo so they could see firsthand what had been added to his room's door. They discussed things for a few minutes and settled on a plan of action.

"Got it. We'll print some stuff out here at home and give it to you in class tomorrow."

* * *

Ashleigh lay in bed with the lights out even though she had hours of studying to do. Her headache was back. She'd never been diagnosed with migraines, but this sure felt like one—at least how she imagined one would feel. Yet, she knew the real cause. She had been subconsciously clenching her jaw and grinding her teeth from stress. As a result, her temples throbbed, and touching them sent pain rocketing across her head.

Why? She kept reliving her visit with the dean. His comment had upset her. *"Didn't you fit that description?"* kept reverberating through her mind.

White. Privileged. Cis-gendered. Heterosexual. Normal weight. What did that guy, that Aric Afton, know about feeling hated? And he was a Christian to boot. They were the worst. Judgmental. Critical. Holier-than-thou Bible thumpers.

As a trans woman, she understood what hate felt like. Still, the dean's comment struck a whole bundle of raw nerves. Had she ever fit that description?

True, she had grown up male, loved by her parents. She'd even gone to church and knew all the usual Bible stories, or myths as she liked to think of them. It wasn't until she was almost ten when two older female cousins dressed her up as a girl and practiced their makeup skills on her that she realized she enjoyed being a girl. She found excuses to go to their house, and they continued their role-playing until her female mannerisms began to feel natural. By the time she turned 16, she had amassed a secret wardrobe at home. At 17, along with her cousins and some of their gay friends, she ventured into public as Steffi, as her cousins called her, for the first time. It was an exhilarating and freeing experience.

Sadly, that was also the experience that led to the most painful period of her life. A neighbor and friend of her mom had seen them and recognized Steffi as her friend's son in drag. That woman reported her sighting, which led to her mom rummaging through the house and finding her things. Sam came home from school two days later to find Steffi laid out on his bed.

Steffi was discarded into the household garbage, only to be retrieved in the middle of the night and hidden elsewhere. Attempts at counseling followed. But Ashleigh's resistance mounted. For the final session with the psychologist, Sam stopped by his lesbian cousin's home, transformed, and reported to the meeting in her full personae, using her chosen name of Ashleigh. The psychologist told her parents that he could not help someone who refused the help and dismissed Ashleigh from his care.

The ultimatum came next. It was their home, her parents had said, and while under their roof, Sam could stay, but there could be no Ashleigh. By then, Sam had graduated and had legally become an adult. Under great duress and feeling totally rejected by her parents, Ashleigh left them, leaving everything pertaining to Sam in the bedroom where he, now she, had grown up.

"Didn't you fit that description?" echoed once again through her head. She covered her head with her pillow but could not block it out.

There was a knock on her door.

"Go away. I have a headache and don't want to see anyone right now."

"Ashleigh, it's us. Sorry. We can come back."

She recognized Bobbi's voice. By us, he meant Lateesha and Toni were with him. Maybe the diversion would help.

"Just a minute."

She arose from bed and adjusted her robe. Then, covering her eyes, she turned on a light and waited for her eyes to adjust and the wave of discomfort to wane. She took a deep breath and opened the door. As she expected, the trio stood there. She stepped back to usher them inside.

"Sorry you're not feeling well," said Lateesha. "We thought you'd want to see our handiwork."

"I do, but I'm not up to heading upstairs to see it right now."

"We understand. I have pics." Bobbi offered her his phone where a photo of the whole door was now displayed. "Swipe left to see the others."

Ashleigh did just that and smiled. "Nice job. That should get his hackles up. On to the next phase."

TWENTY-SEVEN

Aric packed up his books and loaded his backpack for class. He'd already eaten breakfast and wanted to get to class early. He'd had a few ideas on how to re-do the door to his room but didn't have a printer capable of producing them. He couldn't wait to see what the others had come up with.

He turned off his Bluetooth speaker, which had been playing Spotify's Skillet Mix channel. He had waited for *Nickelback*'s "How You Remind Me" to finish before doing so—nothing like being reminded who you really are. He smiled inside. Had Bob actually been listening as he, too, prepared for the day?

Aric opened the door and turned back to his roommate. "Have a good day. Will you be back at lunch, Bob?"

The guy frowned as he added mascara and eyeliner to his otherwise masculine look. When no answer was forthcoming, Aric gave a subtle shrug, left the room, and closed the door.

He raced down the stairs and headed toward class. He arrived 15 minutes early and claimed seats for the group. He pulled up the small writing surface hiding at the side of his seat and tapped its surface with his fingertips as he waited. His friends arrived moments later, appearing as eager as he'd been to meet up. Jess and Chris led the others. Aric lowered his desk and stood to greet them. Jess' smile shone even brighter that morning, if that was possible.

"Hey," said Chris. "I see you survived another night."

Aric laughed. "Probably fared better than Bob did. I left this morning just after listening to *Nickelback*'s 'How You Remind Me.' I think he might actually have been listening, too."

Jess' eyes widened. "Wow. That would be something." She grabbed her pack and opened it. "I think you're going to love what we came up with for your door." She laughed. "We brainstormed with some others in the Young Adults group. Some of those guys are amazing. So creative."

Aric leafed through nearly a dozen signs and graphics. He noticed all had pieces of double-sided tape on the back. Chris nodded as he inspected them.

"Yeah, we figured we might have only a short time window to do this. So, with the tape, all we need to do is peel off the remaining plastic and put it in place."

Aric smiled. "These are great. I can't wait to see the reaction."

Finally, the weather over East Texas had returned to seasonal averages. With a week or so remaining in deer season, Dillon had a hunting party to guide the next day, which would be a pleasant break from the routine on his ranch. The warmer weather would be to their advantage—the animals wouldn't be hunkered down against the cold but more active and needing to forage.

The group was scheduled to arrive within the hour, so he worked on assembling the supplies they would need. The guest bunkhouse had already been cleaned and stocked for their overnight stay. He looked forward to helping them find deer and letting them be the ones doing the shooting. He'd had enough shooting to last him a while.

He offered three types of hunt—safari-style from high rack vehicles, from the comfort of one of their modern blinds, or the old-fashioned spot and stalk hunt. With only one hunting party on the premises, they could choose. Personally, he enjoyed the latter. There was something primal about stalking one's prey. It required a developed skill that most hunters would never learn.

As he pulled a handful of orange vests from his storage cabinet in the bunkhouse, he heard a car drive up. Expecting his guests, he walked out to greet them but was surprised to see Eduardo.

"*Buenos días*, my friend," said Dillon. "This is an unexpected visit."

Eduardo nodded. "Sorry to barge in like this, but I didn't want to use a phone. He approached Dillon and kept his voice low. "I hear you turned off the phone."

From his emphasis on 'the' Dillon understood right away which phone he meant. He replied with a slow nodding of his head.

"Why? We need you, man. Someone's got to protect our country when the feds refuse to."

Dillon huffed and shook his head. "Did they send you?"

"Naw, I got word you quit, and that bothered me. Why?"

Dillon took a deep breath. "Did you ever kill anyone when you were on active duty in the Middle East?"

His young friend shook his head. "I honestly don't know. Nothing up close and personal, but I was in some serious firefights. Never found any bodies afterward, so I don't know if I killed anyone or not. Then I got assigned weaponry like that XM25, and everything I did was long-range. So, if I ever killed someone, I never knew it."

Dillon understood. War, like hunting, had become remote, distanced from the prey. Drone operators sat in comfortable "blinds" well away from the front lines, sometimes even halfway around the globe, and took down an enemy visible only on a monitor. Those on the front lines, as he once had been, had weapons that could take out a person or vehicle a thousand yards away, often precision-guided by a laser.

"Well, I have. In hand-to-hand combat. I relived it almost nightly for over a decade until I accepted Christ as my Savior and Lord. The nightmares disappeared, only to return after I . . . well, let me just say after my first mission with The Remnant."

He had almost given away his role in destroying the dirty bombs and the men with them. He trusted Eduardo to keep a secret. They shared a big one. But, why tempt fate? Why burden him with that one?

Eduardo looked toward the ground and shuffled one foot. "Sorry. Got some buddies dealing with PTSD, too."

"It's more than PTSD. Murder is wrong. In the Bible, a murderer was condemned to death not just by the people but by God, too. God granted the state the right to put evildoers to death, not individuals. So, killing an enemy while in service to the country can be justified."

He didn't want to open the debate about why the U.S. was in the Middle East. After serving there, he couldn't see past the idea that they were there to protect Big Energy and the oil industry, not the U.S., and to add to the coffers of arms manufacturers. So, who was truly at fault? The various terrorist organizations they were told they were fighting, or the U.S. for having invaded their countries? That was a controversy he chose to steer clear of.

"And here's where I'm conflicted. The people we're battling really are an enemy. The drugs they smuggle in have done great harm to our society. A dirty bomb, if the rumors we've heard are correct, would do great harm. But . . . we're *not* sanctioned by the government. We're not 007, licensed to kill. Do I want to keep drugs, criminals, and terrorists out of our country? You bet. Do I want to be a vigilante to do so? Not so sure. I *want* to see the government doing its job and securing our borders. Since there seems to be a political agenda behind letting these people and the drugs into the country, maybe I *should* help keep out the invaders. Or maybe the real enemy is in Washington, D.C. I just don't know which way to go on this, and until I have more clarity, I'm staying out."

Both men turned their heads at an approaching SUV.

"Hey, here comes my hunting party. Gotta take care of 'em."

Eduardo nodded. "Maybe we can talk again. And I hope you get that clarity. It's a war, and I believe we're called to fight in it since our government won't. Stay in touch."

Aric had drafted one of the basketball team members who was in class with Bob to keep him abreast of the guy's presence there. They had hoped to add the new "decorations" to Aric's door during the mid-morning break, but Bob had left class, and they couldn't ascertain where he'd gone. Lunch hadn't worked either. The guy had gone straight to their room and eaten lunch while reading there.

Team Aric finally had their opportunity at the end of the day.

As had become their routine, they all walked toward the dorm after class. For Chris and Jess, it was on their way to the lot where they parked their car. For the others, it was a time of fellowship and discussing what they'd covered in class.

"I'm bummin," said Aric. "We never had a chance to fix my door. Guess we'll try again tomorrow."

"Maybe, or maybe not. Look."

Jess pulled at Aric's sleeve and pointed ahead to the dorm entrance. Bob was climbing into a car. Aric couldn't make out the driver, but did it matter?

"Slow down and don't look obvious. Let's see which way they head."

Seconds later, the car pulled from the curb and did a U-turn. Aric still couldn't see the driver through the glare on the windshield, but that direction led to one of the exits from campus. Unless they turned around and came right back, he figured they'd have time to do the deed.

"Yes!" He pumped a fist in the air. "You guys have time to do this now?"

Four of the five nodded. The fifth pointed to a waiting car. "Sorry, would love to, but there's my ride. I don't want to keep her waiting."

"No problem," replied Aric. "See you tomorrow."

The quintet hurried into the dorm and progressed up the elevators to the fourth floor. With all five of them working together, they had the door redone within ten minutes. A round of high-fives followed.

"Thanks, guys. I'll give you a full report tomorrow."

TWENTY-EIGHT

The colonel sat in the kitchen sipping a fresh cup of coffee brewed the way he liked it, oil black and ready to strip paint. They hadn't made much progress locating Saucedo and his crew, but they had connected the dots between him and cartel leader Roberto Benito Felix Beltrán, known by the moniker "El Espectro." The man had earned the nickname by having informants everywhere that allowed him to ferret out his opponents. The legends he promoted held him to be a specter listening to every conversation, watching every move, and finding every weakness of his enemies. The myth also held that traitors died of fear, but the bodies that had been recovered revealed .40mm slugs buried in the tissues. Wounds to the genitalia, heart, and head were his trademark, probably in that order.

Adam's UltraNet software had provided a veritable gold mine of data on both men. Finding that information had been easy. Finding a prosecutor and judge willing to tackle such a case in Mexico would prove not to be.

"Colonel, we got 'em!" Mike J had rushed from the safe

room to find him. "You were right. That building in Guerrero started humming like a hive just after siesta time. C'mon and take a look."

Colonel S followed his friend and fellow patriot back to the "lair" where Mike J sat down in front of his computer.

"I'll project it on the screen."

Colonel S turned his attention to the large-screen television mounted on an adjacent wall.

"Where are these images coming from?"

"I hijacked a CBP drone for a flight over the town but didn't want to take control of it for too long and make the operator suspicious. So, I tasked a satellite to give me updates every 15 minutes. When the activity picked up, I made another pass over the town with a different drone."

That was a tactic they had used many times. Drones from Laredo and others from Eagle Pass covered a lot of territory for the CBP. They utilized both. To use one drone consistently might raise suspicions if the operator noticed diversions over the same spot.

As they watched, sure enough, trucks and ATVs appeared as if preparing for a run across the border. The colonel checked his watch. *True to form*, he thought. Dusk was this guy's favorite time, and the shipment would likely move out in time to reach the river shortly before the sun set. From their location, he calculated that they would drive south on Federal Highway 2 for a short distance before cutting east to the Rio where the wall construction had ended.

Adam interrupted their viewing. "Hey, this Saucedo character has someone on the payroll at the CBP Office of Field Operations in Laredo. I'm looking into the banking and other accounts of agents there. Shouldn't take long to get an ID."

"We need to be careful then. That field operations office is adjacent to the CBP Marine and Air Operations offices where the drones are controlled. We can't afford for this mole to become suspicious about hijacked flights over his boss' properties."

The colonel nodded. "I've been there before . . . at the Laredo airport. The buildings are at opposite ends of the airfield, but I'm sure they must work pretty closely together. We might need to switch to the air operations out of Eagle Pass as first choice."

"Can do," replied Mike J. "Speaking of air operations, look at that."

All three men focused on the screen where a young man walked out of the building carrying a drone and backpack and placed both on the front seat of a waiting truck.

"Guess we're not the only ones using aerial surveillance."

"Looks like a DJI Matrice 300 Quadcopter," said Adam.

The other two looked at him wearing surprised looks.

"I had to get a drone to stake out that lab in Wisconsin. You know, the one I told you about. Anyway, these are used by police departments and for search and rescue because if equipped properly, they have a 55 minute flight time, an airspeed of 51 miles per hour, if no wind, and an operational range of five miles up to nine miles if terrain and buildings don't get in the way. I didn't get this one, but it's a nice unit. Also has 4K resolution with its camera."

The colonel was impressed with Adam's knowledge of drones more than the drone specs themselves. Such a unit was of no use for them. They needed the large, military-style drones that could fly for miles and long periods of time. That's what they piggybacked their surveillance onto. The CBP's Predator drones fit that need perfectly. Rumor had it that the new administration—taking office that very day—would be grounding the CBP's air fleet. That would prove to be bad news . . . for both their clandestine operations and the country.

Dusk came early in mid-January, even in south Texas. The colonel checked the time. Those trucks could begin to move out at any time.

"How much longer can we commandeer this drone?"

"I'm going to have to relinquish this one now. I can't override the operator's signal any longer." Mike J typed some commands on his keyboard, and the screen went blank.

"What a lousy time to lose it. We need eyes in the sky."

"Give me a minute."

Moments later, a new image appeared on the screen.

"Wow, where's this coming from? We might even be able to count freckles at this resolution."

Adam and Mike J did a high-five, as Mike J laughed.

"Colonel, you aren't going to believe this one. With some intel from Adam, we now have control of a Chinese spy satellite crossing over south Texas."

The colonel smiled. The presence of such satellites from each country was no secret. The U.S. had its high-altitude spies over China and Russia, and those countries in turn had theirs over the U.S.

"Ever hear swearing in Mandarin? It's quite animated, and I'm sure this operator is doing just that right now."

"Hey, look," said Adam. "That's Saucedo himself. They must be getting ready to move out."

The three watched as men climbed aboard the trucks carrying the ATVs and drugs. Mike J initiated text messages to their team that had assembled at the end of the wall in anticipation of intercepting the shipment that evening. As they drove out of town, however, they didn't turn south on Highway 2. Instead, they drove past the 1702 San Bernardo Mission ruins and straight east toward the river.

It dawned on the colonel where they were headed.

"Mike, is Ingersoll's phone still off?"

The man nodded.

"Do we have any way of contacting him?"

"Just his regular phones, why?"

"Text the team. The smugglers are headed for the Ingersoll ranch."

"Hey, Aric!"

He turned to see Mitch running toward him down the hall. In just the short time Aric had been in the dorm, the two had gotten to be good friends. The guy wasn't a believer, but it was a good sign when someone like him followed Biblical principles even when they didn't know it. The Bible says to make your 'yes' mean yes, and your 'no' to mean no. Mitch had shown that. When he had said he'd help cover Aric's back, he'd meant it.

The jock caught up with Aric at the door to the stairwell. Together they began the descent to the dining hall.

"Saw your roomie leave a short while ago. He really looked unsettled. What'd you do?"

Aric felt surprised. "Nothing new. At least, not that he's

aware of yet. Did you see the door?"

Mitch shook his head. "Wasn't paying attention. Gimme a minute." He ran back up the one flight of steps they'd descended and off toward Aric's room. Aric returned to the stairwell door and watched as Mitch started laughing before he even got there. Moments later, he was back at Aric's side.

"Oh. My. Gawd. He's gonna have a fit." Mitch gave him a clap on the back. "Gotta say, though, some of that might get you reported for hate speech on this campus."

Aric shrugged. "That was mentioned. They might have a hard time with that since it's all straight from the Bible. Last I looked, this used to be a Lutheran institution. Criticizing the Bible won't sit well with a lot of alumni."

"Maybe, but they have a way of shooting messengers around here." He paused. "Look, I know nothing about Lutherans except there are conservative ones and liberal ones. Better make sure you're dealing with the right ones."

He made a good point. Aric didn't know the details of the college's Lutheran roots or even if it considered itself a Lutheran college anymore. He was familiar with the Lutheran Church-Missouri Synod back in St. Louis. They believed in the inerrancy of the Bible and were both Biblically and socially conservative. If these folks were members of the "lost-cause Lutherans," as he'd once heard the liberal Evangelical Lutheran Church of America called, he might indeed find himself in hot water. Or boiling water, if the school's leaders had no religious roots at all.

"Too bad I won't be able to see his face when he gets back." Aric figured he'd either be in the dining hall or in his room studying, maybe already sleeping, when Bob got back.

"*Au contraire*, my friend. Let's grab some food and take it back to my room. We can keep the door open and watch for him." He paused. "Even better, I'll set up my GoPro camera to watch your door. We can get his reaction no matter what time he arrives." He rubbed his hands together. "This is gonna be epic."

TWENTY-NINE

After a family-style ranch dinner, Dillon started a bonfire for his guests and lined up chairs for everyone around it. Making S'mores never got old, although admittedly he only ate a couple whenever they made them, not the five or six he used to devour.

"Jim, I think you guys are in for a treat. We're late in the season, so all the bucks are hard-antlered now. I rode through the reserve yesterday and spotted a handful of 8 to 10-pointers and one with a rack I'd put on my wall any day. I only got a glimpse, so I couldn't count the points." He raised his tin cup of coffee and took a sip.

"Lookin' forward to it. You never fail to give us a good hunt. That's why we come back every year." Jim raised his cup in a toast. "Here's to an unforgettable hunt."

Jim Spencer and his three hunting buddies—Walt Fischer, Derek Grimes, and Sean Reyes—did indeed come back annually. They always got a load of venison to ship home, but trophies had not been as easily taken. Their traditional hunting time had been early in the season when many of the bucks still wore velvet in the early stages of antler development. This year they wanted trophies, as well as the meat.

"I got a question," said Sean. "When you ride through on an ATV doesn't that tend to make the deer skittish for a few days?"

Dillon nodded. "I guess it could, but can't say as I've noticed that. When I said I rode through, I meant on my horse, Derringer. I can go places on horseback that I can't on an ATV or Jeep. Which brings me to a question. What kind of hunt do you want to do tomorrow?"

"We haven't quite decided," said Derek. "Do you need to know tonight?"

Dillon shook his head. "Nope. We're good to go with whichever style you choose. We'll have an early breakfast, so you can tell me then."

Sean looked up again. "So, I figured you did your scouting by drone."

The mention of that word pricked Dillon's ears. "Drone? Why'd you think that?" Dillon almost held his breath waiting for the answer.

"As we were unpacking the SUV, I saw one over that way." He pointed toward the deer preserve. "Figured you, or someone here, was checking out the herd." He craned his neck back and forth, and then stood and took a couple of steps in that same direction. "In fact, I think I see it again."

Dillon jumped to his feet and walked in front of his guest. This was not good news. He looked out over his property. Sure enough. It looked like the same quadcopter he and Eduardo spotted over their buildings.

"Fellas, any of you got military experience?"

All four men's eyes widened at that question. Dillon could understand their position. Why in the world would he ask them that? Three of the four nodded.

"You might want to get your guns . . . and ammo."

Dillon ran into the house and opened his gun safe, from which he retrieved his Remington 7600 and a box of bullets. He inserted four into the magazine. By the time he returned, two things had happened. The drone had moved closer, and his guests had their guns at their sides. They all looked concerned.

"What's up, Dillon?"

He pointed to the sky. The light was starting to fade. He couldn't wait much longer. He sat down on the ground with his knees up. Using his knees to support his elbows, he took aim at the drone. The 7600 was a great hunting rifle for deer and elk, but at the distance he had to shoot, the rifle's accuracy was iffy. He wished he had the M110C, but that had to remain hidden. He took a deep breath, steadied himself, and fired, leading the drone along the direction it flew. The device shattered in midair.

"Whoa, great shot! But why—"

He stopped to think. There were several roads through his ranch that the cartels could use to move drugs from the river. Only one had the cover needed to hide their movement, and that road was less than half a mile away. The drone appeared to be scouting that path but had moved close to the house, perhaps to scope out the house and buildings for any activity that might hinder their operation. That was his guess. Had they seen Dillon and his guests at the bonfire? Surely, it would stand out in the waning light. Perhaps it was the fire that led it closer to them, like a bug drawn to a light.

With that realization, he acknowledged that maybe he had been premature in turning off *the* phone. Right now, that device remained hidden in the toolbox of his tractor inside the equipment barn. Maybe The Remnant was already aware of what was taking place. Would the cavalry be arriving soon?

He did have his personal cell phone on him. He needed to call the CBP immediately and then text Eduardo. As he dialed, he said, "Fellas, prepare yourselves. That drone was a cartel drone. I think we're about to have unwanted company."

Their departure from the new warehouse and Guerrero itself was uneventful, as was the drive past the old mission church to the river. Once at the Rio, they waited.

"Jose, get the drone," Raimondo said to his young techie.

"*Si, jefe.*"

As the young man flew the four-propellered aircraft—the quadcopter, as the man called it—Raimondo watched from his side. The images from its 4K camera were outstanding, although some fog along the river made the images hazy.

"To the left, I think," he said. Looking at aerial maps on his phone was one thing, but finding the route at ground level was different. The dated images on Google did not show foliage or changes due to flooding. This rancher maintained only one route to the river for his personal use, and that road led directly to his home. The other gravel roads were used sporadically to take his cattle to water. The one that Raimondo sought was one of those.

"There. Follow that one away from the river. I think that is the one we must use."

He watched the road as it wound up through a narrow arroyo toward the road where they would meet the trucks. It appeared to be the path he had chosen. If so, they would encounter a gate in short order. A second gate would be found about a quarter-mile farther, and a final gate would open onto the county road.

"*Si*. There is the first gate. Another 400 meters and we should see another."

As he recalled the map, they would be getting closer to the house. Would the occupants become aware of noise coming from the road? They could only silence the ATVs so much. As for the drone, they had been staying only seven to ten meters above the road, high enough to clear the brush but low enough to avoid being seen from the house.

"Take the drone up and turn the camera northwest. I want to see what is happening at the house."

"*Si, jefe.*"

The drone rose to 50 meters, and the camera swiveled to find the house. The image steadied upon the house and its immediate grounds. Only one man could be seen, and he appeared to be piling wood onto a pile. That was of no concern. He would likely call it quits at dark.

"Back down to the road. We need to follow it all the way to make sure it is the right one before it gets too dark to fly."

His technician complied, and soon they came across the second gate, followed by the third and its access to the county road.

"*Jefe*, it is getting too dark to fly so low. I risk damaging the drone by flying into branches or a tree obscured by the shadows."

Raimondo nodded. "Take it up to a safe height. In the low light, it is unlikely to be spotted."

The drone was now at 60 meters and heading back to them when the camera noted a glare in the northwest. They turned the camera again toward the house. A large bonfire flared before them, and there appeared to be people moving around it.

"Closer. I need to see who is there." If it was simply a fire to burn scrap with the same man attending to it, he would not worry. Even if it was a family event, he felt no concern.

"There are five men there, *jefe*. They appear to be making S'mores. Yummm." The man smiled.

Raimondo buffed him across the back of his head. "Focus." He had to admit that it did sound good. While being a popular campfire treat in their two northern neighbors, the U.S. and Canada, and less common in Mexico, he had made them himself on more than one occasion.

One of the men stood up and seemed to look their way. Had he spotted the drone?

"I should fly back quickly, *jefe*. They may have seen us."

"No, wait. I want to see what they do."

Another man, the one he had seen preparing the fire, ran toward the house. The other men hurried toward a different building.

"Now, *jefe*?"

"Wait."

The four men returned to the fire, each carrying something that he couldn't quite make out. It was as if they were trying to hide the objects from the drone. He focused on those men, trying to identify what they carried.

"*El diablo, jefe*. The other man!"

Raimondo turned his attention to the ranch owner in time to see him bring his elbows to his knees as he sat on the ground. He had a rifle. He now understood that that was what each of the others had, too.

"Get away, now!"

At that moment when the pilot used the controller to increase the drone's airspeed, the video feed blacked out. The controller flashed that they no longer had communication with the drone.

The young man cursed. Raimondo knew that drone had been his baby, his pride and joy, and now it was gone.

For Raimondo, it was but another tool of his trade. An expendable tool. What were a few thousand American dollars compared to the many times it had led his men safely across the border? This time, however, it had brought potential calamity. Had the drone not been spotted, they had a high chance of success in getting their product safely to the trucks on the other side. Now?

He could not afford to lose this shipment . . . for many reasons. His last mission had failed and cost El Espectro $15 million. This shipment's value was over $20 million. His life was not worth $35 to El Espectro much less $35 million. He could not fail this time, or it would be his last.

He called his lead men together.

"Change of plan. The drone was spotted, and there are armed men at the ranch. Rito, you will still ride with the ATVs. Jorge, you will join them. Only the two of you and the four drivers. Take extra ammunition."

If he was to fail, he wanted to go out on his own terms, as a warrior.

"Juan, Reynaldo, and Luis, you will go with me and the rest of the men. There is a road that goes directly to the house. We will go and deal with those men, and anyone else at the house."

THIRTY

Despite the new focus of his work with UltraNet, Adam kept abreast of what was happening to Aric. By tapping into the campus security system, he had a view of his brother's hallway. That had enabled him to record the two individuals who had "pranked" his room, but he hadn't needed to use that video. He'd been proud of little brother standing up for himself, and the move to call Special Agent Wiese was brilliant. Way to go, Aric!

What had concerned him, however, was that the security officer in charge of monitoring the cameras across the campus had not just chosen to ignore what was so clearly evident with those two individuals breaking into another student's room, but he also protected those two by deleting the video. When asked, he blamed the gap on a glitch in the camera—or so his formal report stated. What he couldn't erase, however, was the key card data. Adam made sure of that.

UltraNet kept tabs on everything the college's computer systems maintained about Aric. He saw that the roommate he'd met on "move-in Saturday" had been transferred to a different dorm already. Why was not a question he'd likely answer. He knew that another roommate had been assigned but hadn't had the opportunity to run a deep-dive background check on the kid.

Now, as he checked in on the dorm's security cameras and saw what had transpired on his brother's door, he wished he had made that background check a higher priority. He took a deep breath and sighed as he massaged his forehead with his hands.

"What's up?" asked Mike J.

Adam frowned. "Well, I'm keeping tabs on my little brother. Ever since he got dragged into my conflict with Wallace Chamberlain, I've felt responsible for him. So, I try to run interference for him when I can, without his knowing about it." He explained to Mike what had happened with the so-called prank and how Aric had dealt with it.

Mike J laughed. "Resourceful kid. I bet that security officer about wet her pants when she ended up talking with the ranking FBI agent in the state."

Adam smiled and nodded. "What's happening in Texas?"

They were geared up to pull an all-nighter if that's what it took. Adam understood that they had promised Dillon Ingersoll that they'd cover his back. If they failed, their network would likely fall apart.

"I was hoping to piggyback on a drone over the ranch, but it looks like CBP is already on it. Ingersoll must have contacted them. The cavalry's been alerted and diverted back to the ranch, but they're a good hour away. The bad guys are still massed at the river. Looks like four ATVs and 22 men."

"What can I do?"

Mike J shook his head. "Not much at this end. I just need to keep watching as things unfold. I don't want to use the regular phones because that could expose our operation, but if I need to contact Ingersoll to warn him, that's what I'll have to do."

Adam nodded. "Let me handle it. If it comes to that, let me know. I can route a text through so many servers, only God could trace the route."

Mike J's countenance brightened. "Hey, will do. I'm liking UltraNet more and more. Glad you're on board."

Adam turned his focus back onto Aric's predicament. Clearly, the campus had assigned him a gay roommate. Why? And who had initiated it?

He set up the parameters for UltraNet and let it loose. The first answer came back in seconds. A RA named Ashleigh Love had initiated the request. What could he find out about her? New parameters for another search were entered. Who was Robert Jannsen? He would soon know.

While he waited, he decided to change the odds in Texas. The file he had amassed on "Agent White," including the details on a bank account in the Cayman Islands, was what every law enforcement officer dreamed of. Of course, the authorities couldn't just accept it from an anonymous source, so the file included every link they'd need to check things out themselves. It was time to eliminate Saucedo's inside man. With a press of a key, the file went to the nearest U.S. Attorney, local law enforcement in Laredo, and multiple patriot groups in the region. The latter would make sure the former didn't brush this under some cactus.

As he finished up with that task, notifications began to

arrive about Ms. Love—make that Mr. Samuel Cooke —and Jannsen. Once upon a time, the information he now reviewed would have been scandalous and shocking. Now, most would yawn and ignore it.

How far our nation's morality had slidden. Aric had once told him that if God didn't judge the United States for its killing of the unborn and its acceptance of homosexuality, He would have to apologize to the followers of some pagan god named Moloch and to Sodom and Gomorrah. On that point, he and Aric had no disagreement.

Another notification beeped, and he took a look. *Well, well, well*, he thought. He thought he'd found everything pertinent to "Doctor Meredith Fry." It now appeared that he hadn't. He knew that Meredith Fry had been born Isabella Cooke, but now he learned that her father was Samuel Cooke's uncle. Isabella had a long list of arrests for indecency, petty thefts, and more. She had become known for grooming young women into the lesbian lifestyle and teen men into transgenderism. Apparently, that had included her youthful cousin. She had disappeared after one of her young consorts was found dead from hanging himself. While she was implicated in the note the boy had left behind, she was never found.

Of course, he had already found the links that led Isabella to become Fatima Khan and later to become Meredith Fry. The doctorate she claimed to have was as phony as her background story. That had been his threat to her over a week earlier. He had told her to back off in her war against Lynch Cully. She had. He had no reason to unveil her secrets . . . until now.

She was somehow instrumental in the conflict brewing against Aric. She also had a connection to the security guard who liked to look the other way when it came to the sometimes illegal actions of the LGBT+ and Antifa crowds. He didn't have the details of that connection, but he would by daybreak. What he did have on the guard, however, was enough to indict him on drug dealing and human trafficking charges.

It was time to pull the plug on that guy, and when he found the connections to "Dr. Fry," she would fry, too. He smiled at his pun.

He readied his file on the guard. Like the file on the dirty border agent, it held all the links needed to make life easy for the detective who caught this case. This time, however, he needed to add a little fire under the feet of the police department. He had no time for them to dilly-dally. In 24 hours, the appropriate material would be leaked to the Wisconsin press and various social media outlets. Considering the charges the man could face, the public pressure would be immediate.

With a single keystroke, the file was sent.

The colonel paced as the three of them watched the infrared images from the drone. He took note of the time: 6:12 p.m. The sun had just set, so the last rays of light would disappear soon. Saucedo would make his move soon.

Every so often, the drone would pass over the Ingersoll home and buildings. Its camera had switched to infrared, which appeared much like viewing things with night vision goggles. The five people they had seen near a blazing fire, had become six, and the fire itself was dying. That sixth person had emerged from the house, and Colonel S worried that the man's wife was now exposed along with the men. That the man's family was in danger ate at him. This was not acceptable.

The drone's camera returned its focus to the river. The smugglers were now breaking into two groups. The ATVs formed one band, and they counted six men there. They could only assume the men were well-armed.

"What are the others doing?" he asked.

"Not sure yet. They've come together as a group. It looks like someone's talking to them."

"Saucedo?"

"Can't tell under infrared, but that's a fair assumption."

"Can you commandeer the drone to go over the house again?"

Mike J nodded. "I could, but I don't want to yet. The operator seems to be checking the house every five or six minutes."

That struck Colonel S as odd. Why would the CBP keep tabs on the house? Something didn't feel right.

"Who's the operator?" asked Adam. "Why would they care about the house unless they have agents on their way there and are checking to see if they've arrived? Wouldn't they keep in touch by radio?"

They already knew that the CBP's response team had been dispatched in hope of intercepting the shipment but not necessarily sent to the Ingersoll homestead. That's when it hit him. Adam was onto something.

"Adam's close. Who's the operator, and where is the

control originating?"

"Well, I can tell you right off that its control is coming from Laredo." Mike J paused. "Oh crap, are you thinking what I'm now thinking?"

"Could be. What if our operator is the dirty agent?"

Mike J tapped some keys. "All I can find is an operator number, 13502. No name."

"Adam?"

"On it, Colonel."

A minute later, Adam confirmed his worst suspicion. "Agent White" had control of the drone. He was keeping tabs on the house because he wanted to keep Saucedo abreast of what was happening there.

The drone once again swept over the homestead. The six people had now become nine.

"Mike, where are our people? Are these our guys? Where'd they come from?"

Mike checked the locations of The Remnant's phones. "Our guys are still a good thirty minutes away."

Who were these extra people?

"Uh-oh," said Mike. "Looks like the ATVs are starting up one road. It goes straight to Eagle Pass Road."

"The others?"

"They're moving out, up the road that leads to the house."

The colonel took a deep breath. They were running out of time. Those men would get to the house before their team could get there to reinforce them. They would have to use commercial carriers to warn Ingersoll.

"Adam, we need to let Ingersoll know what's coming his way."

Adam nodded. In the time it took the colonel to finish one lap in his pacing, Adam replied, "Done. I also took the liberty to alert the Laredo police, CBP, and county sheriffs about the situation."

The colonel nodded and sighed. Notifying Ingersoll was one thing. Alerting the authorities was another. They would wonder where the notice came from, how the information was obtained, and more. He wished Adam had consulted them first. This could put them in the cross hairs of the feds, something they truly didn't need. But what choice did they have? Adam had made the right move. The Ingersolls and whoever was with them were *not* expendable.

Raimondo disconnected his call and looked up despite knowing he'd never be able to spot the CBP drone. Good thing his man had control of the device. He had learned long ago that intelligence was critical to success. Once again, it was going to pay off.

"*Escuchen*! Rito, go slow. The people at the house know something is up. There are nine people there now. We will secure them, so you have time to meet the trucks. Our man in Laredo has diverted the border agents to a different location."

His lead man nodded. "*Si, jefe.*"

"Go!"

He watched Rito and the others mount the ATVs and move toward the path he had pointed them to. They moved along at a crawl. *Perfecto*, he thought. That would give them the time they needed to deal with those at the house, as well as minimize any noise they might create to alert those people.

He might no longer have the benefit of surprise, but the timing was his to command.

He collected the others and described the topography they would face as they moved up the ravine toward the house. He instructed his leads to divide into three squads, two of which would break off into different arroyos leading toward the buildings. He would stay with the third squad taking the main road.

"The owner of this ranch shot down my drone. I believe they are armed, so be careful. They might just be ranchers, but to shoot my drone took skill. You would be an easy target."

His men took off at a trot ahead of him. They hadn't much time.

THIRTY-ONE

Adam looked at the other two. He had made the right choice, whether or not they agreed. He knew that decision could cause ramifications for The Remnant, but he wasn't going to let nine people get slaughtered by a cartel.

"I know. I should have asked about contacting the authorities. The Remnant is your baby, and I might have just thrown it out with the bath water."

The colonel shook his head. "No. You made the right call. We need to get all the help we can muster to help the Ingersolls. Can you determine how far away the CBP response team is?"

Adam turned back to his computer and put UltraNet to work. A minute later, his gut twisted, and the blood drained from his face. What would happen now?

"What's wrong? You look awful." The colonel gave him a quizzical look.

"The dirtbag sent the response team to the wrong place. They won't make it in time."

"What about helicopters? Can we initiate a dispatch for

them?"

Adam considered that. "I think I could swing that, but even with that, I don't think they'd get there. Two, three minutes to get into the air. Probably 15-20 minutes to get to and pick up the team, and another 20 minutes to get to the Ingersolls."

"Do it anyway."

Adam worked the system to dispatch the needed CBP helicopters and then watched the colonel resume his pacing.

"Okay. Mike, can we gain control of the drone? We need to even the playing field."

Adam spoke first. "I can help with that. Mike, use these control parameters." He gave the other man instructions on what to do.

"Oh wow, that's cool. Why didn't I see that?" After entering the commands, he had full control of the drone, but to the CBP it no longer looked like a glitch. "Agent White" still appeared to be in control. Mike J re-targeted the cartel's men. The ATVs were moving slowly toward the road, while the others were moving toward the house. As they watched, one team of three men split off to the northeast.

"Hey, Ingersoll's phone just came back online."

Dillon looked at his guests with dismay. They didn't deserve to be dragged into this mess. But then, if the federal government would do its job, he and his family wouldn't be facing it either.

"Guys, I'm sorry you've been caught up in this. Your deer hunt may have just turned into another Alamo, although I hope with no loss of life."

He proceeded to tell them of the recent drug shipment being stopped by persons unknown at a neighbor's ranch and of seeing this drone over that ranch just a few days later. When that drone skedaddled back into Mexico, they had become convinced it was a tool of that cartel.

"The cartel can't use that crossing anymore because the destroyed trucks block their way. I suspect that drone was scouting my place as a new crossing point. The ranch lane it was over goes from the river directly to Eagle Pass Road. And since it's dusk, I'm convinced another shipment of drugs is coming this way. This seems to be the cartel's favorite time of day for moving their goods."

Of the four men, only Derek looked uncertain. He was the only one without military experience.

"Derek, why don't you stick with Sean?"

He pointed to the barn. "Sean, that barn over there overlooks the road coming up from the river. There's a small loft with a ventilation vent that pops out to the inside. The walls up there are reinforced and will protect you."

The four men gave him looks of surprise and questioning. He realized he should have digressed at the beginning.

"Yeah, my hands and me, we've anticipated this for years."

As he spoke, he heard footsteps coming from behind. His son-in-law Jose and two full-time hands had arrived on foot and were well armed. He had texted Jose earlier with their Code Red alert. Jose, in turn, had rounded up the others. All were game for a fight, and they'd run this drill before. Now, with the hunters there, they were four men stronger.

"Fellas, this here's Jose, Cody, and Raul. Cody, why don't you show Sean and Derek the barn and then take the point on the other side of the road." Cody nodded. "Jose, take Jim and Walt and get them settled into the nests in the bunkhouse."

Just then his personal phone notified him of a text.

Drone shows 4 ATVs and 6 men on lane to county road. 10 men coming up the road toward the house. All armed.

Dillon took a deep breath. *Thank God*, he thought. *They haven't abandoned me even though I left them.* They had promised to cover his back, and they were being true to their word. That meant a lot to him. He resolved to retrieve *the* phone before heading out.

"Hold up, guys. Drone overhead confirms there's an armed force coming our way. There's four ATVs with six men headin' up the east lane. And we got ten men coming up our drive from the river." He didn't have to share everything, like who had alerted him.

Jim spoke up. "If there's a CBP drone up there, where are the CBP agents? Don't they have some kind of rapid response team? Why are we being put in harm's way? This isn't what we signed up for, Dillon."

Dillon nodded, removed his Stetson, and rubbed his hand through his hair. "Jim, can't say as I signed up for this either. I told you what I know. You guys can jump into your SUV and head out if'n you want. Come back later for your gear."

Walt shook his head. "Not on your life. I took an oath to defend this country, and that's what I'm gonna do. If we abandon you, that cuts your numbers in half." He looked at his friend. "C'mon, Jim, we can't leave them behind. How would you live with yourself if something happens to them all?"

Sean nodded in agreement. Derek still looked uncertain. Jim shrugged and acquiesced.

"Fellas, don't have much time for debate here. Only takes about 20 minutes to hike up here from the river. We need to get settled into the protective nests we've created and get ready. Guys, we're giving you the most secure ones."

"Nests? You've mentioned that twice now."

Dillon nodded. "I was a Marine sniper. Sometimes we were on the move and shooting from a bunch of positions. Other times, we hunkered down to wait for a specific target. We'd build what we called a nest for protection from both being detected and possible return fire. Like I said a moment ago, we figured this day would come and we might have to protect our property, so we built a series of protective nests to shoot from. They'll give us the high ground and advantage over the invaders."

Raul motioned with his hand for attention. "Boss, we need to get ready. Those ATVs could already be gettin' close to the choke point."

Dillon nodded. Those drug smugglers were going to get the surprise of their possibly soon-to-be-shortened lives.

THIRTY-TWO

As the others ran off to their defensive positions, Dillon ran to the equipment shed. Once there, he pulled *the* phone from its hiding spot in the tractor and turned it on. He had mixed feeling about using it. After all, he'd made the decision to leave The Remnant. Why should he expect their help in return? Yet, right now he needed all the help he could get.

He typed in a text.

Thanks for the heads up.

In return, he received a call. A familiar voice spoke, "The team of ten has split into three groups. Four are coming up the road and two groups of three have split off into two arroyos to try to flank your compound. We're watching your heat signatures from above. Will keep you posted."

"Thanks. If you're aware of this, where's the CBP rapid response team?"

"The smugglers had a man inside the CBP. He was operating the drone and relaying info about you to the smugglers. We took control of the drone away from him to reverse that flow of info and alerted the police about him. He directed the response team to a location in the opposite direction from you, so they're a good half-hour away."

"What about your team?"

"We were misled, too. But we caught the smugglers' movements and saw them heading your way. At this point, our men are still 20 to 30 minutes away. Can you hold them that long?"

Dillon had to think about that. He knew the men in the hunting party were skillful in handling their rifles, but shooting a deer and shooting a man were worlds apart.

"I'm pretty sure we can. I have a hunting party of four here. Three of them have military training, but shooting people instead of deer was not even on their horizon an hour ago. And my guys and me, well, we've prepared a few surprises just for this scenario."

"The ATVs are about a quarter of the way. The men on foot are halfway there."

"Then, I gotta run."

"We'll try to keep you posted."

"Thanks."

Dillon hung up and ran out of the shed. "C'mon, Raul. We don't have much time."

Together they ran toward the east road. They needed to beat the ATVs to the halfway point . . . in the dark. They had the shorter distance but not the advantage of a motorized vehicle or headlights. Once upon a time, he'd found double-time marching to require little effort. Now, he was huffing and puffing. Yet, he *had* to push on.

They made it. He could see headlights slowly wending their way toward them. He estimated they were still some 200 yards away.

"Raul, unroll the stinger and head to the east nest."

"Got it."

Raul ran down along the side of the lane to the choke point and pulled a metal spike strip across the lane before taking up his position in the east side nest, while Dillon stayed to the west. He'd gotten the spike strip from his brother, a deputy sheriff in a distant Texas county. The device could be relied upon to take out the tires of the first ATV and block the road.

A shot rang out through the dark and from the subsequent sound, Dillon envisioned chips flying from one of the boulders as the bullet hit it. He heard a whistle and knew that Raul was safely inside his nest.

They'd rehearsed this. Over a year earlier, they had created a choke point in the road. Boulders had been moved to both edges of the road where the sides of the arroyo became too steep for even an ATV to climb around them. That forced a vehicle, whether pickup, ATV, or tractor, to move between the rocks. If they tried to drive up the small canyon's sides, they would flip back upon themselves. If the men tried to move up the sides, they had no cover. The only cover for them, besides the ATVs, were the boulders, but Dillon had a booby trap for that scenario, too.

The darkness was another advantage. Dillon and Raul had night scopes on their rifles. If it became an 'us vs. them' scenario, the two men had little doubt who would win. And, as it stood, the smugglers had now fired first.

The ATVs were maybe 100 yards away when *the* phone vibrated with a text notification.

ATVs almost to your position. Captured a muzzle flash on their side. You okay?

Dillon replied,

Fine. Have surprises waiting for them. What about the others?

The answer came in an instant.

Bad guys almost to edge of compound. The two teams appear to be waiting for the main team on the road. They haven't moved out of the arroyos.

Dillon tried to envision the exact whereabouts of those illegals. He estimated that they were roughly 20 feet from their own surprises, or maybe they'd already stumbled upon them, or into them, as the case would be. Maybe the traps had ensnared them, making it appear as if they'd stopped in the arroyo. The main team on the road was his primary concern. The Ingersoll family used that road too often to install special defenses, but those men would have no cover once they came within about 50 yards from the main barn.

His thoughts were interrupted by a sudden pop! pop! blam! pop! All four tires on the first ATV had succumbed to the spike strip. With its heavy load, it now sat disabled and blocking the road. He could hear loud swearing from behind the boulders.

Gunfire erupted from the vehicle's occupants, but they were shooting blindly. They had no idea where Dillon and Raul were hidden. Through his scope, Dillon could see that one man wore night-vision goggles. He and Raul were behind sandbags. As long as they remained there, the goggles wouldn't register them.

An instant later, Dillon was reminded that even a blind squirrel finds a nut now and then. He felt the slug hit the sandbag on his left before he heard its impact. He raised his rifle and returned a single shot. The man with goggles went down holding his right thigh. Another man grabbed him under his shoulders and dragged him behind the boulders and disabled ATV.

Suddenly the roar of an engine filled the arroyo, and the driver of another ATV tried to gun it and head up the side of the ravine. As expected, it flipped backward upon itself, and Dillon could hear the driver's scream.

A moment later, another man tried running up the hillside firing randomly while another gun provided cover from the boulders. A shot rang out from the east nest, and the man tumbled backward.

The fight hadn't been fair from the start, in Dillon's way of thinking. The two of them against only six smugglers. Now there were only three in fighting condition. It'd be like shooting fish in a barrel if he let the events take their natural course, but now he heard gunfire from the direction of the compound. They needed to end this.

He pulled his personal phone from his pocket and called up an app. With a press of his finger, the app remotely detonated four devices hidden in loose dirt on the other side of the rocks. Firecrackers began to explode and light up the shadows. This was accompanied by the release of three substances—the first, a gummy adhesive activated by the oxygen in the air. The second, the contents of a dozen small canisters of skunk scent, and the third, glitter. Those scent particles and glitter would stick to the adhesive, and attempts to remove the resulting goo with one's hands would make it impossible to operate a weapon . . . or an ATV for that matter. The glitter was just for "fun."

In hindsight, Dillon and his men had had way too much fun watching and being inspired by the YouTube videos of glitter bombs for porch pirates. Little did the inventor of those devices know they'd be stopping drug smugglers someday.

With a slight breeze from the northwest, Dillon and Raul were spared from the stink, but yelling and cursing came their way without interference. Dillon felt confident that those men weren't going to get far and that their loads were going nowhere. He gave a distinct whistle, and moments later, Raul crouched behind him.

"Boss, I think it worked." He chuckled.

"I agree, but we need to get back to the others." As if to punctuate his words, several more gunshots were heard from the area of the house and barns.

They moved cautiously this time. Although they knew the trail well, they had no idea whom they might encounter along the way. As they came near the end of the closest arroyo—to them, farthest from the house—they slowed and knelt on the ground. Dillon used his night scope to look for others. He scanned toward the house and saw no one. He had similar results looking down through the gully. He looked at Raul and saw him doing the same thing.

"Do you think the tiger traps worked?"

Raul shrugged.

They continued toward the compound. As they neared the next arroyo, the one closest to the house, they noticed the first dire casualty. The man on the ground looked as if he'd been stabbed by a dozen ice picks. Dillon knelt next to him and felt for a carotid pulse. The man was still alive, but he struggled to breathe. Dillon risked using the light on his phone to inspect the victim. He discovered a large puncture in the man's left chest wall. He suspected it had punctured and collapsed the man's lung.

Raul shook his head. "Don't know how he got out, but if this guy's the example, the traps worked, and the others might not have fared as well."

Dillon nodded in agreement as he extinguished his light. The two arroyos were outside the ranch's grazing lands and had little use to him. However, they had been identified as vulnerabilities in a situation like this. Because of that, they had dug an eight-foot deep, ten-by-ten-foot hole along each one. At the bottom, they had placed dozens of pieces of scrap plywood studded with four-inch smooth shank common nails. Stretched across the top was a canvas tarp dusted with dirt. A fall into the pit was intended to result in incapacitating injuries. Yet, while the risk of death was low, it was not zero. A fall leading to a puncture of an artery or both lungs could be fatal.

As they neared the bunkhouse, both men held back. The two hunters nested inside hadn't been part of their practice runs. He didn't want them to see him and Raul moving and start shooting. He let loose his whistle again. Jose, Jim, and Walt hustled around the front side of the bunkhouse.

"Hey, boss. I think we're good. Looks like we took down three men coming up the road."

Dillon pushed everyone closer to the building. "There were four coming up the road. Where's the fourth guy?" The last thing he needed was for the last man to run out from the nearby shrub oaks, guns blazing. "Jose, go check on Cody and the others. Turn on all the flood lights."

Before Jose could leave the group, light flooded the area, and the chop-chop-chop of a helicopter filled their ears. Seconds later, two thick ropes fell from a UH-60 Blackhawk 40 feet above them, and six tactical CBP agents fast-roped down to the ground. With guns raised they approached the group.

At that moment, the floodlights washed the area with light. Cody and the others came around the corner. Cody had followed their drill and turned on the floods.

"Hey, Dillon, we—" They stopped in their tracks when they saw the armed federal agents. Each man raised his free arm but did not drop his rifle.

Dillon spoke. "Agents, I'm Dillon Ingersoll, owner of the ranch. You guys are a bit late to the dance."

"Drop the rifles!"

Dillon nodded and complied. The others followed his lead.

The man who appeared to be the lead agent approached him. "ID?"

Dillon reached slowly to his back pocket and pulled out a well-worn leather wallet, from which he produced his driver's license. He handed it to the agent, who nodded to his men to stand down.

'What happened here?"

Dillon briefed the man and asked Cody to do the same for their end of the action. After completing their reports, the agent spoke into his radio, and the helicopter veered away and used its floodlights to scan the east lane. It didn't take long before it was back and touching down near the barn.

Within the hour, they recovered 12 bodies—one dead from the ATV rollover, eleven in serious condition with multiple puncture wounds— and three men whom none of the agents wished to get near. Eager to rid themselves of these three, they ordered a special van and hazmat gear to transport them to the detention center in Eagle Pass. All four ATVs had been abandoned, and the drugs recovered. The agents estimated the shipment at over $20 million. No trace of the 16th man was found.

Raimondo had followed his squad, albeit at a bit slower pace. He wasn't as well conditioned as they were. Trotting up the gravel road was not in his job description, if he had one. He hustled, but the three men he followed were soon 100 yards ahead of him.

But there was something else that held him back. Something was wrong. He hadn't received an update from

Agent White, and he had no idea why. The man should have been keeping him abreast of the movements of the men near the barn.

As the implications of that failure dawned on him, he fell back even further. Then he heard screams from the east. Not one man, but many. There had been only a couple of gunshots, but those were more distant, likely from his men on the ATVs. No, these screams confirmed to him that something was wrong, deadly wrong.

He'd made a mistake, he now realized. He'd scouted out the road for the ATVs, but not the routes for his men heading to the house and barns. Of course, the drone had been shot down, but he should have prepared in advance. In his eagerness to make up for the loss of the previous shipment and to get back into the good graces of El Espectro, he hadn't fully scouted this route.

By instinct, he ducked at the sound of the first gunshot ahead of him. Who had fired? His men or the rancher's? With caution, he moved ahead, but he could see little. Soon, the barns and other outbuildings came into view. He saw no movement. He eased forward until he came to the edge of the scrub that hid them from the house. He was still far from the buildings, and that last 50 yards to the buildings was a potential death trap. No cover whatsoever.

Another gunshot echoed around him, and he heard a body fall to his right. He strained to see across the open space. Was that another body on the ground 100 feet away?

Where were the others? The other two teams should have moved in from the east and southeast. Then he recalled the screams he'd heard. Now, only the silence of a mid-January night in Texas met his ears. In his heart, he knew those men were no longer capable of aiding him.

He turned and hurried back toward the river. As he again heard the sounds of running water, his cell phone chirped. A text from his U.S. team.

Trucks intercepted by unknown assailants. All disabled. Drivers all escaped. Will regroup. Status?

He was glad to hear the drivers had managed to escape. Trucks were easier to replace than men. Should he respond? He shook his head as he thought about it.

As he crossed the river, he found only his SUV and Jose, his drone operator. The trucks had left. Why? They should have remained behind to pick up the ATVs after they unloaded and returned to the river.

A sense of dread filled him acutely. The only reason for them to have left was that the ATVs had been stopped and would not be returning. That implied that the drivers had been alerted about such. And that, in turn, implied that El Espectro probably already knew that he'd failed once again. He needed to disappear pronto.

"Jose, *vamos*. We must get back to town quickly."

"Where are the others?"

"Likely dead."

Jose nodded his head. Raimondo noted that the young man no longer appeared timid. If anything, his previous demeanor had become serious and confident.

"El Espectro already knows."

With that, Jose pulled a handgun from behind his back, aimed, and shot Raimondo. The sudden feeling of fire in his chest knocked him back, and he stumbled over a rock and fell backward into the river. He felt his body being rolled over and over into deeper water. There was no tunnel of light, only darkness. Terror, regret—deep, deep, deep regret—and a profound sense of being separated and alone for eternity filled his consciousness before it all dimmed.

THIRTY-THREE

Ashleigh laid her head on the pillow. She couldn't read another sentence, without having to reread it three times. Had she absorbed anything from her textbook over the last 20 minutes? She hadn't been sleeping well, so she needed a good night of uninterrupted shut-eye.

When the pounding on her door awoke her, she checked her phone. Five minutes! She'd only been asleep five minutes. She wanted to pretend she wasn't in and ignore whoever it was, but she was on "probation" as a RA. If the person at her door discovered she had ignored the knocking and reported it, that might be the end of her college "career."

"Ashleigh, you in there? It's Bobbi."

She was awake now. "Just a minute" She hated unplanned visits for which she was unprepared to present herself. She donned a robe and combed out her hair. Electrolysis had dealt with Sam's beard, but it had also left her with a slightly blotchy complexion. She grabbed some foundation but put it down. *What the heck*, she thought. *It's Bobbi.*

She opened her door to find the guy pacing back and

forth, three steps forward then three steps back. He appeared beyond upset. Maybe agitated was a better description.

"Ashleigh, you gotta come see this. I . . . I . . . I'm beyond words."

He grabbed her hand and began to pull her toward the elevators. She resisted.

"Wait a minute, Bobbi. Come see what?"

"My door."

Uh-oh, she thought. What now? "Okay, give me a minute. I'm not going out like this."

She reentered her room and shut the door. She pulled on a skirt and top, added a light application of foundation to her face—enough to even out her complexion, and gave a quick swipe of mascara to her lashes. Good enough, she figured as she inspected her appearance in the mirror.

A couple of minutes later, she stood with Bobbi outside his room.

Over the rainbow flag was a sign quoting the Bible. *"I have set My bow in the cloud, and it shall be a sign of the covenant between Me and the earth. Genesis 9:13"* Under that were the words "He's coming back soon to reclaim His bow. Will you be ready?"

Under the sign stating "On The Right Side of History!!!" was a new placard saying, " . . . said everyone in Sodom and Gomorrah. *'Then the Lord said, Because the outcry against Sodom and Gomorrah is great and their sin is very grave. Genesis 18:20'* "

On top of a poster promoting multiple genders was a sign saying, "*So God created man in His own image, in the image of God He created him; male and female He created them. Genesis*

1:27" The rainbow-colored poster saying "Is it Gay in here, or is it just me?" was countered with the words, "Yep. Just you!" followed by another verse. Over the poster promoting a drag night party in one of the dorms, was a sign with "*A woman shall not wear a man's garment, nor shall a man put on a woman's cloak, for whoever does these things is an abomination to the Lord your God. Deuteronomy 22:5*"

Every poster and sign that Bobbi and friends had put up on the door had been countered with Bible verses. Ashleigh had seen some of these verses before, but not all. Seeing them again plunged her deeper into her depression.

"I can't do this anymore. I expected him to cave and bolt like the other guy. He's so friendly, and he plays this music when he's studying. Not loud. I mean he's respectful when I'm in the room, but the music, I . . . It's like it's boring into my soul or something. I feel . . . I can't explain it, but like I'm a condemned person."

She fought her emotions by allowing anger to take over. Anger at God and the Bible. Anger at Aric Afton for disrupting her life and those of her friends. Anger at what she saw on the door.

Bobbi reached out to start tearing down everything on the door, but Ashleigh stopped him.

"Don't. Leave it up until I can show it to the dean firsthand. This is hate speech. Aric Afton's going to regret this."

Ryan stood up from their dining table after their nutritious, but less than gourmet, early evening meal. Sarah was an outstanding cook and baker because her passion resided in those talents. He loved dinners at home, when he had been able to join the family—a feat nearly unheard of over the past many months. He looked forward to that pleasure once again, but tonight wasn't that night.

Plan B had included Sarah's calling her realtor friend, Monica. So, after two days of flurried activity to finish the garage door's repainting and front door's replacement, at the bureau's expense, their house went up for sale. Two days later, in Portland's red hot real estate market, they had two offers. The first was $35,000 over asking price with a contingency that the buyer had to sell his home first. The second was a cash offer for $30,000 over asking price. That seemed like a no-brainer until they learned that the buyer wanted possession in two weeks.

Two weeks! The challenge was on!

In just over 48 hours almost all of Sarah's kitchen had been wrapped and packed. Sarah's list of items to discard dwindled to become a list of one—the dining table they used as their makeshift work and packing table. The Salvation Army had been blessed with the rest. The things on her list of items to sell had found their way to the garage, and a garage sale was set for the upcoming Saturday, two days away. The boys had gotten into the act by adding toys to the sale, some of which had already been reclaimed.

Some of what they had given away included bedroom furniture. The rest of their bedroom furnishings sat in the garage for the sale. Their most prized possessions—those things they wouldn't want to lose plus the few things they owned of real value—had already been packed into Ryan's repainted SUV, along with critical paperwork they would need. Sarah and the boys had driven that vehicle to a friend's home where they were all now sleeping. *God bless the Holders*, thought Ryan, for extending them that hospitality. That friendship was one of a handful of relationships that Ryan and Sarah would truly miss.

Ryan, having sent his family away for the night, saw light at the end of the tunnel. They would be ready to pack a truck in one week's time, but right now he was running on fumes. Five hours of sleep two nights earlier and four hours the previous night had led to more daytime caffeine consumption than even his overtime shifts during the worst of the riots. He needed to recharge.

He set his phone's timer to two hours and headed to his recliner in the basement. He knew that if he lay down on the couch, it would be dawn before he awoke. The recliner was his go-to place for short naps. Plus, his office was next to be packed, so he would be right there when he awoke.

As he was about to fall asleep, his phone pinged with a text message. Thinking Sarah needed something, he grabbed his phone and checked it. Besides, the phone would continue to chime every 15 minutes until he read it, so he knew he needed to open and read it if he ever wanted to get that nap. It simply said:

Stay tuned to Kenosha news over next few days. Your job opening is coming.

He was too tired for that news to hit home, or to concern himself with the anonymous sender. He quickly fell off into dreamland.

Sometime later, he awoke with a start. What? He checked his phone. It was nearing midnight, and the timer had gone off hours earlier. He'd slept through it. So, what woke him?

Then he smelled it. Smoke!

Fully alert, he ran up the stairs to the kitchen. No fire there. A flicker of light in the dining room caught his attention. He took only one step into that room before realizing the entire front room was ablaze. He dialed 911 and reported the fire.

He dampened a dish towel and covered his mouth and nose. The smoke now stung his eyes, but he had to see what was happening. How bad was it? The front room curtains were fully lit, and the couch now flamed up. Their small kitchen fire extinguisher would be of no value.

He shut the door between the kitchen and dining room and hurried to carry out as many of the boxes in the kitchen as he could. Sarah's gadgets and utensils took priority. Dishes could more easily be replaced. He could now feel heat from the door to the dining room. He didn't have much time. With the last of those boxes moved outside, he ran to the family room and grabbed his fourteen-pointer. There were too many memories wrapped up in that old deer trophy to let flames consume it. Coughing and choking on the smoke, he made it outside and could hear the sirens and see the flashing lights of the approaching fire trucks.

Assured that those belongings he'd been able to salvage were safely away from the building and out of the firemen's way, he ran around the side of the house. Flames now leapt from windows on the second floor, as well as those of the front and dining rooms on the first floor.

The firemen raced carrying their hoses toward the house. They ignored him as they seemed focused on their job. As the fire lieutenant approached him, he glanced at the house once again and saw on their freshly repainted garage door, the words "execute killer cops!!"

THIRTY-FOUR

Ashleigh awoke with a vigor she hadn't experienced for some time. She ate a quick breakfast consisting of a protein bar and a glass of kombucha, prepared for class, and left early hoping to catch Dean Schmitz before class started.

She hadn't anticipated the snow that had settled into the area overnight and was so caught up in her mission, that she'd failed to check the weather. She struggled to stay warm in the outfit she'd chosen but refused to turn back for a wardrobe change. She needed to catch the dean as soon as possible. The "decorations" on Bobbi's door could be removed anytime now. Yes, she had photos, but the impact would not be the same as a first-hand viewing.

She saw Dean Schmitz walking ahead of her toward the admin building. At least *he* was reasonably bundled up against the weather.

"Dean Schmitz!" He didn't appear to hear her over the wind. She yelled, "Dean Schmitz! Do you have a minute?"

This time he turned toward her and stopped. Together they stepped into the entry of the admin building to evade the wind.

"What is it, Ashleigh?" He appeared agitated. "I have an important meeting this morning."

"Dean, I have a case of hate speech that you need to be aware of. Bobbi Jannsen's dorm door was targeted last night. I believe his roommate had something to do with it." She held out her phone with the photos of the door. "I think you should see it personally, to get the real impact of it."

He scrutinized the images and took a deep breath. "Ashleigh, I'm sure it's impactful, but I have a more pressing problem right now. Send me the images."

She felt let down and realized that that emotion seemed to occur daily in her life. "Yes, sir. Do you think you'll have some time today to stop by? It's room 412 in my dorm."

He shook his head. "I honestly doubt it, but I'll try. Talk with you later, Ashleigh."

He scurried on toward his office. As she followed him with her gaze, she saw another RA and two female students sitting outside his office. *Wonder what that's about*, she thought.

Back outside in the weather, with extra time on her hands since the dean was busy, she decided to rush back to her room and change clothes. As she did, she ran into another RA from the dorm where the RA outside Dean Schmitz's office resided.

"Hey, Simone, what's up with Haley? I saw her with two students at Dean Schmitz's office."

Simone looked about and leaned toward her. In hushed tones, she said, "Don't say anything, but it appears one of the campus security officers might have been trafficking young women from campus here. Pimping them. And a female professor from the sociology department might somehow be involved."

"Whoa. Thanks, Simone. I hope that's just a rumor. That's scary."

"I don't think it's just a rumor. Will Moore saw the Kenosha police take Officer Too-Friendly into custody this morning."

"Wow. Like I said, scary, but I'm happy to see him go."

Every woman on campus knew Officer Too-Friendly, and many had fallen victim to his handsy behavior. But actually pimping women from the school? That was beyond comprehension.

Then a thought caught her off-guard. He'd hit on every woman she knew on campus, even the open lesbians. Yet, he never so much as came near her. Why? Only a handful of people on campus knew her backstory—Dean Schmitz and two members of his staff, Lateesha, Ashleigh's own on-again-currently-off-again partner, and one other. Even Toni and Bobbi weren't members of that inner circle, although she often wondered if they suspected. So, why?

The answer to that question hit her like a plunge into Lake Michigan in January—Simone's comment about a female sociology professor. There were two, and one of them she knew all too well. Had Isabella—now Meredith—told him to steer clear? Had she protected her from his advances, perhaps by revealing her secret? She needed to find her cousin, Meredith Fry, sooner, not later.

Aric and Mitch had had a good laugh over watching Bob

go berserk upon finding the door as it was. He could dish it out but couldn't take it, was Mitch's comment. Seeing Bob return with that weird RA wasn't unexpected. She looked livid by the time she left. When Bob came into the room after that, he said nothing. He tried to ignore Aric altogether. He even went straight to bed, turning out the lights on his side of the room. It was like he needed to avoid Aric.

That performance recurred in the morning. Bob said nothing to Aric upon awakening, dressing, or leaving the room. Aric didn't know what to expect. Were Bob and his comrades preparing to up the ante, or had Aric and his friends cowed him? Aric mentally prepared himself for a new level of intimidation.

Mitch had placed the video on social media, only to find himself in "Facebook jail" less than two hours later. Instagram and Twitter likewise suspended his accounts. That had earned Mitch multiple high-fives and congratulatory comments in the dining hall at breakfast.

Aric braced for the snow and wind as he headed out from the dorm toward class. Upon entering the classroom, he saw that Chris and Jess had beat him there. Their faces lit up at seeing him, or maybe he only noticed *her* smile brighten at seeing him. He took another look. No, Chris was smiling and laughing, too.

"We saw the social media posts before they were taken down. That was hilarious. The guy can dish it out, but he can't take it," said Chris.

Aric laughed. "That's exactly what Mitch Johnson said."

"And that gal he brought up to look, she's a RA or something, right?"

Aric nodded.

"Well, she looked like she was about to become incontinent by the time she left."

Aric chuckled. "I guess that's a polite way of saying it. Bob has been giving me the silent treatment since he discovered our work. I'm not sure how to gauge that. He's either working on his next plan or really teed off."

"Or maybe those Bible verses hit him hard," said Jess.

Aric hadn't considered that. "You know, I hope so. He's not such a bad guy. I don't know what got him started down the road he's taken, but if those verses get him to question that route, that's great."

They settled back into their seats when Professor Carter entered the room. Aric found the class a welcome diversion from the drama surrounding his roommate. Near the end of the first morning session, someone entered the room and gave the professor a note. After reading it, he looked directly at the three of them, stopped talking, and walked over to them. He handed the note to Aric.

"I assume this has to do with your dorm room."

Aric gave him a look of surprise. Doctor Carter shook his head.

"Yes, the video went viral. I have no comment."

Aric wasn't quite sure how to take that. He opened the note, read it, and passed it on to Jess. All three of them were to see the Dean of Students upon being dismissed at lunch. Aric felt his gut go hollow. The three of them looked at each other with wide eyes. Chris offered a subtle shrug.

Upon the end of the morning class, the three bundled up for the weather and trudged to the admin building, where they presented themselves to the dean's office. There appeared to be something serious going on that involved the dean, and yet, it didn't seem to involve them. Aric felt surprised when the dean called them into the office just minutes after they arrived. He ushered them to sit down.

"I'll get straight to the point. Some very serious allegations have been made about you. The accusations were made against you Aric, but after a review of the security video, campus security identified all three of you. That's why you're all here."

Aric remembered Mitch's comment about hate speech. He had passed it off as a trivial thing but in thinking about it, he knew he had to be prepared should the issue arise.

"And what is that allegation, sir?" asked Aric.

"You've been accused of posting hate speech on your dorm door. Hate speech can not only get you expelled from here but can also get you charged criminally."

"I think we all understand that. I take it you've seen my door."

"Well, not in person, although I was asked to. I do have photos."

"And what do you see in those photos, sir?"

The man didn't answer right away. After some thought, he said, "The door was decorated to promote diversity and the LGBT movement and placed over those decorations were Bible verses that condemn the LGBT lifestyles. It's those words that are seen as hate speech."

"So, the Bible is now considered hate speech?" asked Chris. "The Word of God has inspired billions of people over thousands of years, but now it's considered hate speech?"

Aric was glad to see Chris also speak up. He didn't want to be the self-elected spokesman for the trio.

"Dean Schmitz, do you consider the Bible hate speech?" asked Aric.

That seemed to catch the man off-guard. "What I think and what my duty as dean requires don't always match up. What I think here is unimportant."

Did the man actually just say that? Aric pressed on.

"Sir, what you think here is very important. Do you support free religious speech, speech that's guaranteed by our Constitution, or not? If not, you're opening the college to a major lawsuit."

The man furrowed his brow. "Are you threatening the college?"

Aric quickly shook his head. "Not at all, sir."

Jessica sat forward in her chair. "Dean Schmitz, if someone's roommate used their shared door to promote something the person didn't agree with or found offensive, is that okay? And if that person posted something on the door to express his beliefs in opposition to his roommate's position, does that automatically become hate speech?"

The dean pondered her questions.

"Dean Schmitz, the LGBT crowd brought this upon themselves," said Aric. "I was originally assigned a roommate named Tom Wise. We got along great. But I spoke up in support of Professor Cully's right to free speech, and the LGBT leaders decided they didn't want me in *their* dorm. They intimidated Tom into moving out and then moved Robert Jannsen into my room expecting his behaviors to drive me out. I've treated him with respect despite my personal beliefs against his crossdressing and other behaviors. He then decorated our door without my consent or knowledge of what he planned to put there. He expressed his beliefs. I simply countered with mine. And now, even though the stuff he posted could be considered offensive to a Christian, it's my posting of Bible verses that is considered hate speech."

"They did the same thing to a guy named Brad Wilson last semester, only he just moved out, so you probably heard nothing about it," said Chris.

The dean raised a brow to that revelation. Jess nodded.

"This has become their modus operandi for censuring those that disagree with their lifestyle."

The dean took a deep breath and then said, "The college prides itself on its stand for diversity. We can't have and won't tolerate hate speech on campus."

Aric mentally shook his head at the man's falling back on the institution's published rhetoric.

"And we don't like hate speech any more than you, sir. We don't see God's Word as such. It presents absolute truth in a world of relative truth . . . if that can even be called truth. Putting the words relative and truth together creates an oxymoron. We have no trouble with diversity either, sir, as long as that's what it really is. Sounds to me like some on this campus speak up for diversity until that means including Christians and the Biblical worldview. For the LGBT crowd, it's my way or the highway."

The dean looked at each of them in turn. He started to speak but was interrupted by a knock on his door. His secretary leaned her head into the door.

"President Kletzger is ready to see you now."

He nodded and turned his attention back to the trio. "I have to go. I'll have to think about what you've told me. I'll be in touch."

"What about the door, sir?"

He paused. "Take it all down so it doesn't continue to cause a commotion."

The trio left the office and headed down the hallway.

"I think that went okay," said Chris. His sister nodded.

"Unless he caves. Too often today, folks tend to virtue signal instead of truly standing up for what they believe. For me, the jury is still out."

After a brief discussion, they hurried from the building and made a beeline to Aric's room. The dean's comment about causing a commotion hit home as they left the elevator and saw a crowd of students outside Aric's room, pointing, commenting, and taking photos. Nothing was said to them as they cleaned off the door, but Aric sensed that the "commotion" was just beginning.

THIRTY-FIVE

Adam paced inside the safe room at Mike J's home. He'd spent breakfast time with his kids and Rachel, and after the kids had been shipped off to school, the two had taken time to discuss their relationship. Adam had had high hopes about the two of them getting back together, getting remarried, and becoming a family once again. Today, he learned that she was torn. She had met someone else during their separation, but she saw that the old Adam, the man she'd loved and once married, was back. She acknowledged the value of being a family, of not having their kids being split between two households. She just needed more time.

"Hey, *mi amigo*, everything okay?"

He'd been so distracted that he hadn't noticed Mike J reentering the room. He stopped and nodded. He still hoped everything would be okay, but he wasn't going to burden his new friends with that. He also determined that he wasn't going to dig around to find out the guy's name. He'd not asked because he feared the temptation would be too great to unleash UltraNet on him.

"Colonel S is on his way." A perimeter alert sounded as he said that. "In fact, that might be him coming up the drive now."

A few minutes, the man joined them in the lair. "Mornin'. You two doing okay? It was a long night. I'm getting too old for that kind of night again."

Mike J laughed. "Yeah. You can still outdo most millennials in the gym."

The colonel shrugged.

"Have we heard anything from Ingersoll?"

When the colonel had left in the middle of the night, the consensus was in hoping that the man would agree to return to their fold.

"I'm more than impressed with his ingenuity. We sure could benefit from his help," said Mike J.

"That's an understatement. Can you imagine digging traps like that and . . . what'd he call it? The choke point . . . in the one road he saw as a potential smuggling route."

Adam turned his focus to the conversation. "Well, the guy's lucky his traps caught armed men and that he stopped a major shipment of drugs in the process. No prosecutor in his right mind will bring any charges against him. But what if those people had been families with women and kids? What if they were the victims of those traps? In the country and on his property illegally or not, there'd be a group of patriots in jail right now. It's not an example we should endorse."

The response was as if he'd thrown water on a fire. He'd extinguished their enthusiasm.

After a moment the colonel replied, "You have a point, a good point. Just like you did the right thing last night in contacting the authorities down there. It's good to have you on board."

Adam nodded to acknowledge the compliment. "Thanks."

"So, do we have any word on Saucedo? Was he one of the wounded?"

Mike J answered, "No. His name wasn't on the list at CBP. I reviewed the drone video from last night. We were so focused on Ingersoll and his people that I didn't notice one person head back toward the river. The camera was focused on the barn and house, so whoever that was left our field of view. Since he's not on the list, I can only assume it was Saucedo and that he made it back to the river."

Adam spoke up. "I had UltraNet set up to monitor the cartel leader, Beltrán. Looks like he got word of the incident just minutes after the ATVs were stopped, as we understand the timetable anyway."

The colonel nodded. "Then I will assume that Saucedo is no longer a problem for us. He's probably dead in the river already, or his body's been tossed into the desert someplace. Best scenario for him was that he made it to the river and kept running. Beltrán isn't going to keep him around after losing two shipments of drugs." The colonel stood up from the chair he had claimed, and added, "I'm gonna grab some coffee from the kitchen. Anyone else need a cup?"

Mike J raised his empty mug for the colonel to take, but Adam shook his head. "No thanks. I'm good."

Adam returned to his computer and accessed his dark web account for UltraNet. One bit of news brought a smile to his face. To no one in particular, he said, "Good news. Agent White has been arrested."

"That's great," said Mike J from behind him. "Anything

else?"

"Not yet."

Adam turned his attention to his kid brother. *What the ..
. he thought.* He checked the security feed from Aric's dorm floor. The door's "additions" remained, and a few students stood outside gawking. Social media saw a video of his roommate's reaction go viral. That video included an angry-looking Ashleigh Love. What caught his attention, however, was the registration with campus security of a complaint from said RA of a hate speech crime. That complaint had been forwarded to the Dean of Students for review. He made a mental note to set up a hack of the dean's accounts to follow that review.

The dean had his hands full. Of that Adam was sure. The trafficking of female students from the college by a campus security officer was under full investigation by the Kenosha Police Department and Wisconsin State Patrol. It was now time to light a fire under the college president about Dr. Fry, as well as her relationship to a certain transgendered RA. Guilt by association had never been Adam's style, but when it came to Aric, it was a boundary he was now willing to cross.

Before that, however, he had one other task to accomplish. He hacked into the campus security employment applications and made sure Ryan Krueger stood out at the top of the pile.

After changing into warmer clothing, Ashleigh went directly to the sociology department looking for Meredith. She knocked on the professor's office door with no response. She checked the department offices and found no one there to assist her.

She checked her phone and realized her time had run out. She needed to get to class. She couldn't afford another tardy or missed class session. Plus, she still had hours of makeup work to do over the weekend.

She sat in class, filling her seat with a warm body but not taking in much of what was being said. Her thoughts kept meandering back to Meredith. Was she truly involved with that security officer in trafficking women from the college? While Ashleigh didn't want to believe that, something deep inside her knew it to be true.

Growing up, Ashleigh had been influenced by her cousin, Isabella. Izzy, as they called her then, had been the first to dress Sam up as a girl. Izzy's flattery of "her" went beyond Sam's expectations. He'd never had such compliments as a boy. In fact, as a boy, he saw himself as less than average. So, her effusive applause for Steffi, as Izzy called Sam when dressed, felt good. She was affirmative of Steffi to the point that Steffi sought out that praise and fell into the LGBT+ crowd that Izzy seemed to dominate. When Steffi "lost her virginity" to one of the gay boys in the group, she considered her identity to be sealed.

Now, to use a term she truly hated, she recognized that she had been groomed. She couldn't begin to imagine where Sam would be today had Izzy not taken control of his life.

"Ashleigh, can you tell us one of the roles of central banks regarding the flow of money and payments internationally?"

Ashleigh remained lost in her thoughts.

"Ashleigh?"

She snapped to as she recognized her name the second time.

"I'm sorry, Doctor King, please repeat the question?"

The professor did and Ashleigh commented on their role in setting exchange rates. That seemed to satisfy the prof, but Ashleigh still received the "evil eye." Anyone with a first-year understanding of finance knew that. This was a third-year course. She needed to pay attention. The four credits in international finance were required for her major.

After 20 or so minutes, she found her attention drifting again. Izzy had gotten into trouble with the law. Mostly misdemeanors as Ashleigh understood it. Until one day after she'd turned 18, Izzy simply disappeared. Someone had told her that she'd taken the name of Fatima Khan, but the two remained estranged. When a professor named Meredith Fry appeared on campus during Ashleigh's freshman year, and she recognized Meredith as her cousin, all sorts of questions arose in Ashleigh's mind. She had chosen to stay quiet and not question Meredith Fry's appointment as an associate professor, but rather to use her as a resource.

In hindsight, maybe that had not been the correct decision. She felt her gut plummet, and the blanket of her depression engulfed her. What if Ashleigh would now be considered complicit in hiding her cousin's fraud? Because of the cost, she had never gone to the length of having breast implants and gender revision surgery. She was still legally male, as anyone who paid attention to her driver's license would discover. The idea of going to prison—a men's penitentiary—left her unable to think.

She had to find Meredith.

THIRTY-SIX

Aric and his friends reported to class after lunch only to find it had been canceled. No explanation was given, but there were already rumors floating about campus about a major shakeup that involved the security office as well as the sociology department. The facts that class was canceled and that his professor was the chairman of that department lent credence to the murmuring. Still, Aric took them for what they were, rumors.

He decided to return to his dorm room to study and said farewell to his friends. As expected, Bob was in class, and the room was a quiet haven for reading. He had always been able to read and study with a low volume of background music, so he tuned into the Skillet Mix channel once again and turned to the current chapter in his text.

He was lost in the vagaries of the municipal versus state court systems when he heard the lock on the door click. He looked at his clock. It was only mid-afternoon. Bob should still be in class.

"Hey," said Aric as his roommate opened the door. Bob

made an immediate 180-degree swing to leave. "Don't let me scare you off."

Bob turned back to Aric. "I, uh, see you, or someone, cleaned the door off."

Aric nodded. "Yeah. Me, with the help of friends."

"That wasn't very nice. What you put up there, I mean, not the cleaning part."

"Well, it wasn't very considerate of you to decorate it as you did in the first place."

Bob shrugged. "At least it wasn't the hateful stuff you put up."

"Hateful? Tell me something, do you believe in God?"

Bob waggled his head. "I . . . I guess so."

"Do you believe the Bible is God's Word to man, kind of like a manual for living?"

"Not so sure about that. I think it's just a bunch of letters from dead, Cis-gendered, wh . . . , uh, patriarchal men."

"You were about to say white men, weren't you?"

Bob shook his head, but the denial wasn't convincing.

"Not one of them was a white man, by today's or any other terms."

"Well, if God exists, He's loving and won't condemn anyone for how they live."

"Yeah. God is loving, but do you know how God defines love? Throughout the Bible, God speaks of love as being obedient to His ways. In the first book of John, it states *'For this is the love of God, that we keep His commandments.'* It's not some gushy, Hollywood-styled emotion or acceptance of everyone's lifestyle. It's being obedient to God. And, actually, the Bible doesn't support the last half of that sentence at all.

Today's world lives by relative truths. What you experience defines truth for you. But God gave us absolute truths. Like the Ten Commandments. Don't murder. Don't falsely testify against someone. Don't covet. Not, it's okay to covet under some circumstances but not under others. Ninety-nine percent of what we put up on the door came straight from the Bible. They're part of the absolutes God has given us, and those absolutes are the basis for our western common law, much of which is ignored today."

"Yeah, well, what if I don't like it?"

Aric shrugged. "Your choice. He gave us free will to choose His ways or our own."

"And if chose my own?"

"Well, maybe that's something you should look into yourself. My telling you wouldn't be the same, and you probably wouldn't believe it if it came from me anyway."

Bob gave him a vacant stare.

"What's that music?"

"A local group called *Skillet*. Well, calling them local is misleading. They tour internationally and have platinum and gold albums. They're also Grammy nominees, but they live here."

"Oh."

Aric sensed there was more behind that question than was being offered.

"If it's too loud or bothers you, let me know." He turned his attention back to his textbook.

"That's okay. I kinda like their style."

Inwardly Aric smiled. *Go Coopers*! he thought.

"Can I ask you a question? Sorry, I don't mean to

interrupt, but I'm curious."

Aric looked up and said, "Go ahead."

"What's the deal? I mean, you're not like any other Christians I've encountered. Why?"

Aric didn't want to give away the fact that he knew what Bob was up to in trying to scare him out of the dorm. He considered his response with care but needed better direction.

"Why what?"

"Well, most guys, Christian or not, would freak out having a crossdresser like me as a roommate. You haven't. You treat me with respect. You remain calm. And as I think about it, even your response to my door decorations was, well . . . maybe I should say it seemed to be a measured response expressing your beliefs, not an emotional response based in homophobia or hate."

Was Aric actually hearing this from Bob? Maybe the guy had more between the ears than he let on.

"I don't hate you, Bob."

"Bobbi, please."

"If you insist, but when I hear that nickname, I think of a preschooler or someone growing up in the shadow of his father with the same name. It just sounds immature, and I don't think you're like that. Same thing for the nickname Robby. Makes me think of a little kid."

"Oh." He paused, and started to say something, but stopped.

"Can I ask you a question, Bobbi?"

"Umm, you can call me Bob if you want. Sure."

"How did you start crossdressing?"

The guy's eyes widened in surprise. From the look on Bob's face, Aric figured no one had ever asked him that.

"You really want to know?"

Aric nodded.

Bob sighed. "My folks were high-profile lawyers. I was an only child and raised by a nanny until my teens, and then I pretty much raised myself. When I was ten, my nanny dressed me up as a girl for Halloween. My mother fawned over me. My dad laughed and pretended I was his little girl. Something just kinda stuck. I don't think of myself as a woman stuck in the wrong body or anything like that. It's just been something I find fun and provocative." He paused again. "You know, even my friends have never asked me that question." He gave Aric a curious look. "I don't know why I told you that. Please keep that between us."

Aric felt surprised at the guy's candor, too. He pressed his right thumb and index finger together and zipped them across his lips. "My lips are sealed. Bob, the Bible tells us to make our yes mean yes and our no to mean no. So, when I tell you that anything you tell me in confidence will go no further, I mean it. If I were to break that confidence, I'd be letting not just you down but Jesus as well, and I don't want to do that. He's going to judge us all someday, and I don't want that on my already long list of mistakes."

Bob's curious look became curiouser and curiouser. At that instant, a thought entered Aric's mind. The Bible spoke of God giving His people words of knowledge, among other things. Such words were pieces of insightful knowledge for that given moment, information the receiver would have no way of knowing. Aric had experienced this only one time before, but he was convinced that the thought he'd just had fit that category.

"Bob, sometimes God gives us knowledge of things we'd have no way of knowing. Usually, that info is for that specific moment in time." Bob now looked a bit fearful. "You're not bisexual as you boast about, are you? In fact, you're still a virgin, aren't you?"

Bob's mouth dropped open, and his eyes widened. "I-I-I . . . Y-y-you say God t-told you that?"

Aric nodded. This conversation was getting weirder by the minute and more intimate than he could have imagined. All Aric could do was trust God to lead this on.

Bob turned away from him, and Aric couldn't tell what might be going on inside the guy's head. Aric imagined that if he were in Bob's shoes, he'd be freaking out right now. Bob turned back to him.

"You say . . . you're telling me God told you that? Like, how is that possible?"

Aric nodded and then shrugged. "God knows everything about you and can do anything He wants. So, passing that info on to me wasn't exactly difficult."

Bob looked defeated and plopped down onto his bed. He took a deep breath before sighing. "And if I answer that, it stays between us."

Aric again did his best bobblehead imitation.

"True on both counts." He blushed. "I'm interested in women, but they don't seem interested in me."

"Really? You don't come across as stupid. Yet, you haven't put two and two together? Why would the ladies express interest in a guy who presents as a gay cross-dresser? Trust me. I grew up with three sisters. One, they don't like competing for best wardrobe. Two, they sure don't want to be with a guy who looks better than they do in a dress. And three, why invest time in a guy who's playing on the same team as them?"

Bob offered up a wan smile. "Points taken."

Aric recognized that he had to give a bit here, too. "Since we're playing true confessions here, you might as well know that I'm a virgin, too. But for me, it's a badge of honor. God gave us marriage as a sacred vow. Sex outside of marriage is sin according to God, and that's true whether it's heterosexual or homosexual."

Aric stopped. He didn't like being lectured any more than most people, and he was beginning to feel like he'd been preaching too much fire and brimstone. But then, Bob opened the door to this conversation, not him. Aric had to believe that God's hand was in this. Why else would He have given Aric that word? He reflected on the conversation and what he'd said to Bob. Had any of his words had an effect?

"Bob, look, if you're uncomfortable with me as a roommate and want to move out, I understand and won't be offended." He thought it somewhat apropos to offer the guy the opportunity to do just what Bob had planned on Aric doing.

Bob jumped up from his bed and said, "I'll think about it," as he headed toward the door.

As the door closed, Aric remembered it was Friday night. He needed to call Jess and see what she was up to after dinner. He also recalled that the Drag Night Party poster that had been on his door listed tonight as the date. Yet, Bob left the room in full drab. Was it simply too early, or had some of Aric's words found a mark?

Ashleigh attended the afternoon class only to be dismissed an hour into it. She quickly learned that all classes had been dismissed early that day, but among the students, the reasons for such ranged from bizarre to far-fetched. She checked her email to find a notice that was sent out to all RAs and student government leaders. An emergency meeting of all faculty had been called, and classes were canceled for that afternoon. At least she knew where she'd be able to find Meredith.

She came to a decision point. Did she go to her room, study for an hour, and then hunt down Meredith? Or should she camp outside the auditorium where such meetings were typically held to wait for her? She chose the latter. After all, the meeting could last 15 minutes or maybe go on for hours. If she waited in the dorm, there was a better than 50-50 chance she'd miss Meredith again. That would drive her to new depths in her depression.

When she arrived at the hall that held the auditorium, security prevented her from sitting in the lobby.

"Sorry, this is a confidential meeting. You aren't allowed to sit out here or near any of the doors to the auditorium." The officer pointed down a hallway. "There's some seating down there. You'll be able to hear when the meeting adjourns."

Ashleigh had no choice but to comply. She discovered the chairs in a small alcove and found the area to be quiet enough that she could read and still be aware of the end of the meeting. She saw that as a win-win situation.

For the next 20-plus minutes, she found herself immersed in her text. She was surprised at her ability to focus on her school work under the circumstances. Her focus was disturbed by the departure of several faculty members whose murmuring and dissatisfaction were evident even at the distance where she sat. She could make out no specific words, however. As she turned her attention toward the auditorium, it became clear that there were many disgruntled people. A few even began yelling.

Soon the doors opened, and the attendees began to flow out. Ashleigh quickly gathered her things and made her way to the lobby. To say these people were unhappy was an understatement.

She looked for Meredith and saw her through a throng of people at the front of the room. However, as Meredith began to move toward Ashleigh and the people parted, she saw the reality of the situation. Meredith was handcuffed behind her back and being led out by plainclothes police officers, their badges hanging from their belts. As she passed by, she gave Ashleigh a look of despair.

Tears of desperation flooded Ashleigh's eyes. She needed to find a restroom before her fear caused her to wet herself. As she turned toward the restroom sign, a familiar voice spoke up behind her—Dean Schmitz.

"Ashleigh, don't leave campus. The police want to question you."

THIRTY-SEVEN

Mike Southworth, the colonel, sat at home reading in his historic home's restored library. On a winter's day, there was no other place he enjoyed more. A mug of coffee or hot tea—switching to a glass of red wine in the afternoon—and a good suspense novel. All in front of a roaring, natural wood fire.

And after the emotional stress of the recent encounter at the Ingersoll ranch in Texas, he needed a break. Evidently, so did the cartels. The recent losses by the Los Zorros cartel, plus the word of mouth spreading among them all that their secret activities were on display to someone who could inflict such losses on them, appeared to have scared the competing cartels into an unusual period of calm. No doubt all of those criminal leaders were searching for moles and other informants in hopes of securing their activity from exposure. Personally, he'd loved it if such rumors curtailed *all* cartel movement. Wishful thinking.

Thanks to Adam and UltraNet, they were developing a database of bent cops, corrupt politicians, and paid-off federal agents in the pockets of the major cartels. Once they had an airtight case against one of them, that data would find its way to a trusted U.S. attorney. Perhaps if they started seeing more of those people in prison orange, the cartels would continue to find themselves losing more men and money than they gained. Again, wishful thinking. Cutting off one head of the Hydra resulted in two more growing back.

The colonel's thoughts were interrupted by his phone. Caller ID informed him that it was Lynch Cully.

"Lynch, good to hear from you. How're things north of the Cheddar Wall?"

Lynch chuckled. "Keep up the cheese jokes, and I'll start sending you the jalapeño and ghost pepper curds instead of your favorites." He paused. "So, how are things with you?"

The colonel read between the lines. The way Lynch asked that question told him there was more behind it than the plain words he spoke.

"Just having a quiet day reading in front of a fire. Mary's off with friends shopping. Again."

In his mind, he could see his friend smile. Mary's penchant for bargains was well known to Lynch and his wife, Amy. As an "adopted" grandson, their little guy, Joshua, was frequently on the receiving end of such shopping forays.

"My love to her, and please tell her Josh has more than enough clothes right now."

"As if that would ever stop her." Both men laughed.

"So, I hear that Adam Afton has moved back to St. Louis. Have you run into him by chance?"

Again, Lynch's tone suggested he already knew that answer, or suspected he knew it. How should he answer his friend? By chance? No. Their meeting was well planned.

"Why do you ask?" Oops. Maybe he shouldn't have responded like that. Lynch was astute enough to see such a diversion as an affirmative answer.

"Oh, a couple of reasons. First, some information on one of the professors in my department here mysteriously ended up in the hands of local and state police. She happened to be a personal nemesis of mine trying to cancel me on campus and get me fired for being friends with Brad Graham. Seems she's a fraud and human trafficker working with a campus police officer to pimp out a handful of girls from the college. She's been arrested on multiple racketeering charges of fraud by identity theft, human trafficking, endangerment of a minor, and more."

"Well, good. Sounds like she deserves to be behind bars."

"Sure. Can't argue with that. It's the way she got caught that got my attention. On the side, I talked with a detective friend in the local police, and he said they received an anonymous file with all the details. It was so well laid out that it took them all of two hours to confirm everything in the file. I know when I was a detective, I would have loved an informant like that. Thing is, only one person I know . . . no, make that two people I know could accomplish that. Adam is at the top of my list."

The colonel didn't want to drag Lynch into a situation that could cause trouble for him down the line. Still, he wouldn't lie to one of his best friends.

"Am I allowed to plead the fifth here? I mean, does plausible deniability have any role here?"

He didn't directly answer the question but expected Lynch to get his answer. There was a delay in his friend's reply.

"Okay, I get it. But that brings me to reason number two. Other friends, still employed at Homeland Security, contacted me about certain events on our southern border. They told me about CBP drones being tasked by someone outside the organization. For the most recent incident, whoever controlled the drone aided a rancher defending his property from drug smugglers and stopped a shipment of Fentanyl valued at over $20 million. In this situation, another mysterious file was delivered anonymously about a corrupt CBP agent. Had all the hallmarks of the file our local police received."

As Lynch paused, the colonel began to see the handwriting on the wall.

"While these particular DHS employees appreciated the help and valued what was done, they're worried about vigilante activity there, particularly with the new administration's love of open borders. They asked if I knew of anyone capable of such actions and if so, asked that I warn them that they are on the radar of the new leadership. Again, I could think of only two people with the skill and resources to pull these things off—Adam and Mike J."

Again, he wanted to protect Lynch by not giving him too much info.

"Tell you what. I'm scheduled to have lunch with Mike J on Monday. I'll share your concerns with him. Same with Adam if I see him, but I don't think he's in St. Louis."

The colonel knew the man wasn't. He had left that morning to return to Wisconsin.

"Mike, look, you know me. I'm a patriot. I don't agree with the new administration on 98% of what they want to do.

Based on their rhetoric and campaign statements, we're going to see fuel prices skyrocket, illegal immigrants flooding into our country, and supply chain and employment problems unlike any we've ever faced. Inflation is likely to jump, and they'll drive us into recession. They desire to bring down the U.S. with their goal being a global society modeled after Communist China."

"I agree with everything you just said."

"I figured you would, but there's more going on here than meets the eye. The Book of Revelation speaks of a beast that rises from the sea and is given its power by Satan. And there's another beast from the land that promotes and pushes people to accept the first beast. That imagery is modeled after the beast from the Book of Daniel, and the first beast is the state, this global government they want, while the second is Big Business, Big Pharma, Mainstream Media, and progressive religion—anyone else who acts as a cheerleader of the state."

The colonel had been taught that the first beast was to be an individual, the Antichrist, while the second beast would be an individual who would become known as the False Prophet. This idea of the state and its supporters being those beasts was new to him. And yet, it made sense.

"So, you're saying there's no Antichrist, with a capital A, or False Prophet?"

"Yep. In the Bible, earthquakes represented two things. A theophany where God came physically to Earth, or a global shift in government. The great earthquake of Revelation 6 symbolizes this major shift to global governance. The shaking has begun, and we've entered the period so many call the Great Tribulation, the seven trumpet judgments."

"Hmmm, I'm going to have to study that a bit, but I trust you've done your homework."

"I have. Mike, I have no reservations about your patriotism or Mike J's patriotism. I don't know Adam Afton well enough to make a call on him, but if he's behind some of this stuff I'm hearing about, then I don't doubt his patriotism either. But Christianity is not one and the same as nationalism. Christ is not an American. I'd hate to see friends get so wrapped up in what some call Christian nationalism that they run afoul of those in power. And that power is becoming more and more entrenched with these globalists." Lynch paused. "Or worse, they face judgment before the throne of Christ for these actions."

Mike didn't like what he was hearing, but the warning came through loud and clear. Maybe it was time for The Remnant to quit while it was ahead. He and the other two were destined for some serious discussions.

THIRTY-EIGHT

Five days had passed since Adam left St. Louis. His return was instigated by Rachel's request for more time to consider his request to renew their vows and become a family again. He found it emotionally difficult to live and work just minutes away from them, yet not be part of their lives 24/7. So, he returned to his lakeside place in East Troy.

With cold, leftover pizza in hand for breakfast, he watched as a dozen local kids cleared the ice on the lake and prepared it for hockey. *So much for effective education via computer monitor*, he thought. These kids wouldn't be in "virtual class" that day for sure, and if both parents worked, who was policing their truancy?

In thinking about classes, Aric had called the night before. The afternoon classes at the college had been canceled for the week, so he was going to drive over to see his big brother at lunchtime. He had someone he wanted Adam to meet. He wouldn't say who, but, of course, Adam already knew. He would act surprised.

His phone rang. Colonel Southworth.

"Hey, Colonel."

"G'mornin', Adam. Have you thought about what we discussed a couple of days ago?"

The colonel and Mike J had communicated with him about concerns and a warning from Lynch Cully. He hadn't had to think very hard about it. The Remnant was their baby. He'd been brought on board to expand their operations. He wasn't needed to reduce them.

"I have. I think Cully is a smart man, and he wouldn't issue a warning without cause. He probably knows more about what DHS knows than he let on. It would be wise to listen to him. If things change, we don't need to work in the same room to do what we did. Plus, working at a distance will make us harder to detect and find." He stopped to take a last bite of pizza.

"It sounds like we're all in agreement. The Remnant is now officially in hibernation."

Adam swallowed his last bite and said goodbye. Looking out the window, he noticed the pickup game had already started on the ice. He turned his attention to his computer and continued work on the various corrupt individuals he'd been investigating. Maybe playing blazing saddles in Texas would call attention to the activities of The Remnant, but no one would find *him*. Only software like UltraNet had a chance at that, and he would know about it long before it could become operational.

As lunchtime came, he stopped his work and prepared food for his guests. He'd been careful to choose foods that both Aric and his girlfriend liked so it wouldn't appear staged. Just before one p.m., he heard a car pull up into the drive. He glanced out the window and saw his brother's vehicle. In the passenger seat was a very pretty girl, more beautiful than the photos he'd seen on social media.

He opened the door before they reached it.

"Well, well, well, little brother, you mentioned a guest, but I wasn't expecting a beautiful lady. Hi, I'm Adam."

"Gee, way to spoil my introductions. Jess, this is my *old* brother Adam. Adam, this is Jessica. We met in class."

Adam laughed at the introduction as he ushered them inside. "Old*er* brother, not old brother. But I guess I deserved that."

Aric put their coats in the nearby closet, and the trio moved into the living room, not that Adam spent time there. He *lived* with his computers.

"I made something to eat. Hungry?"

Aric nodded. "We skipped lunch to get here sooner. Smells good."

Jessica agreed. "It does smell good. You didn't have to go to any trouble. Aric said we'd probably have pizza."

Aric laughed. "He's fueled by pizza."

Adam decided not to mention breakfast.

"Well, not this time. Haven't seen little brother in almost a month so I fixed one of his favorites." He opened the oven and pulled out a casserole dish of fettuccine Alfredo with grilled chicken and bacon, along with a bake-at-home loaf of Italian bread. "Ta-daaa."

As they ate, Aric and Jess filled him in on all the happenings at school. That sociology professor who staged the protests on move-in day had been arrested and indicted on multiple racketeering charges. A campus police officer had been in cahoots with her and was also arrested. The school had been on a reduced schedule as campus security, along with the state and local police, interviewed each and every student on campus about the duo. Rumors were floating about that the college itself might be in trouble for not carefully checking the woman's credentials when they hired her. Of course, he had learned in class that a corporation could only be held liable for an employee's criminal actions if the employee was acting on behalf of the company and the company knew about said activity. Neither was the case regarding the college.

"Hey, do you remember that weird RA who gave you grief about your mask when I moved in?"

"I do."

"Well, word's out that she's a he, and he's a cousin of the arrested professor."

Jess added, "We haven't heard about any charges against him, so he must not have known anything about it."

Adam, too, had found no connection between the two other than being related.

"So, how's Tom, your roommate?" Of course, Adam already knew about the change there. He simply couldn't let on that he'd been "spying" on Aric.

"Tom moved out. I thought I already told you about that."

He went on to explain the situation with Tom and the new roommate, Bob. He talked about the guy's crossdressing, the door, and everything except what he'd been told in confidence. He mentioned being called in by the dean about the door, and that he'd later learned that Bob had asked the dean to drop any investigation and told him that they had worked things out.

"You want to know the best part? Jess and I talked about this on the way here. As of yesterday morning, all the women's clothing, makeup, etc. were missing from his closet. He left his closet door open in his rush to get to class, and I noticed it was all gone."

Jess nodded. "We're praying that he finds an interest in the Bible and maybe starts reading it."

Yes, the previous week had been a whirlwind of activity on campus, and Adam had initiated it all. Not that he could tell anyone and lay claim to it.

However, all was not rosy, and he couldn't, or wouldn't, tell Aric about it.

Ryan and Sarah had had a good cry over losing the house. Now they understood how devastating it was to lose almost everything you owned. They also recognized that it was God's grace that had urged them separate their valuables and important papers first, as well as to accept the Holders' hospitality just one day before. Neither wanted to contemplate what might have happened had they been sleeping there that night. For both, the incident made them realize they needed to right with God. Each had been raised in a solid Christian family, with a loving church, but had drifted away upon moving to Portland. The fire made them rethink their priorities.

Although they had lost 90% of their possessions, what stung the most was losing the house sale. It could take weeks to get the insurance settled, and until then, they could even raze what remained of the house and put the empty lot up for sale. Instead of having over half-a-million to spend on their dream home, they'd be lucky to clear $200,000 once the expense of clearing the lot was incurred.

Still, there had been good news. In the aftermath of the fire, Ryan had received a call from the college with a job offer on their security team. He had totally forgotten the cryptic message of that night, but later learned bits and pieces of the scandal facing the college. And, once his sense of humor returned, he teased Sarah that there was a silver lining to this—they no longer needed a 26-foot truck to move. One of U-Haul's large trailers would fit the bill. Plus, at some future point, they'd have fun buying all new stuff.

The light faded fast as Ryan pulled his SUV, with the trailer in tow, into his in-laws' driveway. Sarah and the boys were right behind him. The farm appeared no different than the last time he'd been there. How long had that been? Seemed like forever with all the overtime and lost vacation days due to the riots in Portland.

No sooner had he come to a stop when Sarah's family rushed out of the house and descended upon their vehicles. Even Sarah's sister and her family were there. They helped Ryan take in the luggage they would need for the next few weeks—all three bags.

Ryan couldn't believe they'd finally made it. Instead of two weeks, they could have left in one. But all of the insurance paperwork and assessments had kept them in Portland. They'd left no sooner than they had originally planned. He had a couple of days to settle in and consider housing options before he'd have to report for duty. The family, of course, insisted they stay there, with them, but Ryan wanted to be closer to campus.

After a belated dinner from the fatted calf—grass-fed and no bovine hormones, he slid into a recliner in front of the fireplace in his in-laws' family room. He was beat. He looked around the room.

"Everyone, it's good to be back home, but I'm exhausted. I can choose to go to bed now or fall asleep in this recliner. Either way, I'm not going to be much company."

Sarah walked up next to him. "Honey, go to bed. You put in a marathon to get us here, so you deserve it." She kissed him on the forehead and helped him to his feet.

As he stumbled up the stairs toward their guest room, his phone notified him of a text.

Welcome to Wisconsin and congrats on the job. Hope you didn't mind a few tweaks to your application. We need to talk.

THIRTY-NINE

Adam wasn't concerned about Aric on campus. Little brother had made enough friends on campus that any attempt to hurt him there would not be without consequence to the attacker. Following his being identified as *the guy* from the Cully protests, his email account started receiving accusatory and negative emails. Adam had traced them back to a public library in Kenosha, but his attempts to find out who sent them had been stymied. At the times when each email had been sent, an account linked to one elementary student or another had been logged onto the computer in question. It went without saying that these kids were not "attacking" Aric. Someone else was hijacking these kids' accounts or computer time.

He even looked at the library's security video. Too many people came and went to effectively isolate any individuals as the culprit . . . or culprits.

Adam had decided to simply monitor the issue since the emails, while negative, were pretty benign. Aric had been through enough turmoil and drama and now had enough on his plate. Adam saw no need to let these emails cause him any distress. Aric hadn't, and wouldn't, see any of these emails because Adam had set up UltraNet to intercept them before they arrived in his account.

Yet, since the arrest of Meredith Fry aka Fatima Khan aka Isabella Cooke, Aric's email account had started receiving more ominous threats. Several foreboding texts spoke of bodily harm. And then, this morning, they devolved into the first actual death threats.

Adam paced within his workroom. Perhaps he should have allowed Aric to see some, or all, of the emails as they escalated. Then, upon receiving a death threat he could have alerted the police directly and would have been able to show them the previous pattern of threats. For Adam to alert Aric or the authorities now would also inform Aric that he'd been covering for him, protecting his back. Adam would have to come clean about his monitoring of Aric's life. That would not go over well.

Adam sat back at this computer and checked Aric's whereabouts. He had class this morning, but the afternoon classes were still on hold as police needed the time to interview students. Where was Aric now?

The movement of Aric's phone showed that he was heading toward downtown Kenosha. Why? The speed of its movement showed that it was in a vehicle. Adam watched as the movement slowed down and stopped. He double-checked. He was in the parking lot for the yacht club in the harbor. Was he getting lunch there with someone? No, the phone, that is, Aric, began to move out along the harbor.

Adam didn't like that one bit. Whether alone or with

friends, his kid brother was in the open. If someone was truly targeting him, the harbor at the end of January was a perfect place. Few people around as witnesses. Icy conditions could be blamed for a slip and fall. Adam felt the need to intervene.

He pulled out a burner phone and dialed a number that he'd only texted before.

"Hello."

"Ryan Krueger, we need to talk, but right now I need a favor. Where are you?" Adam hadn't taken the time to check.

"Who is this?"

"A friend. You've been receiving my texts."

"So, again, who is this? I don't work with anonymous voices at the other end of a phone call or text message."

"Call me Adam. Look, someone important to me started receiving death threats this morning. He goes to the college—"

"So, contact the police. I don't work there yet."

Adam hadn't anticipated his resistance.

"Look, without me you wouldn't be working there at all."

There was silence on the other end for a brief moment.

"Okay, I guess I should thank you. What can I do?"

"I'll explain everything when we get together to talk, but right now I need to make sure he's safe."

"Okay, but I'm at my in-laws' farm. Call campus security. They can check on him within minutes. It'll take me half an hour to get there."

"He's not on campus. His phone's location shows him at the Kenosha harbor, moving away from the yacht club toward the lighthouse. I don't know if he's with friends or not, but if this death threat has any validity, he's out in the open and vulnerable."

"Same thing. Call the police."

"I'd rather not. That could get messy. I'll—"

"I know. You'll explain when we get together." He paused. "Okay, what's his name?"

Adam gave Ryan the details, and Ryan assured him he'd leave right away. It would still take him 30 minutes to get to the harbor. In the meantime, Adam stayed tuned to Aric's phone location.

Ryan hunted down Sarah in her mother's kitchen. The two were baking together, something that made Ryan's heart glow. He knew how much she had missed that while living in Portland.

"Babe, I need to go to town. Be back as soon as I can."

She turned and gave him a look. "You didn't say anything about going. The boys were looking forward to playing in the snow with you."

The area had received several inches of snow a few days earlier, and the temperatures had remained cold enough for it to stick around. He had promised their boys an epic snowball fight.

"I haven't forgotten. I shouldn't be long. While I'm there, I'll pick up some materials on homes for sale."

He walked over and kissed her on the cheek. *Must have been a sloppy one*, he thought, as she wiped it away and brushed flour all over her cheek. He grinned at her appearance.

As he got on the road heading toward Kenosha, he

thought it best that the police help out. He had a friend in the force he could call and avoid the formal channels.

"Ryan, my man, I hear you're back in the county."

"I am, Rick, I am. Have a job lined up at the college."

"Oh, wow, we're all over that case. So, you're taking that spot, eh? How'd you land that one? Half a dozen guys here have applications there."

"Guardian angel, I guess. Hey, you on duty?"

What else could he call the mysterious Adam? And to learn that several local officers had been passed by for him made his job offer even more amazing. Who was this Adam?

"I am. On patrol on the south side."

"Any chance of getting someone to do a welfare check on one of the kids from the college. He's by the harbor, heading from the yacht club toward the lighthouse. Apparently, he received some kind of death threat and folks are worried. I'm heading there now as a favor, but I'm a good 20 minutes away."

"I can check to see if there's a patrol in the area, but to be honest, we've had so many accidents due to icy roads, we're backed up. You might beat us there."

"Gottcha. Well, I'm passing the I right now. I guess it's a good sign if there've been no calls of disturbances from that area."

I-94 divided the urban and suburban areas to the east toward Lake Michigan from the rural areas to its west. Traffic always picked up on the I's east side, so Ryan hoped it wouldn't be too bad.

"Gimme his name, and I'll see who's around. I'll let you know."

"Thanks, buddy. We need to get together for a beer soon."
Ryan passed on Aric's details.

FORTY

Tears flooded Ashleigh's cheeks as she drove toward Kenosha. She had been cleared of any wrongdoing or complicity with her cousin by the authorities, but their interviews had made one thing clear. Her cousin had ruined the lives of dozens of children and teens. Isabella, she found out, had directly contributed to the death of one young boy. Like her, or him, or whatever kind of freak she'd become, Isabella had groomed the boy for her world. After months of conflict, the boy dressed himself up as a girl and hung himself from a tree in the family's backyard. A note found blamed Isabella. Days later, Isabella disappeared.

Fatima Khan, too, had a police record. She simply continued Isabella's legacy under a new name.

Upon further questioning, Ashleigh discovered that Meredith Fry had been a real person, with a real doctorate in sociology. She'd also had a real drug problem, which Fatima was more than happy to supply. The actual Dr. Fry had died of an overdose on drugs given to her by Fatima. Fatima saw the opportunity to start a new life and assumed the identity of the dead woman.

All in all, Ashleigh felt used. She, he, Sam had been nothing more than a social experiment to Isabella. When Isabella's experiment had finished, she simply left him, her, to do battle with the parents. All of the grief Ashleigh had encountered—leaving home out of rebellion, the financial stress, homelessness, the constant fear of being found out and ridiculed, all of it—was the end product of Isabella's disturbed mind.

 Now, what was left?

Nothing.

She exited her car and made her way to the pier leading to the Kenosha lighthouse. She'd left a note for her parents in the car—a note asking their forgiveness and blaming Isabella. She did not expect to return.

After reaching the lighthouse, she had second thoughts, but the depression overwhelmed her. Her secret was out. Others on campus stared at her. She saw them whispering about her and turning away when she looked at them. A handful of nasty notes had been left on her door. Even Lateesha, Bobbi, and Toni had stopped coming around. And Bobbi, it seemed, had decided to become Bob.

What kind of life would she have if she stayed? No, she wanted her grief and the depression to end. The world, her parents, and her so-called friends would be better off without her.

She looked toward the sky, and said, "God, I left you long ago. I'm not even sure You're real. But if You are, please don't let me die without You."

With that, she took two steps and jumped into the icy

depths, expecting to be yet one more drowning casualty at the lighthouse.

Aric felt blessed. His relationship with Jessica had bloomed into more than he thought possible. Having the afternoon off gave them time to be together, and she chose to spend it freezing their butts off by the harbor. Why?

He found he enjoyed her interest in photography. She had produced some amazing images of sunrises behind the Kenosha lighthouse, as well as full moons. Her landscape photos showed a real talent for composition and lighting. To her credit, several of her photos graced the walls of a local bank's lobby.

And now, while it was freezing, she wanted to take photos of the harbor and lighthouse. He thought the wind on campus was brutal, but here, with no obstructions coming off the water, it was enough to make him want to wait in the car for her. Of course, if he did that, she'd never let him live it down. She'd label him with one of her favorite four-letter words—wimp.

As they walked along the harbor wall, staying well clear of its icy edge, he had to admit the patterns in the ice were beautiful. Every once in a while, she would venture to the edge to take pictures. There was no hurrying her. At the rate they were moving, he'd be one of his least favorite six-letter words before climbing back into the car—icicle.

After about 15 minutes and what to Aric seemed like a thousand photos taken, they came to the pier leading to the lighthouse. The concrete pier looked to him to be just shy of

20 feet wide and maybe 150 feet long. Both sides were topped with ice, although the frozen accumulation on the side opposite the harbor, where Simmons Island Beach sat, was much thicker. She had shown him pictures of ice five to six feet thick on the beach where waves both pushed ice upward and splashed across the top to freeze and pile up. The winter so far hadn't seen the temperatures needed for the massive ice walls they sometimes had. Still, he didn't want to find himself slipping on ice and unable to stop going into the water. Anyone in that water would have only minutes to get out before the cold would stop their muscles from working.

"C'mon, let's make our way out to the lighthouse. Bound to be some great shots out there."

"You sure? Looks dangerous with all the ice."

She gave him a flirtatious smirk and said, "You're not going to wimp out on me now, are you? Look, there's another person out there already. Can't be too bad."

She pointed to the lighthouse, and sure enough, there was a lone figure there.

They helped each other up from the frozen sand to the top of the concrete. There did appear to be a narrow, ice-free path down the middle of the pier, bordering a thick electrical conduit that gave the lighthouse its power. As they had done along the harbor wall, they stayed away from the edges except for moments when she would ease onto the ice to get the right angle for a photo.

On more than one occasion, they had to help steady each other. Aric wondered how that sole person at the end of the pier had made it. Had she fallen in more than one instance? He could tell the person was a female from her garb and hair, but he hadn't seen a face yet. As Jess took another series of images, he glanced toward the woman only to see her stand up, take two steps forward, and fall into the water. No, not fall. Jump. The woman was attempting to take her own life.

"Jess! Call 911! That woman just jumped into the water!"

As Jess looked, he pointed toward the lighthouse. Comprehension flooded her face as she worked her way back onto more solid footing.

Aric hurried toward a nearby life ring. The flotation rings had been installed several years earlier after several accidental drownings off the pier had forced the city's hands. He slipped on the ice twice before finally grabbing one of the rings.

With the ring in hand, he moved as quickly as he could toward the end of the pier and the woman in the water. She appeared to make no effort to save herself. Upon getting close enough, he threw the ring toward her. The wind picked it up, and it landed a good 15 feet away from the woman. He said a silent prayer for God's help. He used the rope to pull it in and tossed it again. This time it landed just a few feet from her.

"Grab the ring! Grab the ring!"

She made no effort. At this point, Aric understood that even if she wanted to, the cold prevented her muscles from following what her brain wanted to do.

"Aric, she can't move. She's about to go under."

Aric hadn't noted Jess by his side until she spoke. "Here." He handed her the rope, quickly emptied his pockets, and stepped toward the edge.

"Aric, don't!" was the last thing he heard as the shock of 40-degree water hit him like nothing he'd ever experienced.

He had no breath. His arms and legs rebelled against moving. He'd experienced the ice-bucket challenge once. That cold hit you the same way, but it dissipated within seconds. The only thing to dissipate in seconds here would be his strength. He focused on moving.

"Lord, please help me do this," he whispered. Seconds later, he was able to take a deep breath and turn to find the woman. Her head was about to go under. He grabbed her under the arms and around her chest, pulled her up, and with two powerful kicks, made it to the life ring, which he latched onto with his free arm. It was at that moment that he saw the woman's face. It was the trans RA, Ashleigh somebody.

"J-j-jesss, puulllll!"

He saw that she was trying, but the waves were too much. One big wave had the potential to pull the rope from her hands. Suddenly a man he did not know was there with Jess. He took the rope and pulled them toward the pier.

"Get into the ring, into it!" he yelled.

Aric struggled to comply, but he was losing muscle control, too. The man started to pull them along the pier toward the beach. The waves seemed to help. As they floated up with a swell, they seemed to move ever closer to solid ground.

He sensed being pulled onto the frozen sand as he lost consciousness.

As Ryan slowly drove down the road next to the harbor, he scanned the area for a guy matching Aric's description. He circled the sculpture in the center of the bus loop at the end of the road. As he did, he spotted a young man with a young woman who was taking photographs. He certainly fit the bill—right age and height.

He pulled into a parking slot between two other cars and climbed out. He decided he would check out the guy and girl, confirm that it was Aric, and head back home, calling Adam on the way. Yet, as he climbed onto the concrete pier, a stunning surprise hit him as he saw a third person, a woman next to the lighthouse, walk off the pier and plunge into the water. The guy with the girl went into action and grabbed a flotation ring, which he threw to the woman.

Ryan's police training and instincts kicked in. As he hurried to help, he slipped several times. He saw the woman on her phone, and then . . . was this guy crazy?

He saw the man hand the rope to the woman and then jump in. Did he have a death wish? Cold water rescues required special suits and training. Of course, it hit him that none of that was available and would arrive too late if called in. It wouldn't be a cold-water rescue, just a cold water retrieval. Of two people. How many people died trying to save someone else? Ryan didn't have that statistic at the top of his head.

Ryan reached the girl and grabbed the rope. She was about to lose it, and losing the rope would end the others' lives for sure.

"Get into the ring, into it!" he yelled.

The guy seemed to be losing muscle control in the icy water, and yet somehow, he managed to pull the center of the ring over him and the woman. Ryan began to pull them toward the shore. Sirens now filled the air around the harbor.

One final swell seemed to lift the two onto the sand as if a heavenly hand had scooped them up and placed them on the shore. Ryan dragged them both farther from the water. Both were unconscious, but both were breathing as the paramedics took over.

FORTY-ONE

Ashleigh awoke in a frantic state. Her hands were bound and something, a tube, was stuffed into her throat. She began to thrash about when a woman took her hand. Her hand felt warm and reassuring. A voice told her to calm down. She was okay. A machine was helping her breathe and her hands were tied to keep her from pulling out the tube.

The voice seemed familiar. Ashleigh tried to open her eyes but some kind of gunk coated her lashes and blurred her vision. She blinked multiple times before she could catch glimpses of where she was. The woman squeezed her hand and moved her face in front of Ashleigh's face. It was her, his, mother.

Ashleigh still felt the confusion. Was she a she, or a he living a delusion?

"Calm down, dad's gone to get a nurse. Now that you're awake, they should be able to take the tube out."

Dad? Tears filled her eyes and ran down his cheek. After all she'd put them through, they hadn't abandoned him.

A voice spoke clearly inside her head. "I haven't

abandoned you either, son."

At that, Sam recalled the prayer he had prayed just before jumping into the water.

Aric recalled gaining consciousness in the ambulance. The paramedic's warming blanket felt like a tropical sun on a white sand beach. He took a deep breath and felt no rattles in his lungs. He figured he hadn't taken in any water. His fingers felt stiff, but at least he could move them now.

As he stared out the hospital window that next morning, the events of the previous day seemed a blur. The cold wind. Jess taking photographs. A woman, no, that RA trying to take his life. Some strange man coming to the rescue. He hoped he'd get the chance to meet and thank that man.

As he continued to stare, a welcome voice filled the room behind him. "How's my hero today?"

Jess! He turned to see not only her but Chris and their parents with her. They surrounded his bed.

"Crazy man is more like it," he replied. He saw Chris grin and nod.

"Not at all," said her dad, Pastor Larson. "Greater love has no one than this, that someone lay down his life for his friends."

"How did you all get in? I was told that visitors were restricted to immediate family and no more than two people at a time."

Pastor Larson smiled. "They know me here, so I pulled some strings."

"But we can't stay long," said Jess.

Aric didn't want to hear that.

They chatted a bit and filled in Aric on some of the aftermath of the incident. After a while, a nurse came in and whispered to the pastor.

"Well, looks like your brother is here, so we'll need to leave."

Jess squeezed his hand and turned to exit the room with her brother.

"Pastor Larson, a moment please?"

Jess's dad waved the others on and stepped back to Aric's bedside.

"Sir, two things."

"Sure, Aric. What can I do for you?"

"Sir, the person I went after in the water is a confused man trying to live as a woman. God answered my prayer and helped me save him. There must be a reason for that. Would you check in on him?"

Pastor Larson nodded. "Happy to, if he'll let me. What's the other thing?"

"Sir, I'd formally like your permission to court your daughter."

Pastor Larson grinned. "You have it. Our family would be honored to have you, and I think Jess has been hoping you'd ask."

Adam was given the green light to go see Aric. He gave no one grief about having to wear a mask. He even tucked his own "Masks Don't Work" favorite into a pocket in favor of one of the hospital's freebies.

Their parents were on the way from St. Louis. So, in the meantime, he was going to be Aric's primary visitor. Or so he thought before he saw Jessica and those he assumed to be her family exit the elevator.

"Hi, Jess," he said as they passed by. He lowered the mask far enough for her to recognize him.

"Adam." She stopped right next to him. "Mom, Dad, Chris, this is Aric's brother Adam. These are my parents and my brother Chris."

Her father said, "Nice to meet you. We just came from Aric's room. He looks great."

"I just got the go-ahead to go see him. I guess you beat me to him."

"Sorry. Didn't know you were in the wings. We'll let you get to him."

"Hope to see more of you," said Jess, as she waved goodbye.

Adam did not doubt that as he watched them exit the building. He was about to turn back toward the elevator when he saw someone else enter the building. Ryan Krueger. Aric often told him there was no such thing as coincidence. Adam would be mistaken to think it was his cajoling Ryan to go to the harbor that ended up saving Aric's life. No, even Adam could see the heavenly hand directing that.

He walked up to the man and extended his hand. "Ryan, I'm Adam. That guy you pulled ashore is my kid brother, Aric, with an A. Thank you."

The man looked at Adam with a look of disbelief. "Are you kidding? If you hadn't pushed me into going there, the result today would look a whole lot different."

"Can we go outside to talk? Someplace where we don't have to wear these things." He pulled at his mask.

Ryan nodded with his head and led the way back out the doors. To their right were several benches. They claimed the first empty one.

"I told you I'd explain things when we talked, and here we are."

"We are indeed. First, I need to thank you. I don't know how you did what you did, and I don't think I want to know, but you gave me the final push I needed to leave Portland. Knowing that the chief, whom I admire, would be protected was a godsend for me. And of course, getting the job here. Wow. I mean, I learned this morning that several really qualified local officers were passed by in my favor. Again, I don't know how you pulled that off, but thanks."

"My pleasure. Can you give me a minute? I need something from my car."

"Uh, sure. I'll wait right here."

Adam sprinted to his car and retrieved a manila envelope from the trunk. He hurried back to the bench and sat down next to Ryan.

"This is for you."

Adam saw Ryan's look of amazement as he pulled out the papers that filled the envelope. Adam knew what was there. He hoped it would fill Ryan's family's needs. Ryan inspected the paperwork.

"Are. You. Kidding. Me? The title to a house on ten acres less than ten minutes from the campus?" He gave Adam a bewildered look. "I don't get it. I mean, looking at the photos of this place, my wife Sarah is going to love it. She'll be so excited I'll need to go home with Depends before I show this to her." He laughed. "But I-I don't get it. Why? We've never met. You don't know us, and we don't know you."

Adam nodded. "But I knew your half-brother, Sam Renner. He died in my arms."

Tears welled up in Ryan's eyes. "You were overseas with him when he died?"

Adam shook his head. "Not exactly. What they told you was a lie." He went on to explain exactly what happened and how both men responsible, Henry "Buck" Buckner and Wallace Chamberlain had received the justice they deserved. "I feel partly responsible for his death, and I swore that I'd make it up to him. I managed to get control of funds of his that the company never disclosed, which were substantial, and put them into a trust. That trust did very well under the Graham administration. With the last election's results, I figured it was time to pull those funds out of the stock market and put them into real estate, for you. The property is paid for, and I think you'll find enough in the accounts to cover education expenses for the boys. You see, Sam used to talk about you all the time. You two got into some real shenanigans."

Ryan's tears were accentuated by his grin. He nodded.

"He also talked a lot about Sarah and the boys, to the point I felt I had a pretty good idea what kind of life you wanted. And that included a place to live, so here you are. Now I feel I've paid my debt to Sam."

With that Adam extended his hand. "Thank you for saving my kid brother. We're even."

As Adam rose and headed toward the entrance, Ryan asked, "Hey, your text said you had another task or job or something for me to do. What?"

Adam turned back and shook his head. "Man, I need help watching out for him. He's bound to get himself into more trouble, and I could sure use the help from an expert in shenanigans." Ryan accepted the task with a grin and a nod.

Acknowledgments

As always, I again want to acknowledge and thank my dear wife, Paula, for her valuable proofreading skills, help, and encouragement. With the retirement of my main proofreader, I've started using *Grammarly* for additional error checking. If you find any errors, it missed them, and let me know.

Plus, a big thank you to my editor, Patrick LoBrutto. His feedback always makes my stories better.

And finally, my sincerest compliments to Adrijus Guscia for his incredible covers.

About the Author

Braxton can't lay claim to wanting to be a writer all his life, although his mother and seventh grade English teacher were convinced he had what it would take. A bachelor's degree in Bio-Medical Engineering led to medical school and a residency in Emergency Medicine. He served for a decade in the U.S. Army Medical Corps with tours such as the Chief, Emergency Medical Services at Fort Campbell, KY, and as a research Flight Surgeon at Fort Rucker, AL. Who had time to write?

By the 1990s, as a civilian, his professional and family life had settled down, somewhat, and his mother once again took up her mantra, "Write a book. You're a good writer." In 1997, a Valentine's Day writing contest convinced him that maybe he could write fiction. He spent the next fifteen years learning the craft of writing.

Now, twenty-plus years after that first hesitant start, he has sixteen novels published, as well as non-fiction books and a children's book, and can't find enough time to write. As a Christian, he writes "true-life" Christian fiction (suspense and thrillers) that many call "cutting edge," as he's not afraid to take on such issues as human trafficking, racism, and more. His characters are real-life as well, with all the flaws and blemishes real people have. As such, his books are never likely to gain acceptance by the Christian Bookseller Association. But then, he never intended to tell stories just to the choir.

Books by Braxton DeGarmo:

Still Here Series:

The End Begins – 1
The Shaking – 2
The Beasts – 3
The Trumpets – 4
The Mark - 5

Non-Fiction Study Guides:

Still Here! Surviving the End Times
Still Here! The Apocalypse is Now
Still Here! Countdown Revelation

MedAir Series:

Looks that Deceive – 1
Rescued and Remembered – 2
The Silenced Shooter – 3
Wrongfully Removed – 4
A Zealot's Destiny – 5
Kidnapped Nation - 6
The Khmer Connection - 7
Resurrected Trouble - 8

Seamus O'Connor Thrillers:

The Militant Genome
Ten Seconds 'Til

Other Books:

Indebted

Children's Books:

The Toucan Who Can Can-can